PRAISE FOR FALON BALLARD'S CHARMING ROM-COMS

'A fanciful, slow-burn grumpy/sunshine tale, ideal
for readers who enjoy escapist romance'
Library Journal

'Laugh-out-loud funny and romantic beyond the scope
of space and time, *Change of Heart* is another total
winner from Falon Ballard. I have never met a
heroine I've cheered for so hard'
Annabel Monaghan

'The perfect blend of wit and romance. I love my
rom-coms with a slice of magical realism and *Change
of Heart* delivers in spades. Imagine *Pleasantville*
and *The Hating Game* had a book baby. I adored
this book; Falon Ballard at her best'
Sophie Cousens

'Laugh-out-loud funny, heartwarming, and with a heroine
who commands every room she enters... I couldn't put
Change of Heart down. I want to live in Heart Springs,
I want Cam Andrews in my corner, and I want this
story to be adapted into an actual Hallmark movie'
Sarah Hogle

'*Change of Heart* is the badass feminist rom-com that
fans of *Pleasantville* and *The Stepford Wives* will love.
It's funny, sharp, and a slow burn that will keep
you on the edge of your seat'
Erin La Rosa

'Falon Ballard injects the Hallmark rom-com with
some much-needed acidity in this Hollywood
co-stars-with-benefits sparkler'
ELLE

'Full of her signature charm, steam, and laugh-out-loud moments, Falon Ballard's newest fully delivers. *Change of Heart* is perfect for anyone who has ever wanted to see the big-city Hallmark villain rewrite the narrative and become the unexpected heroine of her own story. I devoured this in a single, delicious sitting!'
Holly James

'Ballard's lively and fun rom-com will have readers hoping that these two have their second chance'
Booklist

'Ballard delivers a feisty and fast-paced Hollywood fantasy in this addictive contemporary'
Publishers Weekly

'Ballard creates a winning romantic comedy full of simmering chemistry. A fun and sexy ode to rom-coms, full of joy and chemistry'
Kirkus Reviews (starred review)

'Full of winks to the rom-com genre and packed with steamy tension'
Library Journal

'Falon Ballard is a master of chemistry-filled banter and lovable characters!'
Sarah Adams

'Falon Ballard is the queen of sharp-wit and swoony romances . . . I will devour everything she writes and beg for more'
Mazey Eddings

Falon Ballard is the *USA Today* bestselling author of several rom-coms and the cohost of the *Happy to Meet Cute* podcast. When she's not writing a romance book, reading a romance book, or talking about romance books, you can probably find her at Disneyland. Ballard lives in the Los Angeles area.

For more information, visit **falonballard.com**, or follow her on TikTok and Instagram **@FalonBallard**.

BY FALON BALLARD

Standalones
Lease on Love
Just My Type
Right on Cue
All I Want is You
Change of Heart
Toe to Toe

Idle Reputations
Something Wicked

Toe to Toe

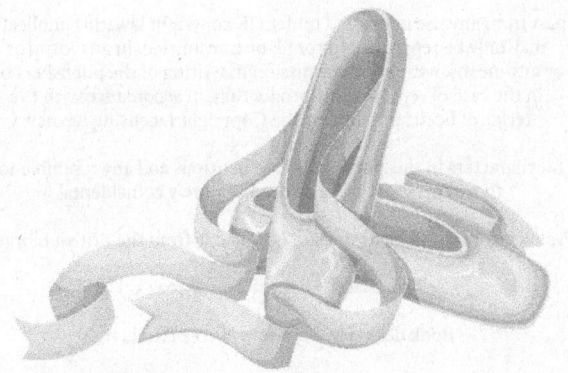

FALON BALLARD

HEADLINE
ETERNAL

Copyright © Falon Ballard 2026

The right of Falon Ballard to be identified as the
Author of the Work has been asserted by her in accordance
with the Copyright, Designs and Patents Act 1988.

Published by arrangement with G.P. Putnam's Sons
An imprint of Penguin Publishing Group
A division of Penguin Random House LLC.

First published in the UK in 2026 by Headline Eternal
An imprint of Headline Publishing Group Limited

This paperback edition published in 2026

1

Apart from any use permitted under UK copyright law, this publication
may only be reproduced, stored, or transmitted, in any form, or
by any means, with prior permission in writing of the publishers or,
in the case of reprographic production, in accordance with the
terms of licences issued by the Copyright Licensing Agency.

All characters in this publication are fictitious and any resemblance
to real persons, living or dead, is purely coincidental.

Cataloguing in Publication Data is available from the British Library

Paperback ISBN 978 1 0354 4024 5

Book design by Shannon Nicole Plunkett

Printed and bound in Great Britain by Clays Ltd, Elcograf S.p.A.

Headline's policy is to use papers that are natural, renewable and recyclable
products and made from wood grown in well-managed forests and other
controlled sources. The logging and manufacturing processes are expected
to conform to the environmental regulations of the country of origin.

Headline Publishing Group Limited
An Hachette UK Company
Carmelite House
50 Victoria Embankment
London EC4Y 0DZ

The authorised representative in the EEA is Hachette Ireland,
8 Castlecourt Centre, Dublin 15, D15 XTP3, Ireland (email: info@hbgi.ie)

www.headlineeternal.com
www.headline.co.uk
www.hachette.co.uk

Toe to Toe

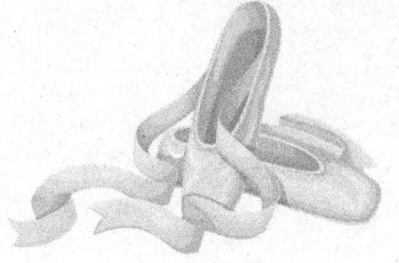

This one is for my readers: Whether this is your first Falon Ballard book or your seventh, none of this would be possible without you.

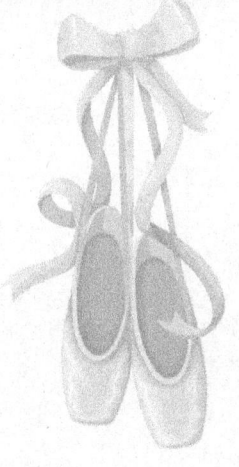

Author's Note

Dear reader,

Thank you so much for picking up *Toe to Toe*! I am so excited for you to meet Allegra and Cord and join them on their journey to happily ever after. Before you begin reading, I wanted to make you aware of some sensitive content you will find on the pages of this book. There is sexual harassment in the workplace on the page, as well as mentions of sexual assault that happened off-page and in the past. Our female main character, Allegra, is a professional ballerina, and while she does not suffer from any diagnosed eating disorder, she is very aware of her eating habits and those behaviors are present on the page. Please, first and foremost, take care of yourself. Happy reading!

XOXO,
Falon

ONE

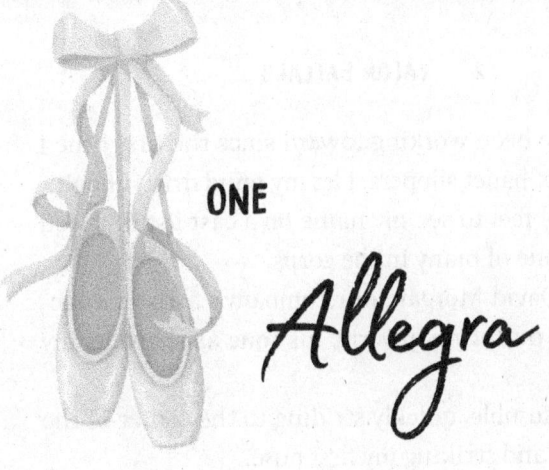
Allegra

I f my life were a color, it would be ballet pink.

And I think I might hate pink.

My reflection in the mirror of the dance studio reeks of it. Pink tights, pink leotard, pink pointe shoes. Even though this is just company class and I can wear whatever I want, I've never gotten out of the habit of reaching for pink, just one of the many habits ballet has ingrained in me.

My arm floats over my head, my heels pressed together and my toes turned out. Every person in front of me and behind me at the barre moves with the same fluidity, the same grace. We hit the same position on the same beat, moving as one entity more than as individual dancers. This part of our day is all about blending in, becoming one.

After class, we move on to rehearsal. We are only a couple of weeks from performances of *Swan Lake*, a show I have danced so many times now that I feel like I could do it in my sleep. At least I have a featured role this time, though it's not the one I wanted.

Hopefully I can dance well enough to finally get the

promotion I've been working toward since the first time I put on a pair of ballet slippers. I let my mind drift, imagining how it will feel to see my name on a cast list in a lead role, not just one of many in the corps.

"Allegra." David Morgan, our company's artistic director, snaps me out of my reverie, his tone as sharp as my lines.

"Sorry," I mumble, quickly striding to the center of the practice room and striking my first pose.

Not exactly the best way to show him I'm ready for a bigger role.

But once the music starts, I forget about David, and the show, and the role I'm desperate for. I forget about the color pink and the ache in my shoulders and needing to ask Mom and Dad for more money soon.

As I begin the steps, the rest fades away.

It's cliché, I know, being swept away by the music. Only caring about the choreography and the movement and the character I'm trying to capture with nothing but a few flicks of my feet and swoops of my arm. But just about any dancer will confirm the truth of it. It's why we're here. Why we can't seem to leave when it would be self-preservation to walk away.

I finish, my chest heaving, sweat beading on my forehead, but I don't let the strain show on my face.

David watches me for a moment that borders on uncomfortable, his eyes raking my body from head to toe, before dismissing me with a nod. "Fine."

I spend the rest of the rehearsal with my back against the wall at the rear of the studio, stretching while my eyes watch our principals dance the dueling duets of Odette and Odile, the good and the evil, the light and the dark.

Part of me wishes I could hate them, wishes I could feel like they've taken something from me that they haven't earned, but nothing could be further from the truth. Every dancer at Ballet New York works their ass off, and watching my colleagues flit effortlessly around the room only inspires me to keep pushing harder. This is the time of our tightly scheduled day when we long to stand out, to be the dancer no one in the room can pull their eyes from. I don't think I've ever been that dancer.

"Don't forget we have a company meeting tomorrow morning at eight," David reminds us at the end of rehearsal as we're changing our shoes and packing up.

As if we could forget. He's been dangling the news of our next show over us for weeks. Apparently, he's going to bless us with something new and original instead of the classics we typically perform. When David first signed on as artistic director of the prestigious company, he promised to innovate and create, but the past few years have brought financial hardships to much of the dance world, and nothing sells tickets like the classics.

It will be refreshing to try something new. Assuming he lets me be a part of it.

"I think most of you are going to be excited with this new project. I can't wait to share it with you." Though he doesn't exactly sound enthusiastic, I know he means it. Mostly because a few months ago, he got totally wasted one night when we all went out after rehearsal and told me he had had a stroke of "creative genius" that was going to put our company back on the map.

I wasn't aware we'd been eliminated from the map, but when your director starts spilling secrets, it's unwise to interrupt the flow.

Unfortunately, shortly after expounding on his own ingenuity and brilliance, he tried to get me to come home with him.

I said no, for so many reasons.

Things have been a little strained for us ever since. He can't come right out and say anything because to acknowledge his behavior that night would be opening up himself and the company to a string of lawsuits neither can afford.

I sure as fuck am not going to say anything because I love my job. And after ten years with this company—between the school and the corps and now as a soloist—I'm due for my chance at principal. And I'm not going to let a little thing like sexual harassment derail me. If sexual harassment derailed every ballerina it happened to, ballet would cease to exist.

So I push it down and focus on the only thing that matters: the dance.

As I leave the building, my phone vibrates from the pocket of the soft pink joggers I pulled on over my tights. The sun has gone down and the early spring air still holds a hint of a chill. I let the sounds of the city wash over me, horns blaring and people laughing as they enjoy dinner on a restaurant patio—maybe the first of the season. I fish out my phone, smiling when I see my sister's name on the screen.

"Hello?"

"Ohmygod, is this the one and only Allegra Hart, star of Ballet New York? Did I actually manage to get you to pick up the phone?" Bethany's voice holds only a hint of sarcasm.

"Haha. I always pick up the phone for you, and you know it." I pull my sweater a little tighter around me as I begin the short walk to my studio apartment, taking a second to appreciate the green buds beginning to sprout on the trees.

"Unless you're in class. Or rehearsal. Or a performance."

I snort. "You think I'm going to just stop a show and be like, Sorry, audience, I know you paid a buttload of money to be here tonight, but my sister's calling to talk about *Real Housewives* and I gotta take this!"

"You and I both know all discussions of *Real Housewives* take place on monthly sister night and must involve wine and popcorn."

Bethany instituted monthly sister nights when it became clear my schedule was not going to allow for many—or any, really—spur-of-the-moment hangouts. We've been holding them since we were teenagers, and I can count on one hand the number of times one of us has had to cancel. Sister night is sacred.

Two years my junior, Bethany is the Hart daughter who didn't have to live up to our mother's expectations, so therefore designed her own life and is living a real adult one. She has a college degree, and an apartment with more than one hundred square feet of living space, and a career with normal hours, and a fiancée. She has a name that belongs only to her, not one borrowed from one of the greatest American ballerinas of the twentieth century.

"Anyway." My building is in sight and I know if I don't get my sister off the phone quickly, I'll be chatting with her for the rest of the night—not that I don't love her and our talks, but I have an even earlier morning tomorrow than I usually do, since David's meeting cuts into my normal preclass workout hours. "To what do I owe the pleasure of your call?"

"I'm calling to make sure you have made arrangements for tomorrow."

Shit.

I completely forgot about Bethany's bachelorette party.

So like any good sister, I lie: "Arrangements have totally been made. I will be there." I don't remember where *there* is, but that's a small detail. I can text my mom and ask her for the pertinent info. Not that she'll be joining us, but she makes a point of knowing everything about us—at all times.

"We're meeting at Six Pact at nine o'clock." Bless her. Like any good sister, she totally knows I'm lying. "Do not be late."

I groan in reluctance. "I think I managed to block out the fact that we're going to a strip club until right this moment."

"First of all, it's not a strip club. It is a male entertainment extravaganza. Second of all, I'm the bride and I do what I want."

"Why does what you want have to include half-naked guys doing a shitty approximation of choreography?" I unlock the front door to my building and cross the lobby. I think about taking the elevator—fuck knows I've earned a break after all the dancing I've done today—but I ultimately veer to the right toward the stairs, knowing it will burn a few extra calories. Maybe I'll even let myself have a drink tomorrow night.

"You enjoy half-naked guys just as much as the next woman who's interested in men, don't lie to me."

I trudge up the first set of steps. "I spend my whole day with half-naked guys, B."

"The rest of us are not so lucky."

"You are marrying a woman, doesn't that mean we can skip the dudes with bad moves and worse costumes?"

"That is biphobic, Allegra Hart. I will not stand for that kind of erasure."

"Pretty sure I'm also bi, sis."

"Pretty sure you haven't had sex with anyone of any gender in years, *sis*."

"Wow. Both rude and irrelevant." I make my way up the last set of stairs to my floor, so close to a hot shower and an icy foot bath, I can practically feel the warm water easing the aches of my muscles. "All right, B, I will be there, but I want it noted for the record that I am attending against my will and I plan to hate every second of the experience."

"That's the kind of love and devotion I expect from my maid of honor!"

I groan again, the combination of the reminder of all the duties yet to come and the relief of finally reaching my front door overtaking me. "I'll see you tomorrow. Love you."

"Love you too!" she chirps before I disconnect the call and shove my phone back in my pocket.

As the front door of my studio opens, its arc swinging wide, I barely manage to catch it before it slams into the counter of my "kitchen." It takes only about four steps before I've crossed from the door into my "bedroom." My full-size bed is covered by a plain white duvet. Two white pillows sit at the top. The whole thing rests against a plain white wall.

I don't spend a lot of time here, so decorating has never been a priority. I promised myself when I made principal, I would invest a little more effort into my living space. Maybe even try to keep a plant alive. But right now I don't have the time or the funds to care. I toss my ballet bag near the front door and drag myself straight to the bathroom, unable to think about touching anything when I'm still covered in a day's worth of sweat.

The water flows over me, and I let out an unholy groan as the pulse beats against my aching shoulders. I spend more time than I should underneath the stream, wondering what kind of announcement could be awaiting us tomorrow. Wondering if I totally blew my shot at principal by turning down David's advances.

Overall, things in the ballet world have gotten much better in recent years when it comes to the wildly unbalanced power dynamics between directors/choreographers and dancers. I know that, were I to report David's behavior, it would be taken seriously. Just as I know it would likely be the end of my time with Ballet New York. Not that they would fire me, obviously. But I would be ostracized—emotionally and mentally pushed out, if not technically.

And besides, it's not like he really did anything so terrible. Yes, he propositioned me, but he didn't persist, at least not much, after I said no. And as of now, saying no hasn't caused any sort of harm.

I need to stop worrying about it. David was so drunk, he probably doesn't even remember.

I reassure myself of this as I tuck myself into bed, curling up with my iPad to watch the latest episode of *Vanderpump Rules*. Somehow the drama of drunk twenty-five-year-olds constantly banging their co-workers feels tame in comparison to the drama of the ballet world. But I allow myself to forget about dance, about promotions, about directors with wandering eyes, about everything.

I'M TEN MINUTES EARLY TO THE COMPANY MEETING THE NEXT morning, wanting to find a seat well within David's eyeline. I want him to be thinking about me in connection with whatever this new project is. Want him to start seeing me in a leading role, even if I have no idea what said role will entail. Whatever it is, I'm ready for it.

We gather in the largest of the rehearsal rooms, crowding into the space, the chatter echoing around us as we wait for David to grace us with his presence.

Lucy, one of the few in the company I would call a friend, plops down next to me on the floor, automatically extending her legs into a stretch, her dark hair falling over her face as she leans forward. "So what are the odds this whole thing could just be an email?"

I smile, but it's tense. Not for the first time, I wish I could have a little sliver of Lucy's ease. A Japanese American woman with bright eyes and bolder sass, she's perfectly happy with her place in the corps, and in general, doesn't stress about things like castings and contract renewals. She dances because she loves it, says she'll do it for as long as it makes her happy, and when it doesn't, she'll stop.

The thought of no longer dancing, no longer being a part of this company, is enough to make the cup of oatmeal and banana I ate after my workout do pirouettes in my stomach.

David strolls into the room one minute before the meeting is due to start. A white man in his midfifties who danced as a member of the company for years before taking over as director, he's finally let his hair go gray and somehow it makes him look younger than when he was dying it a too-dark brown. He's still in impeccable shape, his presence looming both literally and figuratively. He doesn't need to call for our attention; the moment he strides to the center of the room, flanked by his assistant, Brianna, the chatter dies down.

He takes a minute to look around, like a king surveying his subjects. For today at least, his smile seems to indicate he doesn't find us lacking. He claps his hands together once, leaving them joined in front of his chest as if in prayer. "I know we all have busy days ahead of us, so I won't waste any time. As you know, I have been wanting to include more original pieces in our upcoming seasons, and after our board and our season ticket holders see what I've come up with, I can only imagine they'll be demanding more."

Lucy rolls her eyes and doesn't even try to hide it.

I elbow her in the ribs without moving my eyes from David.

"Picture this." He spreads his hands wide, painting the visual for us. It's the most excited I've seen him in ages and our last performance received a nearly perfect review in the *Times*. "A courtesan, destitute and desperate for a chance at a better life. A penniless writer with nothing to offer her but his love. A prince, richer than she can imagine but cruel and heartless. And the impossible choice she must make."

"So the plot of *Moulin Rouge*?" Lucy mutters under her breath.

A quick glance around the room and it's clear that more than one person has caught on to David's not-so-original idea.

But no one dares to question his brilliance.

When we don't burst into applause and cheers, he continues to try to sell us. "Think about it. Ballet is grace and elegance, technique and precision. But ballet has never been sexy. Not until now."

"Has the man never seen anything performed outside of Lincoln Center?" This time Lucy's muttering isn't so under her breath and a few people around her giggle.

And I mean, she's not wrong. It's a little ridiculous to claim that ballet has never before been sexy. But in David's mind, and probably in the minds of most of the people paying our salaries, it's a groundbreaking idea, one that will push all the boundaries.

"Because the choreography of this piece is going to require a different set of skills, I will be holding auditions in six weeks. And as usual, Brianna and myself will be watching during company classes and rehearsals to see who is standing out." His eyes flick briefly to me. "I want to see who is willing to go the distance and give this piece what it needs."

It's a glance so quick I could have imagined it. Or maybe he's just looking at everyone. But I can't help but feel the look was too pointed to be in my head.

But I don't focus on that. I focus on what he's just said. Auditions. There are going to be auditions for this ballet. Normally David doesn't need to audition us—he sees us dancing every day. He knows what we can do, what we're capable of. But if there are going to be auditions, then I have a chance to make myself stand out, stand above the rest of the company.

Of course, I have no idea what he means by "a different set of skills" but whatever it is, I will make it happen. I'll learn how to tap dance if that's what it takes.

David dismisses us, giving us a ten-minute break before we're set to begin class. He's headed for the door, and I know this might be the only chance I get.

I catch him in the hallway. "David? Do you have time for a quick chat at some point today? I just have a couple of questions."

He glances at me over his shoulder, not bothering to

stop walking away. "Come to my office after rehearsal this afternoon."

Brianna, David's assistant and right-hand woman, calls after him. "Is this a meeting I should be there for?"

"No need," David responds, pushing through the door at the end of the hall and letting it slam behind him.

Brianna looks at me. "Would you like me to be there, Allegra?"

I know why she's asking. She can act as backup—or as a witness—if I feel like I need it. But I shake my head. "No. It's nothing big. Shouldn't take more than a few minutes."

I rehearse what I want to say to David as I spin across the floor, nearly losing my balance as I come out of my turns. Being distracted during class and rehearsal is probably not the best way to go about securing a lead role, but tomorrow I will be back to my dedicated self. And when I meet with David this afternoon, I will assure him I will do whatever it takes to be his leading lady.

TWO
Allegra

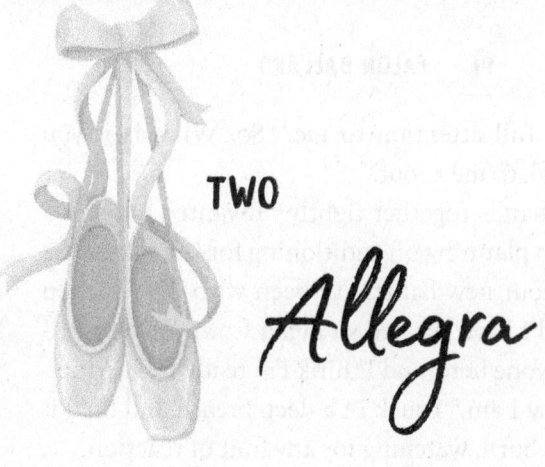

It takes a solid thirty seconds for David to call for me to enter his office after I knock on the door. Normally I wait until I get home to shower and change, but today I made use of the locker rooms after rehearsal. I even took a few minutes to apply a thin layer of makeup, doing my best to appear fresh and natural.

I close the door behind me and wait for him to offer me a seat at one of the chairs in front of his desk before I fold myself onto the cool leather.

"How was rehearsal?" He doesn't bother to remove his eyes from the screen of his computer as he asks the cursory question.

"It was good. Great. The ballet is going to be fantastic, as always." I try to hide my nerves with enthusiasm, but I don't know that I'm succeeding.

"Glad to hear it. The masses do love the drivel."

I wouldn't exactly call *Swan Lake* drivel, but I'm not about to start this conversation with an argument.

After a couple of clicks, David finally closes his laptop

and turns his full attention to me. "So. What is it you wanted to speak to me about?"

I clasp my hands together tightly. "I wanted to let you know that I am planning on auditioning for the role of the courtesan in your new ballet. I've been with BNY for ten years now, and I have learned so much from you and Brianna and everyone here, and I think I'm ready for a principal role. I know I am." I suck in a deep breath and hold it until my lungs burn, watching for any hint of reaction.

He frowns. Then he frowns some more and leans back in his seat, putting distance between us. "You are planning on auditioning for the role of the courtesan?"

I nod, not really sure why that information is so shocking. I haven't hid my desire to move up in the company, and a brand-new ballet is the perfect time for that to happen.

He cocks his head to the side, studying me like I'm a map and he's a man too stubborn to stop and ask for directions. Which he undoubtedly is. "Now, I don't want you to take this the wrong way, Allegra..."

I wait for him to finish, second-guessing my decision to not ask Brianna to sit in on this meeting because nothing good can finish his thought.

"You're a very skilled dancer. Your technique is impeccable. You turn well, your turnout is great, and you have good feet."

"But?" With the accolades he's listed, I should be at the top of the class, not lingering as a soloist after ten years.

"But I don't know that I could ever believe you as a woman who makes her living having sex. Not just makes a living at it but loves it. Thrives on it." He leans forward, his arms resting on his desk as his eyes bore into me. "There's a certain kind of energy that vibrates off a woman like that, and I'm not sure it's something you could portray."

My cheeks flame, the heat so immediate I feel like I just stuck my head in an oven. What the hell am I supposed to say to that? "Well, that is the challenge of performing a role, right? Taking on the qualities of the character that we might not possess ourselves?"

His mouth presses into a thin line. "Sometimes, yes, mere acting is enough. But this is the kind of role a performer needs to *feel* in order to truly embody it, to capture what I'm trying to capture. I'm not sure you have it in you."

"Are you saying I'm not sexy enough for this part?" I wish I could imbue my words with strength and incredulity because truly the audacity of this man is unmatched. But instead I sound as weak as I feel in this moment.

"I would never say something like that to one of my dancers, Allegra. That would be completely inappropriate." He holds my gaze until I can't stand it any longer and look away.

"Right. Of course."

"However, hypothetically speaking, if you wanted some advice before auditions, I would say you should think about embracing your sexuality. Maybe exploring opportunities that have been presented to you that you might have turned down in the past. Going out of your comfort zone."

My stomach spins and I have to swallow the bile that rises in my throat.

So much for him not remembering his drunken request and my adamant refusal.

"Right. Got it." I push myself out of the chair, moving quickly to the door to hopefully disguise my shaking thighs.

I don't bother closing the door of his office behind me. I don't bother stopping back at the locker room to grab my bag. I make sure I have my keys and my phone and I fly through the hallway of the building, rushing down the five flights of stairs and out into the cool, crisp air of the early evening.

I practically sprint through the streets of New York, dodging businessmen and -women on their cell phones and tourists taking up the whole damn sidewalk, making it home in record time. Making it home in just enough time to fall on my bed before I completely lose it.

Shame and humiliation burn through me and I curl in on myself as the tears flow steadily down my cheeks.

I replay the conversation over and over in my head, wishing, hoping that I misunderstood something. That what he said is different from what he really meant.

But the more I think on his words, the worse they feel.

Despite the careful wording, David's meaning is one hundred percent clear. He won't consider casting me as the courtesan because I refused to have sex with him. And he's going to wrap it all up like I'm the one who is falling short, like I don't have it in me to be this character when really what he means is I can't be sexy because I didn't want to have sex with him.

It's so beyond inappropriate, I almost laugh. But nothing about the situation is funny, not really.

Once I've cried myself out, I sit up, wiping under my eyes, my fingertips coming away stained black.

I know my tears are justified, just as sure as I know I can't let myself drown in them. I need to figure out my next step. Lucy would tell me to go straight to the board and who cares if it costs me my career. Bethany would tell me to quit on the spot, try to lure me back to the real world with temptations of paid vacations and a job that doesn't demand permanent damage to my body.

My mom would probably tell me that's just how directors talk to their dancers. She wouldn't come right out and tell me I should have slept with him when I had the chance. But she would probably be thinking it.

I have no one I can go to who will fully understand. No one who can give me the kind of logical advice I really need.

My phone chirps with a text.

BETHANY: Are you home yet? Want me to come by on my way to the show? We can share a cab!

Shit.

The last thing I need to be doing tonight is going to watch a bunch of meathead dudes rip their clothes off for screaming bachelorettes. For half a second I consider bailing, but there's no way I could do that to my sister. She's made accommodations for my schedule on more occasions than I can count, even scheduled tonight's festivities weeks ahead of the wedding so it wouldn't interfere with performances of *Swan Lake*.

ME: I'm home, but I still need to change and do my makeup. I'll meet you at the theater?

BETHANY: Don't be late! You don't want to miss the opening number!

I think calling it an opening number is probably giving the whole thing a little too much credit, but I keep that to myself, giving her message a thumbs-up before dragging myself off the bed and over to my tiny closet.

I have a couple of dresses that I normally wear to our company galas, but they seem a little too stuffy for a bachelorette party at a show called Six Pact. Luckily, I find a short black dress shoved in the back. It isn't all that exciting but it will have to do.

I do a quick makeup job, thankful for all the stage makeup training I've had over the years. My naturally wavy blond hair falls down my back when I pull it out of its typical bun and after a dab of frizz control crème, I decide to just let it be. I slip into knee-high black boots and throw on a light jacket and am down the stairs within twenty minutes, hailing a cab I can't afford so I'm not late for my sister's big night.

Her crew is at the front of the line by the time I hop out of my cab, and I rush over to them just as they're shown through the entrance of the theater. From the outside, it doesn't look much different from any of the other brick buildings in the area, but once we duck inside, it's all dim lights and fog machine haze. There's a lingering smell of sweat, but it isn't the overpowering kind, and it's laced with the scent of booze and cologne.

It isn't until we are shown to our table, mere feet from the stage, that my sister spots me. Squealing, she wraps me in a giant hug; I have to fight back the tears because I didn't know how much I needed one of her signature embraces after the day I've had.

Music is already pumping through the room, but Bethany doesn't hesitate to shout over the noise. "Are you okay?"

I nod, leaning in for another hug under the guise of wanting to speak directly into her ear so I don't have to yell. "I'm good! It's your bachelorette! Are you so excited?"

Her smile beams as I pull out of her arms and tug her

down into a seat facing the stage. A server comes over minutes later and the group of women—most of whom I don't know—orders multiple bottles of alcohol for the table.

I grab the server's elbow before he can leave, noting how firm his arms are. "Can I just get a sparkling water with lime, please?" I wait for the chiding, the teasing because I don't want to drink at a place that so clearly calls for being intoxicated, but he doesn't say anything, just nods and jots down my order with a smile.

Once we all have drinks in front of us, the one person in the group I do know, Sarah, Bethany's best friend from college and her only other bridesmaid, raises a toast to my sister and we all clink our glasses together. It would be a nice chance for me to get to know some of my sister's friends, especially since I know I will be seeing them more over the coming weeks at various wedding events, but the music is so loud that, combined with the excited chatter of a room full of mostly women, I can barely hear my own thoughts.

I make small talk with the woman sitting to my left, one of Bethany's co-workers, occasionally checking in with the woman of the hour to make sure her glass is constantly filled.

All of a sudden, the music cuts and the lights completely black out. The first thing I think is, *That's not very safe.* The second thing I think is, *Holy shit, I have never heard so much screaming in my entire life*—not even when Bethany dragged me to a Jonas Brothers concert when we were teenagers.

We sit in the darkness for longer than is comfortable, the tension mounting, the screaming reaching near hysterical levels.

And then a single spotlight illuminates a man standing

in the center of the stage. He's wearing a full three-piece suit—he even wears a fedora and carries a cane. It's about five more items of clothing than I expected to see, but I guess part of the fun is in the actual stripping.

The notes of a familiar song start, one I never would have expected to hear at a show like this, but "Singin' in the Rain" is pretty unmistakable.

I'm surprised once again when the man begins to dance, because this is not at all what I was expecting.

He's tapping. And he's doing it well.

I am not a tapper and haven't taken a class since I was a kid, back when I danced for fun. But it doesn't take a trained dancer to realize this guy is good.

The shadows cast by the brim of his hat make it hard to see his face fully, but even with the limited view, he's gorgeous. And the way his muscles move under the tight-fitting fabric of his suit. Phew. My mouth has suddenly gone so dry, I think about swigging right from the bottle of vodka sitting on the table.

The end of the song scratches and suddenly we're listening to the beginning chords of Rihanna's "Umbrella." The room explodes as we collectively recognize the riff on Tom Holland's famous *Lip Sync Battle* performance.

The light stays still on the main guy in the center of the stage as he slowly begins to remove his clothing.

I didn't think it was possible, but the screams grow even louder as the man reveals himself, one piece of clothing at a time.

He whips off his belt and unbuttons his pants and even my normally levelheaded and calm sister is losing her proverbial shit. But he doesn't remove his pants, and when the intro of the song ends, moving into the first chorus, the entire stage lights up, revealing twelve additional dancers. All of them are bare-chested, hairless and shiny and so ripped that even I'm impressed by their defined physique.

Bethany grabs my arm, shaking me a little. "Is this not the best thing you've ever seen?!?"

I've seen Kimin Kim and Olga Smirnova guest at the American Ballet Theatre, but rather than reminding Bethany of that fact, I nod and smile, trying to look impressed.

And if I'm being honest, I'm more impressed than I expected.

The first number concludes and the screaming once again ratchets up to extreme levels. I applaud along with everyone else, honestly enjoying the clever choreography.

The show continues, the dancers breaking into smaller groups to perform more targeted numbers. They start pulling guests onstage during the second song, and that's when the performance becomes more of what I had anticipated. I have a hard time seeing what's so appealing about a sweaty man grinding on my lap, but according to the faces of the lucky recipients, I must be missing something.

It's during the fourth or fifth song when an unbelievably gorgeous Black man comes to collect Bethany. She pretends to protest for a half a second before shoving the rest of us out of her way to make her way to the stage.

The guy gently pushes her into a chair and proceeds to writhe all over her before picking her up, wrapping her legs around his head, and lowering her to the ground.

Aside from the sheer weirdness of watching my sister get a lap dance, I'm mostly just glad she decided to wear pants tonight. Also, I really hope these floors are disinfected after every show.

When Bethany returns to her seat after being fully

debauched by a stranger, her eyes are wide and a bit wild. "Holy shit, I can't believe I did that!"

I laugh, tugging her back down into her seat. "I can't either!"

"Is it weird that that was one of the hottest things that's ever happened to me?" She fans her cheeks, reaching for a glass of water and chugging the whole thing.

"Maybe just don't tell your future wife that!"

Bethany shakes her head. "I think even Cassidy would give me this one. The way these guys move is like sex incarnate!"

I laugh again, pouring Bethany another cocktail and shoving it into her hands. The show continues, a few more small group numbers and several more women left panting after their turn onstage. For the most part, the music is loud and upbeat, hip-hop songs with steady beats and intense rhythms.

So when a slower song comes on, the lights once again dimming and leaving just a single spotlight onstage, the room pays close attention.

It's the guy from the opening number, the tapper. He hasn't been in any of the smaller group numbers that I've seen, but it's clear from his commanding presence that he must be the star of the show.

This time when he strips, he takes it all off—or almost all anyway, leaving himself in a pair of tight, short black briefs. With no hat hiding his face this time, my earlier suspicions are confirmed—the man is drop-dead gorgeous. His muscles look like they were hand-sculpted, but it's his face, the cut of his cheekbones, the dark stubble covering a chiseled jaw, the bright blue eyes I can see from my seat, and the dark hair that flops in his eyes as he moves, that leave me momentarily breathless.

And I'm not the only one. The entire audience seems to be collectively holding our breath as we watch him move across the stage. His movement is all at once graceful and sensual, hypnotizing to watch. His lines are straight and perfect, but it's the loose way he swivels his hips that has me absolutely mesmerized.

Holy shit.

This is what David was talking about, capturing sex appeal with dance. Because I don't think I've ever seen anything hotter than the way this man glides across the stage, each movement equal parts effortless and purposeful. He radiates sex, not just from his perfect body, but from the tiniest quirk of his lips, the lift of an eyebrow, that swivel of the hips. How does he make his body move like that?

The realization hits me square in the chest. I don't have what it takes to dance like that. At least not right now.

The inkling of an idea sticks in my brain as the applause echoes around the room. It grows and grows, until I know what I need to do.

I call our server over and order a vodka soda because if I'm actually going to do this, I'm going to need a little liquid courage.

Bethany, who's well beyond tipsy at this point, leans over to clink her glass against mine. "Of course you wait until the very last minute to start having fun!"

Fun I might be having, but when one of the guys comes over to our table and reaches for my hand, I wave him away, directing him toward one of the other screaming women instead. Once he's picked another lucky contender, I let my eyes drift back to the stage. The main guy, the beautiful dancer, is standing in the wings and looking right at me.

My heart stops pumping in my chest.

It should be illegal, to look at someone like that, while looking like *that*.

He quirks an eyebrow and I shrug, hoping I didn't offend him. But a grin splits across his face and just the sight of it makes me shiver.

The stage fills with all of the dancers, clearly coming together for some kind of final send-off moment. I chug the rest of my drink, wincing as the alcohol burns my throat.

The last number of the show is sillier than any of the others: "It's Raining Men" blaring through the speakers as they call back to the opening number with their umbrellas and trench coats.

The show concludes with bursts of confetti and, somehow, even more screaming than before. The houselights rise slowly, giving everyone a chance to reorient themselves, but it isn't long before our servers are coming around to usher us out of the building. I take my time, knowing I need a few minutes before I can put my very loosely laid out plan in motion.

Luckily, it takes a few minutes to get Bethany and the rest of the girls out of the club and into the car waiting for them. God bless Bethany and her planning everything down to the last second because I don't know that I would trust any of them to make it home on their own.

I squeeze Bethany into a tight hug before opening the car door for her. "Text me when you get home, okay?"

"You're not coming with us?" She stumbles into me, her words slurring.

"No, I'm going to take the train so I can get home faster." It's not a total lie, but it also isn't the complete truth. I'll tell her all about my plan tomorrow, assuming it actually works, and assuming she's not so hungover she can't even answer the phone.

"Right. Got an early day of rehearsals tomorrow, I'm sure." It comes out more like *shhhhhhure*.

I don't actually, because tomorrow is Saturday, so all I have is my daily workout and a class, but I don't bother to correct her. "I usually do."

She pats my cheek, her hand lingering for a few seconds too long. "You work too hard, sister of mine. You need to learn how to have some fun. Did you have fun tonight at least?"

I remove her hand from my face and smile. "I did have fun tonight. Just maybe not as much as you." I half lift, half push her into the car, turning to Bethany's co-worker Lyla, the one of the group who's the most sober. "Make sure she drinks some water, please."

The girls all pile into the SUV, shouting goodbyes at various levels of volume and drunkenness. I wait until the car pulls out into traffic before turning on my heel and facing the club entrance once again. It's been about thirty minutes since the show ended, which means I might just have perfect timing. Part of me can't believe what I'm about to do, but the other part, the much larger part, knows I'm willing to do whatever it takes.

Even humiliate myself in front of the most beautiful man I've ever seen.

I take a deep breath and head toward the back of the building.

THREE

Cord

I need a shower. And a drink. And some sleep. Not necessarily in that order.

I probably shouldn't have performed tonight. The week has been long; hell, the month has been long. Paperwork and red-eye flights and tasks I never really thought about when I decided to start my own show.

But I needed to get out there, to remind myself why I started this whole thing in the first place. It's not the screams of the audience—though those certainly don't hurt—it's the rush of performing. The way the light hits your face and the satisfaction that comes with nailing a routine.

Despite the exhaustion, I feel more awake than I have in a long time.

I say my goodbyes to the rest of the guys, promising to join them for a postshow drink next time, even though we all know I likely won't.

Pushing out the backdoor into the cool night air, I pause when I hear Warren engaged with a fan. I'm not in the mood for a run-in, so I hover in the doorway and listen.

"I promise I'm not a fangirl, I just really need to speak to one of the performers."

I roll my eyes. Like Warren hasn't heard that line before.

"As I said, that doesn't happen here. The performers don't speak to audience members after the show." Warren's voice is calm but firm. He's been with me since I opened Six Pact and I hired him because he has the gentleness of a kindergarten teacher and the strength of a bull.

"Right. And I totally don't want to go backstage or anything. I just really need to talk to one of the guys. I'm a hundred percent sure he's going to want to talk to me."

I huff out a silent laugh. I doubt that. We have a pretty strict no fraternization policy here, but even if we didn't, most of my guys are in serious relationships.

"Who exactly are you hoping to talk to?" Warren asks.

"Um, I don't know his exact name, but he's the main one. The tap dancer."

That piques my interest. Not just because she's obviously talking about me, but because of how she chose to describe me.

"Not usually the first descriptor that comes up when people are describing Cord." Warren echoes my thoughts.

"Cord! Yes, that's the one. I really need to talk to Cord. Not about anything weird, I just have a business proposition for him."

"A business proposition, huh?"

"I'm serious! I get that women probably throw themselves at him all the time, but that is so not what this is about!" The indignation in her tone is so clear I almost believe her.

Curiosity gets the better of me and I chance a peek out the door.

Holy shit.

It's her.

The woman from the show.

Of course it's the woman from the show, idiot, I think. But I didn't know it was *the* woman from the show. The one I noticed right away. Not because she was overly invested, but because she seemed like she would rather be anywhere other than sitting in the audience watching us perform. Which is unusual.

Warren sighs, abandoning his post at the door to cross the sidewalk to the woman. "Look, miss, I'm sure you have the best of intentions, but please trust me when I say Cord is not going to want to hear what you have to say. Whatever it is you are planning to offer him, he's not interested. So why don't you save both of us some trouble and just be on your way?"

"I'm not going to be interested in what, exactly?" I push the door open, getting my first clear look at the woman.

She's on the taller side, thin, but clearly toned. Her blond hair hangs in waves down her back and she tosses it when she sees me standing there. Not in a flirtatious way, like it's bothering her and she wants it out of her face. Her breathtakingly beautiful face.

"I was just telling this young woman that she needed to leave, sir." Warren reaches for her elbow, but she takes a step back to avoid his touch.

"And I was just telling him I'm not here for any shady kind of sexual proposition."

I saunter down the two stairs leading from the backdoor, landing just a few feet away from her. "That's a shame." I nod to Warren, dismissing him. He retakes his position blocking the door.

I move so I'm standing directly in front of the woman. She's not as tall as I originally thought—she only comes up to my chest. Her posture is impeccably straight, giving her the appearance of height. My innuendo doesn't register, or if it does, she isn't going to give me the satisfaction of a response.

She's beautiful, that much would be clear to anyone. But it isn't her looks that has my breath stilling in my lungs. There's something more there, something about her.

She pushes her shoulders back, despite her already perfect posture. "I do have a proposition for you, it just happens to be a business one."

I pull out my cockiest grin. "Oh? Are you going to introduce yourself first? Typically, I like to know who it is I'm going to be doing business with."

Her gaze catches on my lips and stays there. I grin even wider. "Allegra Hart."

I stick out my hand. "Cord Donovan."

She hesitates before placing her hand in mine. Her reaction is immediate, a quiet gasp that I would have echoed if I hadn't mentally prepared myself for the sensation of her skin on mine. My fingers tighten around hers and she doesn't pull away. "Nice to meet you, Allegra Hart."

Her eyes—a hazel that looks gray in the dark—flutter closed for a half a second and when she reopens them, she pulls her hand from mine, tucking it behind her back. "I would like to hire you."

My smile fades, and an unexplainable wave of disappointment washes over me. "We don't do private parties, but if you call the box office, they can let you know about the different packages we offer."

She shakes her head. "No, I don't mean the group. I would like to hire you."

I arch an eyebrow. "I thought you said this proposition wasn't sexual."

Her cheeks flush and she directs her gaze to the ground, as if that might hide the pink dancing over her skin. "It's not. I'm a dancer, with Ballet New York, and I have an audition coming up that I need some help with."

It's like someone dumped a bucket of ice water over my head.

Of all the things I expected her to say, that was low on the list.

I drop any hint of flirtation or a smile or friendliness from my face about to kindly but firmly let Allegra—fuck, she's even named after a ballerina—know I have no intention of helping her.

But she rushes on before I can shoot her down. "I'm a soloist, and I'm trying to get promoted to principal—that's like the lead role."

"I know what a principal is."

"And our director is putting together a new piece and the female leading role is a courtesan and I want to audition for the part, but according to my director, I don't have the sex appeal to fully embody the character and so it's something I need to work on and I really didn't have any idea how to go about it, but then I saw your show tonight and it hit me—that's what sex appeal onstage looks like, and so I just thought maybe I could hire you to teach me."

My stomach turns as her words sink in. "I have so many questions."

"Okay?"

"Your director told you that you don't have any sex appeal?" An old, familiar ire burns up my chest.

She rocks up onto her toes and rolls back down again, her calves flexing with the movement. "I mean, I think it was more implied than directly stated, but essentially yes."

I scrub a hand over my face. What a fucking prick, not that that comes as a surprise. Directors of ballet companies usually are. "And you saw the show tonight and now you think I can teach you how to add sex appeal to your dancing?"

"Yes?"

"Jesus Christ." My hand runs through my hair this time, pushing it off my face. It's still sweaty from the show and mercifully stays out of my eyes. I let them study the woman—Allegra. There's a desperation in her gaze, one I know all too well.

"I can pay you," she offers, her voice small.

"I don't need your money." God knows I probably have more of it than she ever will with the way corps dancers get paid. There's no way I can do this. I cannot actually be considering saying yes. "This is a terrible idea."

"Because you don't think I can do it?"

"Because you don't know anything about me." And if she did, if she knew who I was, she wouldn't be here asking me for help. She wouldn't want anything to do with me.

"I know what I saw on that stage."

"You didn't seem all that impressed at the time."

The flush on her cheeks spreads down to her chest, and I do my best not to stare. "I'm not into lap dances."

I take a step closer to her. "If you want to learn how to be sexy, you're going to have to get a lot more comfortable with bodies, Allegra Hart. Both yours and others'."

She swallows thickly, but there's a hint of fire in the depths of her eyes. "Does that mean you'll do it?"

"I want something in exchange, but not your money." *What the fuck am I doing right now?*

"What do you want?" She holds her breath, and I wonder just how much she is willing to give up in order to achieve her ballerina dreams.

"I've been thinking about adding a piece to the show with a female dancer. Something a little more romantic, but still as hot as the rest of the show." I haven't been thinking about adding anything to the show, but it's the best I can come up with on the fly. The only thing I can think of that's legal but might still get her to say no to this farcical plan of hers.

"I can't commit to performing on a nightly basis."

"No need. Choreograph it with me, perform it once or twice to test it in front of an audience, and then I'll find a more permanent dancer." There's no way she's going to go for this, lowering herself to perform in a male revue.

"And in exchange you'll help me prepare for my audition?" She bites her lip.

I nod, swallowing the fear that she might actually say yes. I get closer. "But I have to warn you, I'm going to push you out of your comfort zone, Allegra Hart."

Her pupils expand, drowning out the sparkling gray. "Understood."

Fuck.

Well, at least she's got some backbone. I hold out my hand. "Give me your phone."

She complies without question.

I type a text to my own number and save my contact info. "Now you have my number. I texted you the address of our studio. It's only two blocks from here. Meet me there tomorrow at three o'clock."

She takes her phone back and glances at the screen. "You saved your number under Big Daddy?"

I grin. I'm not sure what kind of disaster I've just gotten myself into, but if this is really going to happen, I'm going to have fun with it. I offer her my hand again. "Pleasure doing business with you."

The cockiness drains out of my smile when her hand slots into mine for the second time. The simple brush of her skin shouldn't be so overwhelming, yet I find myself breaking the contact this time. She smells like rosin, and the hint of pine sends me reeling back in time, to a place I never want to return to.

"I'll see you tomorrow," she says, and she doesn't sound any more confident than I feel.

She turns on her heel and walks down the street, away from me, fading into the darkness.

I watch her until I can no longer see her silhouette in the shadows.

A throat clears behind me.

I don't have to see Warren's face to know he's smiling. "One word and you're fired, Warren."

"Sure thing, boss." He chuckles. "You have a good night now."

Something tells me a good night is not in my future, not with the vision of Allegra Hart burned into my brain.

And not with what I just signed myself up for.

Fuck.

FOUR

Allegra

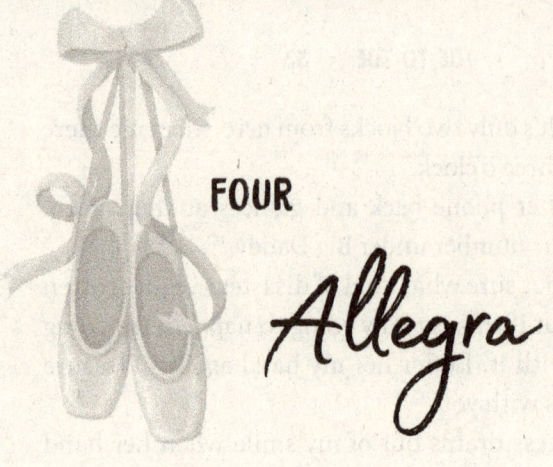

I go to class the morning after Six Pact, but I'm distracted from the moment I step through the door. During each break we have throughout the day, I pull out my phone and type a text to Cord Donovan—I changed his name in my phone the second I got home—canceling our meeting for later this afternoon. Clearly the one drink I had went straight to my head because the whole proposition is ludicrous at best.

But every time I go to send the message, my thumb hovers over the button before moving instead to the backspace, erasing the words I know I should say. I know I shouldn't go meet with him, know I am only asking for trouble. But that doesn't make it any easier to wipe away the one possibility of seeing him again.

Lucy catches up to me as I'm walking out of the BNY building, planning to head to the gym for my workout. "Everything okay, Hart? You didn't quite seem yourself in there today."

I shrug, hoping no one else noticed, though surely if Lucy did, Brianna did as well. Luckily David doesn't come into the studio on the weekends, so at least he didn't see me totally in my head. "Thinking about the audition."

"You going out for the courtesan role?"

"Am I delusional thinking he'll give me a real shot at it?"

Lucy nudges me with her elbow. "If anyone in this company has earned a real shot at principal, it's you."

"That doesn't mean David is going to give it to me."

She mutters something under her breath that sounds a lot like "I'd like to give David a kick in the pants."

For a minute I think about telling her my plan, that in just a couple of hours I'm supposed to be meeting a stripper—sorry, a male entertainer—in the hopes of learning how to convince a man whose advances I rejected that I'm so sexy onstage, he couldn't possibly give anyone else the role.

But the whole thing sounds so stupid, even in my head, that I can't bring myself to say it out loud. I know Lucy would be supportive, though I'm sure she would also have opinions about the whole thing, but it's almost like saying it out loud would make it real, and I don't think I'm ready for that.

Instead of heading to the gym, I go straight back to my apartment, saying goodbye to Lucy, who lives one block farther up the street. Her apartment is way bigger than mine, but she shares it with two roommates. I would happily trade space for peace and quiet, but Lucy is the kind of person who actually likes other people.

I flop onto my bed the moment I walk in the door. Reaching for my phone, I see I have less than an hour to make some kind of decision. But first, I should check on my sister and make sure she's still alive.

ME: So how badly are you hurting right now?

It takes her a few minutes to respond, which is unlike her.

BETHANY: I had to put on my sunglasses before I could unlock my phone and respond to this message.
BETHANY: Why did you let me drink so much? You're supposed to be the responsible one.
ME: I am. I only had one drink and woke up feeling fresh as a daisy.

Not really, since thoughts of a certain someone made it almost impossible to sleep last night.

ME: Was it everything you hoped for and more?
BETHANY: Abso-fucking-lutely.

I laugh out loud. I consider, again, telling her about my whole plan for this afternoon. Bethany always gives me good advice; she's, objectively speaking, the smartest person I know. I also know, instinctively, that she would encourage me to keep my appointment with Cord Donovan, if for no other reason than it's been a really long time since I got laid.

Not that I would sleep with him. Obviously.

ME: Make sure you drink a lot of water today. And eat some protein.
BETHANY: Okay, Mom.
ME: Wow. Rude. May your hangover bleed into tomorrow.
BETHANY: Hey! That is uncalled for.
ME: Call me tomorrow?
BETHANY: You know it.

I send her a pink heart. Indecision is still racking my brain, but the time of my meeting with Cord is rapidly approaching. Chances are he's already left for the studio, so it would be rude to cancel at this point.

At least, that's what I tell myself as I change into something less sweaty. I dress in leggings and an oversized sweatshirt, slipping into my Uggs even though it's not cold enough really. My feet just need a little softness and comfort after a week of rehearsals and classes. I take my long blond hair out of its bun, but I haven't washed it, so I end up tying it right back up.

Eying myself in the mirror, I see I have just enough time to throw on some concealer to deal with the dark circles that never seem to fade from under my eyes.

I should have left myself enough time to take the subway, but I'm cutting it close as is, so I jump into another cab I can't afford. Whatever, it will be worth it if I get the part, and I already need to reach out to Mom and Dad and ask for more money soon anyway.

I'm surprised I haven't heard from my mom today. Usually she likes by-the-minute updates as to how rehearsals and classes are going. I'll take whatever reprieve I can get from her expectations while I can get it.

I arrive at the address in Hell's Kitchen one minute before our scheduled meeting. Eyeing the brick building warily, I pull open the heavy door and make my way up a set of stairs. The landing opens into a huge dance studio, the windows letting in the waning afternoon light, though it has to fight with the surrounding buildings to make its way in. The floors are unscuffed and polished, the mirror on the main wall shiny and minus any cracks. In the far corner of the room, there's a state-of-the-art sound system. The corner closest to the entrance holds several couches that don't look like they came from Craigslist.

It's the nicest studio I've ever been in.

"You made it."

I jump, spinning around to find Cord has crept up behind me. "Jesus, you scared me."

He grins and shrugs. "Sorry."

I turn my attention back to the room because it's easier than holding eye contact with him. Somehow, I feel like staring down a rabid tiger would be easier than holding eye contact with him. "This is a great space."

"Thanks. I finished renovations on it about a year ago."

"You own the floor?" It would be impressive, given the location and the general cost of New York real estate.

"I own the whole building. Our offices are on the next floor up and the top two floors are apartments we rent out to the dancers." He says it without a hint of ego, like all creatives can afford such things.

My mouth drops open. "Wow. The stripping business pays better than I would have thought."

He smirks at my description of his career. "Stripping does pay well, of course, though I consider myself more of a dancer and choreographer. But most of my income comes from ticket sales and franchising fees. Six Pact has locations all over the country."

"So you're the creator of the show?"

"Creator, director, choreographer, business manager. Now I have a team of people helping me, but for a while it was just me."

"Impressive," I say, and I mean it, more than a little envious of the financial security he's created for himself. Most ballet dancers, even the ones known by name, can't hope to make the kind of money Cord is raking in.

"Thanks." He gestures for me to take a seat on one of the cushy-looking chairs. "Shall we get started?"

Suddenly, my stomach spins with nerves. Having the studio space to focus on and talk about has delayed the inevitable—the reason I came here in the first place.

I sit, hovering at the edge of the chair even though it's so comfortable that I long to sink into it. I wait for him to speak, but he watches me with an amused smile tugging on his lips, clearly comfortable to do the same. Finally, I break, the power of his blue eyes too much to handle. "So, like I said last night, I need help."

"With your sex appeal." There's a gentle teasing to his tone, chiding but not unkind.

Still, it doesn't stop the flush from spreading over my cheeks. "Yes." I take a deep breath and force myself to look at him head-on. "I really want this part. I want to prove to my director that I can do this."

Cord's head tilts to the side, causing his dark brown hair to fall across his forehead. "Why does his approval mean so much to you?"

"Because I want to be a principal dancer. It's all I wanted for as long as I can remember. I'm not getting any younger"—I'm only twenty-seven but that's practically ancient in ballet years—"and I feel like this might be my last chance."

"What happens if you never make principal?"

I have to pause before I answer the question, because I honestly don't allow myself to think about it. I don't allow myself to consider what might happen if the one thing I've been working for my whole life never comes to fruition. "I . . . I don't know."

"Will it make you less worthy as a person if it's a goal you never accomplish?" He's not patronizing, but it's a question I can't help but bristle at.

The flush in my cheeks is no longer from embarrassment, but from anger. "I don't see what difference that really makes. I didn't come here for therapy, I came here because I thought you had something to teach me."

Cord nods, seemingly unaffected by my mini-tirade. "Okay. So that's your only concern—be sexy enough onstage that you get this part?"

I ponder his words as I inhale a calming breath, thinking he might want me to say something like *I want this for myself just as much as for the part*, but I don't know that that's true. I mean, sure, it would be nice to feel sexier in my skin and in my body, but the whole concept seems so out of reach and I hate failing. Getting this part feels tangible, even though I know it's a long shot. Anything else would be wishing for too much.

So I nod. "I want this part."

"Okay." Cord rubs his hands along his thighs, encased in jeans that are hugging the thick muscles there. He gestures for me to stand. "Show me what you've got."

FIVE

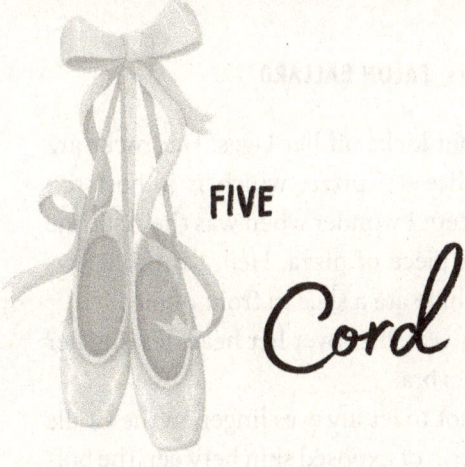

Cord

Allegra freezes, as if my demand is unreasonable. "What do you mean?"

"I need to see what I'm working with. So show me what you can do." I find it hard to believe she didn't expect dancing to be on the program at some point in these dance lessons.

"What, you want me to just get up there and freestyle?"

I shrug. "Sure. Or show me something choreographed, I don't care."

She gestures to her feet. "But I don't have my pointe shoes. I didn't even bring a pair of ballet slippers. All I've got are these."

"You mean to tell me you came to a dance class and didn't bring the proper footwear?"

She glares at me. "I wasn't aware this was an actual dance class."

Damn. She's cute when she's ornery. I don't bother to hold back my smirk. "So take them off and dance barefoot. You mean to tell me a trained dancer with Ballet New York can't dance unless she's got her favorite pair of slippers?"

She scowls at me but kicks off her Uggs. Her socks are covered in cartoon slices of pizza, which is almost too adorable for words except I wonder when was the last time she let herself enjoy a piece of pizza. Hell, I think it was only a year ago that Chloe ate a slice in front of me.

Allegra yanks her sweatshirt over her head, leaving her in leggings and a sports bra.

I fight really hard not to let my eyes linger on the swells of her breasts or the strip of exposed skin between the bottom of her bra and the top of her leggings.

Allegra strides into the center of the room. Though her shoulders are pressed back and her posture is straight, I don't miss the deep breath she heaves as she pulls out her phone and taps on the screen. Once she finds what she's looking for, she slides her phone across the floor and out of the way.

The music starts and it doesn't take more than a few beats before she's completely swept away in it. She loses herself in the choreography, floating around the room like she's dancing on clouds. Her technique is precise, her lines, impeccable. It's clear that she loves it.

I have to swallow forcefully to knock the emotions down. They're rising in my chest, making it hard to catch my breath.

She looks so beautiful, flying across the floor.

But even in just these two minutes, I can see that there is something missing: confidence. Allegra has everything it takes to be a prima ballerina, a principal at BNY if that's what she wants. What she doesn't have is the belief that she's capable of it.

It would be surprising, the lack of faith in her skills and talents, but I've seen it so many times before. Ballet has the tendency to beat the confidence right out of you. And given what her director said to her, the environment at BNY doesn't seem to be focused on building up their dancers. It's more likely that asshole is looking to break her down. Makes it much easier to get away with whatever he wants that way.

I almost wish she'd brought her pointe shoes so I could watch this piece as it's really meant to be danced, but even still, she's breathtaking to watch.

The song ends with a flourish as she hits her final pose. Her chest is heaving, but I pull my eyes away, not willing to be one more man who objectifies her.

I clap my hands, the appreciation for her performance genuine.

Her eyes fly to mine, and there's surprise there, like she expects me to be mocking her.

"Your technique is impeccable." I stand and meet her in the center of the room.

"Thank you." She takes a subtle step back. "Why do I feel like there's a *but* in there somewhere?"

"No *but*. Though we might have our work cut out for us."

"*Though* is just another word for *but*." She bristles at the implication.

"You clearly love to dance, Slippers, but there's something important missing from your performance."

"Pointe shoes?" She doesn't bother hiding the sarcasm.

So there is some fire in her. Good. Now I just need to bring it out.

I shake my head. Reaching out a single finger, I tap the center of her forehead. "You dance here." I move my finger so it's level with her heart, careful not to make contact with her chest. "You need to dance from here."

She scoffs, though I would bet money it's not the first time she's been given that feedback. "Are you going to pretend like you go out on your stage every night and dance from the heart?"

I shrug. "I do. I love what I do, I love being onstage."

"So do I."

I believe her. Who would put themselves through the torture of being a professional ballet dancer if they didn't love it? "But are you having any fun? How do you expect to entertain an audience if you, the performer, aren't having any fun?"

"Ballet isn't supposed to be fun."

I don't hold back my laugh. "Truer words have never been spoken." I tap her forehead again, this time letting my finger linger before it drifts down, dancing over the curve of her cheek. "But my point stands. You're in your head, and we're going to have to work on that."

Something tells me it would be much easier if the problem were with her dancing, and not with her mindset.

I cross to the other side of the room, grabbing a single chair and bringing it back to where Allegra stands, a dumbfounded expression still on her pretty face. "I want to make one thing clear before we go any further here."

She nods, opens her mouth as if to speak, and then closes it again without saying anything.

"If you really want to do this, I'm going to need to push you. You are locked up tight in your comfort zone, and if you really want this, we're going to have to break you out."

She nods again, looking less sure by the moment.

"But everyone has boundaries that shouldn't be crossed. And I need you to promise me you will stop me if I venture too close to yours." I drop any hint of teasing from my voice. This is important, and I need her to know that I am one hundred percent serious.

"Do we need a safe word or something?" Her voice is breathy and her cheeks flush.

I swallow down a breath of my own. "It's not a bad idea."

I close my eyes for the briefest second, tamping down any thoughts of Allegra and activities that might require a safe word. I should not be imagining her spread out on my sheets.

I stifle a groan.

"How about *umbrella*?" she blurts out before I've truly recovered my wits.

Maybe she was paying more attention to my performance the night before than I thought. I let a cocky smile overtake my face, using it as a shield. "*Umbrella* it is." I gesture to the chair. "Now sit."

She does, even as she asks, "Why?"

"Because the first step here is exposure therapy."

"Exposure therapy?" she echoes. "What does that mean?"

I tap on my phone and find the right song. The opening beats of "Pony" thud through the speakers.

The realization of what exposure therapy means dawns on her face. I watch her eyes for any hint of trepidation, but instead, they go wide. Her tongue darts out of her mouth, licking along her bottom lip.

And I realize I might have just made a huge fucking mistake.

"A little cliché, don't you think?" she asks, but the sarcasm has drained from her voice, leaving something that sounds remarkably like wanting behind.

I circle behind her, mostly so I don't have to look her in the eye. "I noticed last night that you did everything in your power to avoid a lap dance." My hands land on her shoulders, pulling her back in the chair. I haven't done a lap dance in quite some time, leaving that portion of the program to the rest of the guys in my show. But I know these moves well, could do them in my sleep if I needed to. So I'm not sure why I feel like I'm doing this for the very first time.

"It wasn't my night. I was there for my sister." The breathiness is back in her voice, laced with anticipation.

"Well, tonight is just about you." I cross back around so I'm standing right in front of her. I need to be able to see her face for this part. "I'm going to put my hands on you. And I'm going to put your hands on me." I don't know if it's a warning or a promise. "What's your word, Slippers?"

"Umbrella."

"Good."

It's the last thing I say.

SIX

Allegra

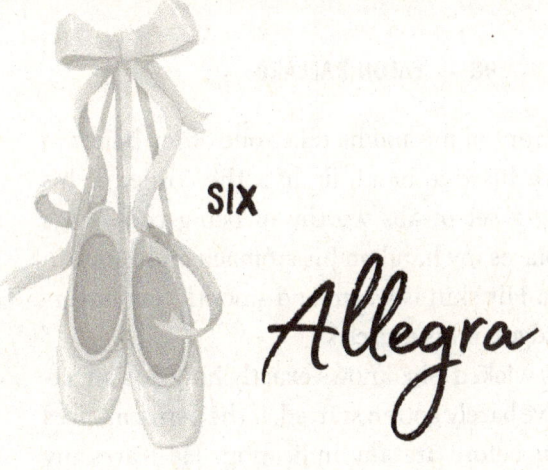

His movement starts slow, finding the intricacies within the music. His hips roll, relaxed and controlled, in a way that makes me automatically think about what else those hips can do. Since they are level with my eyes, it's hard to look away.

I don't want to look away.

The way he moves, the glide of his feet on the floor, the sensuous sway of his body. It's nothing short of mesmerizing. I thought it was captivating last night when he was several yards away from me, separated by an audience and a stage. But here, with him right in front of me . . . I can hardly breathe.

He spins around me and I find my head involuntarily following the motion. His hands land back on my shoulders before they skate down my arms to my wrists. He captures my hands in his, raising them over my head and placing them on his chest. He's still wearing a shirt, but I can feel the heat of his skin through the fabric.

Cord does some kind of handstand on the back of my chair, his arms bending in ways even I can't fathom. He lands back in front of me and he takes one of my hands in his again. With his free hand, he lifts the corner of his shirt, exposing a set of abs worthy of being the show's moniker. He places my hand on his stomach and I suck in a sharp breath. His skin is warm and smooth, my fingers catch on the ridges of his muscles.

His smile is wicked—he knows exactly how he's affecting me and we've barely gotten started, if the performances from the night before are any indication. He leaves my hand pressed flat against his stomach as he reaches behind his neck to tug his shirt over his head.

And look.

Male ballet dancers have some of the most gorgeous bodies I've ever seen.

But Cord Donovan is on a whole other level.

I swallow thickly and he lowers himself so he's practically sitting on my lap, his thighs bracing my hips. When he begins that sensuous hip-roll move again, he's so close to my core that I worry he might feel the heat that's burning me up from the inside out.

He takes my chin in his hand, bringing my gaze up so our eyes are locked.

Somehow, being the sole focus of his blue eyes is even more breathtaking than the feel of his body moving over mine.

He trails a single finger down the center of my chest, down my bare stomach, pausing just above the waistband of my leggings.

He lets it hover there, his grin never faltering. Dropping to his knees on the floor in front of me, his hands grip the tops of my thighs, pushing them open, making room for his broad shoulders.

I can't stifle the gasp because suddenly his mouth is right there. Sure, there are layers of fabric between us, but the warmth of his breath seeps through and I shiver.

He wraps my legs around his shoulders, and I know what's coming, saw it several times during the show last night, but it still catches me off guard when he stands. His face is pressed in between my legs and before I can latch on to something to stabilize me—not that I need to with Cord's strong hands anchored on my hips—he's flipped me around.

Now not only is his face in between my legs, but my face is level with his crotch.

I should be disgusted or appalled, I should be shouting my safe word.

But all I really want to do is tug on his belt, loosen the waistband of his tight jeans.

My back hits the floor, gently, Cord's body shifting and spinning once more. He hovers over me, the muscles in his arms straining as he dips his weight. His hips press into mine and an unfamiliar sensation shoots through my veins.

I want him.

Normally I don't have enough free time or free headspace to want anyone. But right now, in this moment, desire is all I can feel.

My breaths quicken as Cord lands on his knees in between my thighs. He tugs me up into a sitting position, his hands once again placing mine on the bare skin of his chest. He's slightly sweaty, a little sticky, but I like it. This time when he drags them down over his stomach, he places mine on the belt at his waist.

I don't know if he was reading my thoughts, or if every

woman he gives a lap dance to longs for this moment, but I follow his lead, yanking the belt loose from his jeans.

He unbuttons and unzips, directing my hands to circle around, slide in between the fabric of his pants and the cotton of his underwear and latch onto his ass. It's firm underneath my fingers and he grins as they dig in.

His own fingers linger at the front of his pants. He cups himself over his boxer briefs and somehow that simple movement is the hottest thing I've ever seen.

His hand slips into the waistband of his underwear, tugging it down, revealing the slightest hint of dark hair underneath.

Right as the song comes to an end.

The cocky grin Cord has been wearing throughout the entire dance fades. He jumps up from his spot kneeling in between my legs, fastening the button on his jeans and tightening the belt.

He reaches down a hand to help me up and I almost push it away, not sure I can handle another brush of his skin on mine. But I'm also not sure my leg muscles are working properly and the last thing I need is to try to stand on my own and fall flat on my face.

So I slip my hand into his. The moment I'm back on two feet, I drop it.

He takes several steps away from me, his hands coming to rest on his hips as the silence threatens to drown me.

After what is probably only seconds but feels like hours, he swipes his shirt from the floor and tugs it over his head. He runs a hand through his hair, pushing it back from his face. Thanks to the sweat, it stays in place, showing off his perfect cheekbones.

"So," I say, making my way over to the couch. I pull on

my sweatshirt, letting my fingers tangle in the soft cotton hem so I don't have to figure out what to do with my hands. "What comes next?"

Cord clears his throat and for the first time, avoids my eyes. "Look, Slippers, I can teach you the moves. I can show you how to roll your hips and bat your eyes, but it isn't all about the choreography."

"It's not?"

He beckons for me to join him in front of the mirror. I stand in front of him, facing our reflection. He pushes my shoulder blades inward, slouching my posture in a way that feels completely unfamiliar. My sweatshirt slips off one shoulder, but I make no move to right it. "Right now, you think of your body as a tool. It's what allows you to dance. You think in terms of pointed feet and straight lines."

I straighten my shoulders the moment he releases his hand from my back. "What else should I think about my body then?"

"Think about all the ways your body can bring you pleasure." He smirks, watching my breath still in my chest, his eyes lingering on the line of my collarbone. "The taste of a really good meal. The exhilaration of pushing your body and the adrenaline that comes with it. A hot bath after a long day." He trails a single finger over my exposed shoulder, goose bumps exploding in the wake of his touch. "That first touch from a new lover."

I don't say anything because I know if I open my mouth right now, I will either collapse into a pile of nervous giggles or throw up and, honestly, I'm not sure which is worse.

His eyes meet mine in the reflection in the mirror. "Let's meet again in three days. Before then, I want you to find pleasure in your body. Start thinking about it as something more than just a tool."

My inner people pleaser immediately nods, agreeing to his instructions before I have time to consider if I truly even know what he means. It's been so long since I've done anything just for pleasure's sake, unless you count staring at hours of Bravo at the end of a long day, and somehow I don't think binge-watching reality TV is the kind of thing he has in mind.

"Take a picture of whatever it is you end up doing and text it to me."

I raise one eyebrow. "You expect me to send you a photo of myself in the bath?"

If I didn't know better, I'd say that was a flush creeping over his perfect cheekbones, but something tells me it will take more than one semiflirty comment to get under Cord Donovan's skin.

"Let's meet here on Tuesday. What time works for you?"

"After dinner? Maybe eight?" I'm already dreading the added hours after a day full of class and rehearsal, but I remind myself to keep my eye on the prize. It will all be worth it once that part is mine.

Cord nods. "Sounds good." He checks his phone. "Want me to get you a cab?"

I shake my head, knowing I can't afford another pricey taxi. "I'm going to take the subway."

He doesn't offer to walk me to the nearest station, which is good because I don't know if I can handle much more time in his presence.

So I give him an awkward wave and head toward the elevator. "See you in a couple days."

"Hey Slippers," he calls as I step through the doors into

the elevator. "Make sure you bring your dancing shoes next time."

I flip him off right as the doors are closing, but it doesn't cut off the sound of his laughter. Luckily, it does hide the wide smile that spreads across my face at the sound.

I MANAGE TO MAKE IT THROUGH SUNDAY AND MONDAY WITHout thinking too much about Cord Donovan.

That's a lie.

Obviously.

Every moment that I'm not thinking about dance, I'm thinking about Cord. Many moments when I *should* be thinking about dance, I'm thinking about Cord.

It's not just how ridiculously hot he is, or how, when I got home after our first session, I whipped out my dusty vibrator and came harder than I have in a very long time.

It's his words, his directive. His homework I've been completely ignoring.

I've had an entire lifetime of treating my body like it exists purely for ballet's sake. I don't know how to think any differently. I don't know that I *want* to think any differently. I'm so close to getting everything I've worked my whole life for, it doesn't seem like now is the time to switch off that part of my brain.

Still, I am nothing if not a good student, so I spend most of my Tuesday morning company class thinking of something quick and easy I could do to find a moment of pleasure, something I can accomplish before meeting Cord tonight.

A bath is out since my apartment isn't big enough for a tub. And I know myself well enough to know I have a lot more work to do on my mind before I can think about food as anything other than fuel for dancing.

I could go get a pedicure, but my feet are a mess and I know I would spend the entire time apologizing to the nail technician for having to deal with my battle-worn toes.

Lucy and I sit together over lunch and I decide to ask her for her input, as she seems like the kind of person who lets herself feel joy whenever she damn well pleases.

"If you had to do something this afternoon solely for the sake of finding pleasure in it, what would you do?"

Her hand freezes, fork full of pasta halfway to her mouth. "Are you asking me about getting myself off? I'm not opposed to sharing secrets, but I didn't know we were that kind of friends, Allegra."

"Haha." I wad up my napkin and throw it at her. "That's not what I mean at all. I just mean something simple. Something not dance related. Something to just bring yourself some joy."

She shrugs. "I'd probably get myself a latte and stroll around one of my favorite bookstores."

"Hmm. That could work." I don't really like reading, never really had the time for it outside of finishing whatever books were required for my homeschool credits, but it doesn't sound like such a terrible way to spend the afternoon.

Lucy sets down her fork on her plate. "What do you mean that *could work*? Work for what?"

My cheeks flush because the last thing I want to do is tell one of my colleagues that I'm being tutored by a stripper to prep for an audition. On the other hand, I need to tell someone, and Lucy is not the kind of person who would judge me. "So the other night I went to see that Six Pact show, for my sister's bachelorette party."

Her eyes light up. "Fuck yes, I love that show! Ohmygod please tell me you got a lap dance from one of those super-hot hunks and it led to you exchanging numbers and now you're meeting up to have a torrid affair."

"Um, no. Not exactly."

"Darn it. I was hoping to live vicariously." She goes back to eating her pasta. "Okay, so you went to Six Pact and...?"

I cut up my grilled chicken breast into tiny pieces so I don't have to make eye contact. "Well, I did talk to one of the dancers after the show, but not for hookup purposes. I asked him if he would help me work on some things I need to improve before the auditions."

"What is a dancer from Six Pact going to teach you that you aren't learning in class here, or don't already know?"

"How to be sexy," I mumble, shoving a bite in my mouth in the hopes the words get lost.

She sets her fork down again, this time with purpose. "Who the hell gave you the impression that you aren't sexy already?"

"Who do you think?" I can see Lucy is building up to go on a tirade, so I keep talking before she gets the chance to butt in. "Anyway, one of the things he told me to do was to stop thinking about my body as merely a tool for ballet and start thinking about it like a vessel for pleasure."

"Did he use those exact words, *vessel for pleasure*?" She waggles her eyebrows.

"Lucy, you are not helping." I pick at my chicken, wishing it had an ounce of flavor to make it even slightly palatable.

"Okay, okay, I'm sorry. So you need to find something

that brings you pleasure and has nothing to do with dance?"

I nod, wondering if I look as hopeless as I feel.

"Well, what are your other hobbies?"

"I don't have any hobbies. Ballet is my whole life."

Lucy closes her eyes in exasperation. "That is the saddest thing I've ever heard."

"Gee, thanks."

"You're welcome." She pats my hand. "Okay, if hobbies are out, is there some place you like to go and visit? Some place that brings you peace?"

I spear a piece of spinach from my salad. "You're going to laugh at me."

"Highly likely." At least she's honest.

"I love to go to Times Square."

Lucy visibly gags, and I can't really blame her. Lucy moved to New York as a teen, but I've been here my whole life and I should know better.

"I know, I know. It's gross. It's full of tourists and reeks of capitalism and it's everything that's wrong with the city."

"Yes, and?"

I shrug. "There's just something about it. I go there when I feel lonely. You never have to be alone in Times Square."

"Shit, it's kind of poetic when you put it like that." She wipes her mouth daintily with her napkin. "Sounds like you've got your after-rehearsal plans then."

"I guess so."

And so, even though I'm not totally sold on the idea, once ballet obligations are done for the day, I hop on the crowded subway, get off at 42nd Street, and make my way into the throngs of people clogging Times Square. It's evening, dinnertime, right before the night's shows are set to begin, so the streets are teeming with tourists. There's lots of pointing and posing with creepy characters and guys asking if I want to go to a free comedy show. It's some New Yorkers' version of hell, but I can't help but feed off the frenetic energy.

I treat myself to a nonfat decaf latte and find a spot at one of the spindly red tables in the center of the action, where I settle in to play my favorite game: tourist or New Yorker. For the New Yorkers, how long have they been here—less than five years, five to ten years, or lifers? Particularly in this location, it's usually an easy game to win. But sometimes people surprise you.

I take a photo of my latte sitting on the table, the bright lights of Times Square in the background, a kaleidoscope of colors competing with the sunset. First, I send it to Cord, then I post it on my Instagram while I wait for his response, sure that it's going to be ninety percent mocking.

CORD: Cutting it a little close, aren't we?

Okay, so mocking, but not in the way I expected it to be.

ME: My schedule isn't exactly filled with free time. And besides, I got it in before the deadline, that's all that matters.
CORD: See you in a couple hours, Slippers.

I send him the pointe shoes emoji.

Checking the time on my phone, I make a plan for the best use of the two hours until my lesson with Cord. I'm closer to his neighborhood than I am to mine, which means it wouldn't make sense to go all the way home, only to turn around and head right back. I had planned on showering and changing, but what would be the point of that if I'm just going to be dancing more?

Surely I don't need to make myself pretty and fresh for Cord Donovan.

So going home is out.

But as much as I'm enjoying my little New York City respite, I don't want to stay here for two more hours.

I send the text before I let myself think on it too much.

ME: Since I'm already in your neck of the woods, did you want to go grab dinner somewhere?

I immediately regret it, mostly because who under the age of forty says "neck of the woods"? Also because there's a good chance he'll read that and take it the wrong way, like I'm asking him out on a date, which I definitely am not.

CORD: I would love to, but I'm actually in a rehearsal right now. Got a new guy joining the show this weekend.
CORD: You're welcome to come to the theater if you want. We can walk over to the studio together after.
ME: Are you going to make him give me a lap dance?

Not that it matters, I'm already hoisting my dance bag over my shoulder and tossing my empty coffee cup in a nearby trash can.

CORD: Probably.
CORD: Don't worry. It won't be as good as mine.
ME: I'll be the judge of that.

I'm already a couple of blocks closer to the Six Pact performance space when my phone rings. I answer it without looking at the screen and immediately regret it.

"Sweetheart. Did I see that you're in Times Square?"

I hold back the sigh, but just barely. "Yes, Mom. I just stopped for a quick cup of coffee."

"What are you doing all the way downtown? Shouldn't you be in rehearsal?"

Forget it. I let the sigh free. "Rehearsals are done for the day. I'm actually taking some extra classes to help me prepare for an upcoming audition and the studio's in Hell's Kitchen."

She perks up. "Extra classes? That's what I like to hear. As long as nothing you're doing is going to interfere with David's methods."

David's methods can go fuck themselves, I think, but would never dare dream of saying, especially not to her.

"It's not interfering with anything, Mom. In fact, I'm just arriving at the studio. I'll call you later."

"Okay, sweetie. Let us know if you need help paying for these new classes. You know your father and I are happy to give you whatever you need for ballet."

It's a generous offer, and one I'll probably need to take her up on, but for the moment, I shrug it off.

I lie to her and tell her I don't need money before disconnecting the call and shoving my phone in my jacket pocket.

I'm still in the clothes I pulled on before leaving the ballet studio, sweatpants pulled over my tights and a light jacket blocking out the early-spring evening chill, and I'm starting to rethink my choice not to go home and change.

But it's too late now. Besides, it's not like I need to impress Cord Donovan. I don't care what he thinks anyway.

I keep repeating the lie to myself, over and over, until I reach the theater, my stomach fluttering as I pull open the heavy door, knowing Cord waits on the other side.

SEVEN

Cord

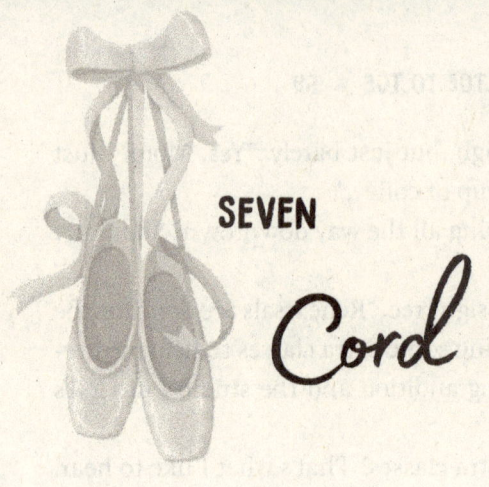

I shove my phone back in my pocket and return my attention to the four men standing onstage with me, three of whom are giving me looks that I don't like.

"Who ya texting, boss?" Noah, my dance captain and the closest thing I have to a best friend, nudges me with his elbow.

Josh waggles his thick black eyebrows up and down. "You're smiling."

"No, I'm not." I purposefully turn my lips down.

"Has the day finally arrived?" Noah throws his arms wide, always the drama queen. His golden brown skin shines with sweat under the stage lights. This is just a rehearsal so there's no need for him to be shirtless, but he takes every opportunity to show his eight-pack. "Has the great Cord Donovan finally found someone to crush on?"

I roll my eyes. "Enough. Let's get back to work so we can get out of here."

"Got a hot date?" Brayden quips with a flip of his hair.

"You're all fired." I nod to Austin, the only one not joining in on the ribbing, but probably only because he's new. "Except you."

Austin smiles and gets back into his opening position.

I point at him. "He's my favorite."

The rest of them grumble but fall back in line. We only make it through the routine once before the door to the theater opens.

Allegra sneaks in on quiet feet and slides into a seat in the back like we might not notice she's there.

Every single one of us notices.

"You made it." I know I need to get ahead of this before the guys jump to conclusions. Though knowing them, there's no stopping them from jumping to conclusions. "Everyone, this is Allegra Hart, ballet dancer extraordinaire. We're going to be working on that piece I told you about. Allegra, this is Josh, Brayden, Noah, and Austin."

They all take the opportunity to abandon their positions and come to the edge of the stage, scoping out the new addition.

"Hello." Allegra waves, her movements small and timid. "Thanks for letting me crash your rehearsal."

"Damn, Cord, you never let anyone crash rehearsal," Josh says. I don't miss the way his hand moves to tug up on the fabric of his shirt, showing off his dark brown skin and ridges of abs.

"Seriously, man," Brayden joins in with another toss of his perfect nineties hair. "My sister came in from California just to see me and you wouldn't even let her through the front door."

"Yeah, well, you know the drill. My show, my rules." I try to sound harsh, but I know none of them buy it. "Let's run the number from the top." I hop off the stage, making my way through the chairs and tables to slide into the seat next to Allegra's.

The guys get set in place, the music starts, and instead of watching my dancers, I'm watching her, noticing every hint of her reactions. She tries to hide it but she's impressed. I imagine it's grudging but she's still impressed.

The song ends and the guys hit their final pose. Allegra's applause is genuine and enthusiastic.

"Any notes?" I lean in, getting a whiff of something floral and soft. I don't pull away, letting myself linger next to her under the guise of needing to hear her response.

She swallows thickly. "The new guy . . ."

"Austin."

"Austin is a half a beat late on most of the steps."

I nod, rising from my seat and strolling to the stage. I pull Austin aside and give him the note. I could have just called out the directive from my position in the audience, but I prefer to address corrections one-on-one, something I decided to do early on and have never wavered from.

I stay by the stage so I watch the number instead of Allegra. The guys run it again, and this time, Austin's timing is perfect.

"Amazing. That was spot-on." I clap my hands together, then check my watch. "Why don't you guys get out of here. I'll see you all tomorrow for the full run-through."

Austin flags me down to ask some questions while Josh and Brayden head backstage. I watch out of the corner of my eye as Noah jumps from the stage and crosses over to where Allegra sits.

Something stirs in my gut, an unfamiliar feeling I don't want to even try to give a name to. I rush Austin out and stride over to break up the conversation between my best friend and my student.

"Is this guy harassing you, miss?" I clap a hand on Noah's shoulder only slightly harder than I normally would.

"Who, me?" The smile never leaves Noah's face as he stands and claps me back so hard I flinch. "It was nice to meet you, Allegra Hart. Looking forward to seeing you dance." He waves over his shoulder as he heads backstage.

I find myself studying her face once again, watching for any hint of interest to spark in her eyes. But she turns them back on me instead of watching Noah walk away. I don't acknowledge the relief that comes with that.

"Did you end up eating dinner on your own?" I ask. I know to tread lightly when it comes to ballerinas and food, but I want to make sure she eats something.

She shakes her head. "No, but I can get something at home when we're done."

"You sure? My place is in between here and the studio. We could stop and at least have a snack before our lesson." I don't know why I offer. The last thing I should be doing is inviting this woman to my home. I don't invite anyone over.

"I'm good." Her voice squeaks a bit, and I smile.

"Okay, shall we head out then?" I lead her to the front of the building and out to the street.

The air has turned chilly as the sun has gone down. Allegra zips her jacket all the way up and tucks her hands into her pockets.

"It's just the two blocks," I say, then kick myself for not being able to come up with anything more intelligent than that.

Luckily the walk is short and the studio is warm, and the silence between us feels comfortable and not stilted.

Allegra tosses her bag onto one of the chairs and takes off her jacket, revealing a light pink leotard underneath. "What do you want me in?"

I halt in my tracks on the way to turn on the speakers, stopped by the vision of Allegra wearing exactly what I want her in. "I'm sorry?"

She gestures to her feet, currently clad in Ugg boots. "Slippers or pointe?"

"Oh. Right." I turn my back to her as if I'm focused on the stereo and not on calming my racing heart. "Slippers are fine for today, Slippers." I flip the switch in the speakers and keep the music low. We're not dancing tonight, but having a background beat will help.

"So what exactly is the plan for tonight?" She kicks off her Uggs and slips into a pair of soft pink shoes.

I sink into the armchair across from her. "First, let's talk about your homework."

Her back straightens. "I completed it, as asked."

"Kind of a last-minute finish there."

She shrugs, but I can see the tension in her shoulders. "You told me to have it done before our next meeting, and I did."

"So what about your afternoon in Times Square brought you pleasure?" I don't know why I'm bothering to interrogate her, it's not as if these made-up assignments really matter—I'm flying by the seat of my pants when it comes to these lessons—but I find myself wanting to hear her answer.

She bites her lip as she thinks. "Times Square is someplace I like to go when I'm feeling lonely. Being there makes me feel safe, I guess."

"Were you feeling lonely this afternoon?" I hate the thought of that, but I hate even more that her answer has an effect on me.

She shrugs again and it's still anything but casual. "Not particularly. But you asked me to do something that brings me pleasure and that's what I did."

The word *pleasure* dances across my skin.

Fuck. I need to get myself under control here.

I lean forward, resting my elbows on my knees. "Can I ask you a personal question, Slippers?" I wait for her to nod before I continue. "When was the last time you were with someone who satisfied you? Sexually speaking, I mean." So much for getting myself under control. I don't know where the audacity for the question comes from, but that doesn't keep me from needing to know her answer.

She sucks in a breath. "I don't date a lot."

"I didn't ask about dating."

She meets my gaze and there's fire in the depths of those hazel eyes. "I'm not the kind of person who enjoys casual sex. It doesn't work for me."

"Is that because you don't feel a connection to the person or because the people you've been with have been bad in bed?" Something gnaws in my stomach at the thought of this woman's partners not doing everything in their power to bring her pleasure.

She considers the question. "Probably a little of both. My job and my schedule don't exactly allow me a lot of free time to go out and meet new people, so it makes dating hard unless I want to date within the company."

Dating within the company, it goes unsaid, is never a good idea.

I sit back in my chair, dragging my hands along my thighs, still clad in warmup pants, doing my best to get my runaway thoughts under control.

"Where did you train?" she asks when I let the silence linger too long. "Noah mentioned he went to a prestigious ballet school and I assume as the director you've had professional training, too."

"What?" I deflect, not about to address that inquiry.

"I was just curious about your training."

"Don't worry, I've got the necessary skills to teach you what you need to know." I hop out of my chair and stride to the middle of the room. "Let's get started."

She follows me, standing center and facing the mirror.

I move behind her. "I'm going to touch you again during our lesson. Do you remember your word?"

"Umbrella." She peeks over her shoulder. "You don't have to warn me you're going to touch me every time. I've been dancing since I was three. Guys are always putting their hands on me."

My mouth pulls down. "Yes, well, in my studio, people ask before touching other people's bodies." I hold up my hands. "May I?"

She watches my reflection, thoughtfully parsing out my words in her head. "You may."

My hands find their place on her waist. "One of the main differences between what you do when dancing ballet and what dancers like the ones in my show do, aside from the entertainment factor, is in the hips."

"Are you trying to imply that ballet is boring?" Her breath catches as my hands trail down to her hips.

"I don't think anyone could argue that ballet is more entertaining than my show."

"Yes, well, not everyone enjoys watching a bunch of sweaty men rip their clothes off. Some people have culture and taste."

"Perhaps we should compare ticket sales and see whether or not that's true." I grin at her in the mirror. "Can you roll your hips for me?"

She tries, I'll give her that. But the movement is stiff, her torso seemingly unable to bend. My hands, still resting on her hips, barely move.

"You've been trained to focus on your lines, but if you really want your performance to be imbued with sex appeal, you need to forget about lines and focus on curves."

She grimaces at that, and I wonder if there's a story there. While Allegra is lean and obviously fit, she does have more curves than the average ballerina. Not that I let my eyes linger or anything.

I shift my hands, spreading my fingers wide over her hips. I force them to stay gentle, not greedy. "Like this." I guide her hips in a circle, smirking at her resistance. "Stop fighting me."

She takes a deep breath and lets it out slowly. Her shoulders sink in an attempt to relax her muscles.

"You're still working against me, Slippers." The words come out in a whisper after a few more hip-roll attempts. I take a step closer to her and suddenly our bodies are pressed together, my hips settled right behind hers.

That floral scent nearly overwhelms my senses and I have to fight not to recognize how perfectly her hips flush with mine, the soft curve of her ass nestling against me.

This time, instead of using my hands to stir her body in

a circle, I use my own hips, the two of us moving as one. I do it again, rolling us in the opposite direction. It's the hottest thing that's happened to me in far too long. "Good. That's much better." I practically choke on the words.

"Much better," she echoes, voice faint and breathy.

That's how we spend the next half hour, my hips pressed against hers, my hands on her waist, as I try to get her to loosen up her muscles and forget all the things ballet has ingrained in her.

Finally, I have her try the motions on her own. She doesn't watch herself in the mirror, as if she's afraid of what she might see.

I let her run through the series of movements, my eyes never leaving her. Once she finishes, she goes back to the beginning, ready to do it all again, but I hold up a hand to stop her. "You didn't look at yourself once the entire time."

She shrugs. "So?"

"Do you normally watch yourself during ballet?"

"Depends. I do most of the time during class, sometimes during rehearsal." She fidgets with the waistband of her leggings.

I move behind her once again, directing us to face the mirror. "Tell me something about me that you find attractive."

She glances over her shoulder with a scoff. "Seriously?"

"I have a point, and I promise it's not just to stroke my ego."

Her eyes flutter. She sighs, studying my reflection. "You have nice eyes."

"Thank you." I grin. "Tell me another one."

"Your smile is perfect, even if it is cocky."

This stirs a laugh. "My parents will be happy to know

the thousands of dollars of braces were worth it. One more."

Her voice softens. "You have really good hands. They're sturdy and your grip is gentle but still makes me feel safe."

It takes me a second to recover from that one. "I'm glad you feel that way with me." I clear my throat. "Now. Tell me three things about yourself that you find attractive."

Her mouth opens and closes, no words coming out for a second. "I don't really see how that's going to help anything."

I step around her so we're side-by-side. "Humor me."

"I guess I don't think about myself that way."

I gesture toward the mirror. "Well, now's the time to start. Look at yourself. If you were a stranger and saw you walking down the street, what would you notice? What would catch your attention?"

She takes a tiny step away from me, her eyes locked on her reflection. Those eyes are so expressive, and they swirl with emotions. I want to parse out every single one of them.

I stay quiet. She turns to meet my eyes, and I see so much of my former self there. I reach out my hand and she slips hers into it. I tug her closer to the mirror, stepping behind her once again. "Should I tell you what I find most attractive about you, Slippers?"

She swallows thickly. "You don't have to do that."

I wonder if she thinks I would be lying, finding things about her for the purpose of the assignment. As if she didn't take my breath away the very first time I saw her.

"I want to." I take her chin in my hands, gently turning her eyes back to the mirror. "Your smile. I admit, you don't give it to me often, but that night at the show, when you were talking with your friends, it lit up your whole face."

She freezes, holding completely still.

"The second thing I noticed, and I'll apologize in advance for my stereotypical man-who-likes-women reaction, is your breasts. They're perfect."

I can't help but notice her nipples pebble under the thin fabric of her leotard, and I have to force myself to swallow.

"And the third thing?" she prompts after a silent minute.

"Your eyes. They're so expressive, yet mysterious."

There's an awkwardly long pause, the two of us staring at each other through the mirror. Not for the first time, I wonder if all of this is a huge mistake.

"Ready for your homework?" I ask when I can take the silence no more.

She nods.

"Our next lesson will be Saturday night. After my show. Up until then, I want you to text me each day with something about yourself you find attractive."

She lets out a sigh, but I already see a wall coming up between us.

I step around her, bringing us face-to-face. "Be honest with me. And be honest with yourself, Slippers. How can you expect others to find you attractive if you don't feel that way yourself?"

"You know, when I asked you for these lessons, I thought you were going to show me something practical I could take with me into my audition."

The corner of my mouth quirks up. "Doubting my methods?"

She bristles. "Just wondering if you really have methods, or if this is all some kind of silly game for you."

I drop my smile. "This isn't a game, Slippers. I can't promise you you'll get this part, but I can promise that when this whole thing is over, you'll understand that you are bigger than ballet." I clench my hands into tight fists at my sides and I don't say anything more. Anything incriminating.

She lets the silence linger for a moment.

"Where are we meeting on Saturday night?"

I cross to the far side of the room, needing some space to breathe. "I'll text you the address. We're going to take a little field trip."

"Can't wait." She tries to sound sarcastic, but I hear the truth in her words.

Because I can't wait either.

EIGHT

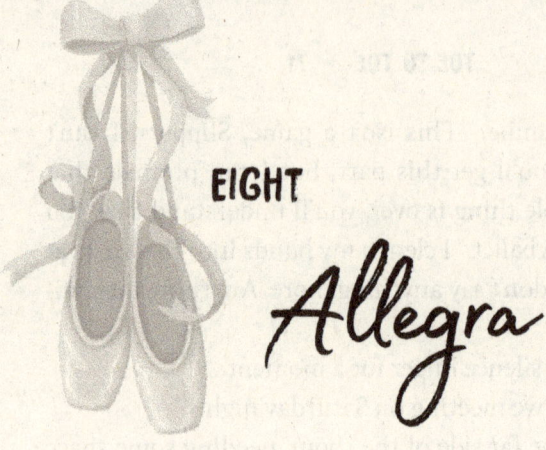
Allegra

I wait until ten o'clock the next night before I complete my homework. I wanted to wait until 11:59, but I'm tired and have to wake up early and sleep is calling my name.

I stand in front of the mirror in my bathroom, examining myself in a way I don't normally allow. I'm not here to paint my face with stage makeup, I'm not studying my body for flaws that need fixing. I look at myself as a stranger might.

My long dirty-blond hair is down, freshly washed after my shower. It spends so much of its time up in a bun, I often forget that it's thick and shiny, that I can let it air dry and wear it naturally, without having to spend a ton of time styling it. After a second of running my fingers through the damp strands, I pick up my phone.

ME: I like my hair. I wish I had more occasions to wear it down, but I like that it's long and shiny.
CORD: That wasn't so hard was it?
CORD: And I agree, your hair is gorgeous.

It's a simple sentence via text message, and yet, it sends a ripple of butterflies soaring through my stomach.

ME: Thanks.
CORD: Hope you had a good day.
ME: You too. Good night.
CORD: Night, Slippers.

The next day I wait until I've stepped out of the shower after a long day of class and rehearsal. We have performances starting in just two weeks, which means everyone is cranky and rehearsals are running longer than normal. I'm tired and sore, but I still take a few minutes in front of the mirror, studying my reflection and doing my best to only think of the positives.

ME: I have a good nose. It's not too big, and not too small.
CORD: Your nose is adorable.
CORD: Hope you had a great day.
ME: It was long, but good. Hope you had a great day too.
CORD: Good night, Slippers.
ME: Good night, Cord.

The following night, I text him as I'm heating up dinner after another grueling day. It hurts just to stand, my legs worked to the point where they've almost gone numb. I don't need to study myself in the mirror because I noticed something during class today.

ME: I like that my legs are visibly toned, that you can see the hard work I've put in reflected in my body.
CORD: Not going to lie, your legs are fucking gorgeous.

The microwave beeps, but it takes a minute before I can tear my eyes away from the screen of my phone. I take my plate of grilled chicken and vegetables to the table.

CORD: I know it's last minute, but do you have plans tonight?
ME: I'm just sitting down to a gourmet dinner.

I snap a photo of my meal and send it to him.

CORD: I hate to tear you away from that culinary masterpiece, but any chance you'd want to go see a show with me tonight?

My heart skips a beat. I didn't know it could actually do that, but I feel the flutter in my chest.

ME: What kind of show?
CORD: An entertaining one 😊

I should say no. Obviously. I have rehearsal tomorrow and a show to prepare for. Not to mention my upcoming audition. I need to be at the top of my game for the next few weeks.

CORD: I think it could actually help with our lessons, if that convinces you.
ME: Fine. I'm in. Send me the info.

I was already convinced, but if there's any way to write this off as a necessary excursion, I'll take it.

I hurry through dinner so I have time for a quick shower, though I don't have much time for hair and makeup. Which is fine. If we're going to a show, we're just going to be sitting in the dark anyway.

When I rush from the subway, he's waiting for me outside the theater, dressed in dark jeans and a blue button-up with the sleeves rolled up. I breathe a sigh of relief that I didn't dress too casually in my jeans and form-fitting sweater.

"Slippers." He grins as I approach.

I roll my eyes at the ridiculous nickname, though I can't fight back a smile, and take in the unassuming brick building behind him. It reminds me of the Six Pact theater and I don't think that bodes well for the rest of my evening. "So what are we seeing?"

"It's a surprise." He offers me his arm and leads me through the front doors.

The interior space is small and intimate. Like at Six Pact, there aren't rows of seats, but tiny café tables and spindly chairs circling the performance area. A host leads us to one, dropping off menus before he departs. When our server comes by, I order a sparkling water. Cord has been perusing the cocktail offerings on the menu, but he asks for the same.

Once our drinks have been delivered, Cord leans his elbows on the small table, leaving only inches of space separating us. "How was rehearsal today?"

"Good, I think." I take a sip of water and wait for him to fill the silence. When he doesn't, I continue. "I don't have a main role in this one, so the pressure isn't too terribly high, but I am dancing an important part."

"What show are you doing?"

"*Swan Lake*. Have you ever seen it?"

Cord makes a face. "A long time ago. My sister used to be pretty into ballet."

I grin. "Your sister seems like a wise and very cool person."

He sits back in his seat though his eyes never leave my face. "She is. We're twins, actually."

"Oh god. Poor thing." I snort. "Her, obviously, not you."

"Haha." His tone is dry, but a smile tugs at the corner of his mouth.

As the lights in the room begin to dim, I realize that this is kind of fun. Aside from my sister, I don't tease anyone else much. I have no interest in Cord himself, clearly, but I can't lie and say this whole thing has been terrible so far.

A single spotlight comes up on the stage. A woman has her back to us, one leg up on a black chair. She's wearing a top hat, long white gloves, and a gorgeous red silk dress. The music starts and it's low and sultry. The woman spins around, dangling her hand toward the audience. She begins to remove her glove, the movements small, almost effortless. And yet, looking around the room, it's easy to see that this woman has the crowd in a trance. We're all fixated on this almost mundane motion, waiting for her to show us more.

And she shows us more. By the end of her number, she's down to her panties and a pair of tasseled pasties.

I lean over to Cord as she sashays offstage. "So, this is the lesson, right?"

He shrugs. "I already had tickets for the show, so I would've come either way. But I think you can see how it's relevant."

"I mean, it's easy to be sexy when you're taking off your clothes." Which is not something I plan on doing in front of David, at auditions or any other time.

He shakes his head, directing his attention back to the stage where the next performer is getting set in place. "It's not about that, Slippers."

I refocus on the performers and try to think about what

he means by that. Obviously there's more to being sexy than just being naked, and being naked doesn't automatically equal sexy. So I home in on those smaller details, the little movements that embody sex appeal. The shrug of a shoulder, a coy smile, a peek of a tease. By the end of the show, I understand the bigger picture—that it's the smallest movements and the confidence that matter most.

I still have no idea how to get my body to mimic those movements, but I think I'm starting to understand.

Cord walks me to the subway station after the show. It's only a few blocks, but I find myself veering closer to him the farther we go. My arm brushes his shirt and a shiver races through me. He deposits me at the top of the stairs, leaning in to give me a quick hug.

His chin is covered in a thin layer of stubble, which scratches my cheek as he pulls away. "I'll see you tomorrow night, Slippers." He waves as I head down the stairs, totally nonchalant as if he won't be replaying that hug over and over in his mind. Not that I will either, of course.

When I get to the bottom of the stairs, I look back to find him watching me walk away and I put a little extra sway in my steps.

"WHAT HAS YOU SMILING LIKE AN ABSOLUTE GOOBER?" LUCY asks, plopping down next to me on the studio floor the next morning as I stretch my aching legs.

We're on a break in between class and rehearsal, the company enjoying the brief respite and filling the room with exhausted chatter. But even the long day isn't enough to dampen my excitement. Cord just texted me the details for our lesson tonight, and I'm borderline giddy about seeing him again.

But I squash that thought as soon as it comes. Cord is just a tutor, a means to an end. Yes, he's one of the hottest men I've ever seen in real life, and one who is proving to be thoughtful and kind as well. But he's also just doing his job. This is nothing more than a business arrangement.

I realize Lucy is still waiting for me to answer her question, a knowing smile on her face. "Nothing much. Just getting excited about the audition."

She straightens her legs out in front of her and reaches for her toes, her lithe body folding perfectly in half. "Excited for the audition, or excited for this very special prep work you're doing for said audition?"

"Can't it be both?" I fiddle with my phone, searching the address Cord had sent me. "Shit." The expletive escapes me and even though I'm a grown adult, I check my surroundings to make sure none of the directors heard me.

"What's wrong?" Lucy sits up, eyes worried.

"Our next lesson is going to be at a salsa club." I meet Lucy's eyes, my own just as worried. "I don't know how to salsa."

"Maybe the whole point of the lesson is for you to learn."

It's a reasonable argument, but it doesn't stop the itch of fear scratching under my skin. The last thing I need is to look even more incompetent and clueless in front of Cord.

I shake that thought right out of my head. The man is my tutor. If I can't look incompetent and clueless with him, then it sort of defeats the purpose of our lessons. I'm only doing these lessons so I don't appear incompetent and clueless in front of the person who really matters: David. I knew when I first approached Cord, there would be a certain amount of failure to be expected, and even if it goes against my very nature, I need to accept it.

I tuck my phone back into my bag as we all stand to get set for rehearsal. "What do I wear to a salsa club?" I whisper to Lucy as we take our places for the beginning of the show.

"Something short and swingy. And definitely wear heels."

I groan at the thought of shoving my feet into a pair of heels after a full day of ballet.

"Actually, I have the perfect shoes in my locker. Remind me to give them to you when we're done." Lucy winks at me over her shoulder before flitting out onto the floor with the rest of the corps.

I focus my attention firmly on the dance in front of me, knowing I need to be fully present in order to not mess up my own section of the show. I'm dancing as one of the four Little Swans, a famous section of the ballet that requires perfect precision and timing.

Thoughts of Cord and salsa dancing and short swingy skirts will have to wait. For now, there's only space in my brain for ballet. I give *Swan Lake* my full attention, and my quartet nails our portion of the dance. When we get an approving nod from David, it feels like a victory.

I HAVE TO MINE THE DEPTHS OF MY CLOSET TO COME UP WITH something short and swingy, and when I slip into the red dress that's tight in the bust and flares around my hips, I immediately feel self-conscious.

But then I take a minute to look in the mirror. I've left my hair down, swinging across my back, and it looks healthy and shiny. I force myself to check out my figure as if I weren't someone who's been dancing ballet since she was three. My breasts are pushed up by both my bra and the dress, and outside of my normal leotard ensemble, I can admit that they look good. The short skirt shows off my legs, long and toned and accentuated by the gold heels I borrowed from Lucy. They're specifically made for dancing and surprisingly comfortable.

By the time my minute is up, I'm almost sad to cover my outfit with my coat, but I know the night air is chilly and I'm going to need it.

I hop on the subway, taking the time to enjoy a little Saturday-night people watching: the couple heading out for a night on the town, the businessman still typing away on his phone, the teenagers chatting and laughing, shoving each other playfully.

Cord is waiting for me in front of the club, looking better than any one man has the right to. He's in black pants that hug his thighs and a black button-down shirt, sleeves rolled up to the elbow as if he knows forearms are my weakness.

"Nice to see you wore the appropriate footwear, Slippers." He opens the door to the club, his hand finding a spot on the small of my back as he guides me into the space.

The entryway is dark, the bouncer flashing a light on our IDs before guiding us to the cashier. Cord hands over some kind of pass rather than cash, which is good because I hadn't exactly budgeted for door fees.

"Do you want to check your coat?" the greeter asks me as she stamps our hands.

"Oh yeah. Sure." I pop the buttons and slip my jacket over my arms, exchanging it for a ticket that I tuck into my clutch.

I turn to follow Cord into the main room of the club.

His eyes land on mine, but they still there for only a second before they drift down to my chest, over my hips, and down to my legs.

I wait for a pithy comment that doesn't come. Instead, my skin burns under the force of his gaze—his gaze he seems unable to break, his eyes tracing over every inch of me with an intensity I swear I can feel. My skin pebbles under his appreciative stare and my mouth goes dry.

Eventually, I clear my throat, bringing his attention back to my face. "Shall we?"

He swallows thickly and nods, turning away from me and walking into the club. I follow behind him, taking the chance to ogle his butt in those very tight pants. At least *I* manage to keep my staring covert.

As soon as we enter the dance floor area, my senses are assaulted. The music is loud and so is the chatter. Brightly colored lights illuminate the walls and the bar, while a disco ball throws glitter over the crowded dance space.

Cord reaches back for my hand, leading me over to a tiny table in one of the corners. It's tucked away but still has an excellent view of the dancers spinning around the floor, a whirl of bright colors and rapid motion, which is good because I can't take my eyes off them. Their feet seem to move at the speed of light, their turns whipping around even faster than the best turner in our company. The movements are so quick they should feel rushed and blurred, but every step they take is sharp and controlled. Partners come together, their bodies moving with each other and against each other.

It's mesmerizing.

And sort of hot.

Okay. Very hot.

I sink into one of the chairs and hope Cord doesn't expect me to get out there on the floor because my body does not move like that.

But something tells me he didn't bring me here just to watch.

"Do you want something to drink?" He has to shout over the music, leaning down so his mouth is almost level with my ear.

I shake my head. Even though tomorrow is Sunday, I still need to get a workout in, plus I'll probably take a company class. Also, I didn't budget for the extra calories.

"I'm going to go grab a drink. When I get back, we're dancing." He starts to head across the room to the bar.

I reach out and grab his arm. "In that case, I'll take a vodka soda." I'm going to need the liquid courage. And surely one drink won't derail my carefully planned week.

Cord returns a few minutes later and I sip greedily. He must see the look of abject terror in my eyes because he doesn't immediately drag me out of my chair. He sits next to me instead, moving his own chair close to mine so we can actually hear each other. "So like I said before, so much of portraying sex appeal onstage is in the hips. And salsa dancing is all about the hips."

I've been too focused on the dancers' feet to pay any attention to their hips, but now my attention is drawn and my anxiety ratchets up a notch further. "My hips don't move like that."

Cord laughs, but it's not unkind. "That's why we're here, Slippers. For you to learn."

I gesture to a couple spinning by us. "Do you know how to do that?"

He takes a long swig of his beer. "Not as well as they do, but I know the basics." He points to another couple, one that appears to be not quite as experienced as the rest of them. "It's really just three steps. Out, step, in."

I watch the couple and see that Cord is right. Amid the spins and turns, it all comes back to the basic three-step combo.

"Finish your drink and then we're getting out there." Cord gestures to my almost empty glass.

Shit. I didn't even realize I was drinking that fast. I swig the last sips, vowing to drink only water from this point on.

The second my empty glass hits the table, Cord is standing in front of me with his hand out, waiting for mine. And like the complete idiot I must be, I forget what it feels like to have his skin on mine. I place my hand in his and let him tug me toward the dance floor.

Cord spins me effortlessly so that we're facing each other, our bodies so close I smell the potent combo of his clean laundry and musk. He keeps our hands joined and his free hand slides around to my back, his palm flat, the expanse of it so wide he brushes the bare skin of my upper back.

I tentatively place my other hand on his shoulder. In reality, it's bare hints of contact. We're in a position I could pass off as professional. We're just dancing together.

But then my eyes meet his and there's something burning down in the depths. Cord's usually cocky grin has faded, his mouth pursed so tightly it looks like he is in pain. Like being this close to me is so awful he can barely contain his grimace.

I let that thought pull me from the depths of my lusthaze. "Are you going to lead, or do I need to?"

With a snap of a finger, Cord is back to his normal self. "Let's stick to the basic step until you get the hang of it."

I step to the right, rock onto my other foot, and then bring my right foot back in. I know I don't have the rhythm, the natural ease, that the dancers around me display so effortlessly, but at least I don't screw up the simple steps. Cord picks up the pace after a minute, and though I have to focus a bit more, I surprise myself by falling into the movement. Letting Cord lead me around the outer edge of the dance floor, so we stay out of the way of the more experienced pairs. Normally I'm dancing to stand out, but here I just hope to blend in and it's a freeing sort of change.

"Good," he says, leaning in close so I can hear him over the blare of the music. "You've got the footwork, now it's time to add the flare."

I don't like the sound of that. "Who needs flare?" I practically yell back. It's easier to scream than to bring myself close enough that my lips might accidentally brush the skin of his ear.

His grin is back, the cocky one. "Come on, Slippers. Have a little fun with it." His fingers dig into my waist, and I do something I might come to regret later: I let him have full control.

I let Cord use his hands to move my hips and spin me around and pull me closer. Even though it goes against everything in me to cede power, I let him have it. I pretend like he is one of my partners in the company, men I am comfortable with, have been dancing with for years. I have no problem letting those dancers put their hands all over me, have no problem letting them lift me and spin me and toss me into the air.

Yet even though we're not messing with lifts and tosses here, dancing with Cord feels more dangerous. Giving myself over to him feels like something I might come to regret.

But I do it anyway, convincing myself it's purely for practical purposes. I need to learn, and Cord is here to teach me.

I'm not sure at what point I start to have fun. But flying around the dance floor with Cord's hand on my back feels not only fun but safe.

Like I know he's not going to let me fall. Or fail.

We dance through four or five upbeat songs, the beats frenzied, the pace so quick even my impeccable cardio ability is put to the test. As if he knows we all need a breather, the DJ switches to a slow song. One not meant for quick spins and turns, but for swaying and pulling your partner close.

I drop Cord's hand, assuming we'll be making our way back to our table to sit this one out. Clearly this is not part of the lesson.

But when I free his hand, he snakes his arm around my waist, collapsing the space between us to practically nothing.

I mean to push away from him, really I do, but my body responds without my permission, both of my arms circling his neck like we're back at high school prom. Of course, I never went to prom because I never went to high school. I was already too busy with dance to worry about such small things, already studying at the Ballet New York School, hoping to one day be a part of the company.

"What's on your mind, Slippers?" His voice is low and close to my ear. I try to hide the shiver it sends racing up my spine.

"Just thinking about how I never went to prom." I answer truthfully before I can think about all the reasons why I shouldn't. All the reasons why Cord Donovan doesn't need to know such personal details about me.

"I never went to mine either."

Surprised, I pull back a little, so I can see his eyes. "How come? I would have thought you could have your pick of any partner you wanted."

He shrugs, that knowing smirk pulling on the corner of his lips. "I could have."

I roll my eyes and adjust my hands. The movement causes my fingers to graze the ends of his hair at the nape of his neck. It's silky and thick and I want to thread my fingers through it.

It might be my imagination, but I think he pulls me in even closer, our hips flush together, less than an inch separating our chests. I'm grateful for that tiny gap so he hopefully can't feel how hard my heart is pounding in my chest. I tell myself it's still recovering from the exertion of all the salsa dancing, but it might have more to do with the way Cord's fingers keep stroking the bare skin of my back. I know I need to pull away to preserve my sanity, but I can't move. I can't see anything but Cord, the rest of the room fading into a hazy blur.

"Allegra, I . . ." My name on his lips is potent, drugging.

"That's enough of that slow stuff, lovebirds. Let's get back to salsa!" The DJ follows his horribly timed interruption with a return to the thumping beats from before. Somehow the music has gotten even louder and faster.

I don't know if I have it in me for more of the quick-paced steps. My body feels like it's been doused in cement, my limbs so heavy I don't know how I'll be able to walk home.

"Ready to go?" His lips brush the shell of my ear and I'm grateful his hands are still on my back, keeping me standing in place.

Nodding, I turn for our table where I've left my clutch. The moment I break our hold, I feel the loss of him. I want his hands back on me, my hands back on him.

But I beeline for the table, swipe up my purse, and head for the front entrance. I pick up my coat and shove my arms into the sleeves as if it can act as some kind of armor, protect me from things I should not be feeling.

Because I need Cord to be my teacher. I don't have room for him to be anything else. And I think his behavior makes it clear he's not interested in anything else with me anyway. Not that that matters. My head needs to be squarely on my audition, my focus can't afford to be diverted for even a few minutes. Becoming a principal dancer requires my full time and devotion. Ballet has to come above all else.

"Can I give you a ride home?" Cord asks once we've made it out of the club and to the streets of Manhattan. He gestures to a black SUV waiting for him at the curb like he's some kind of celebrity.

I shake my head. The last thing I need is to spend any more time in close proximity to him, not while I can still feel the ghosts of his hands gripping my waist and pulling me close. "I can just take the subway."

"It's no trouble, Slippers."

It might be, I think but don't say out loud. "It's okay. I'm fine on my own. Any homework?"

He studies me, his gaze too knowing, and I can only pray he doesn't see how much he affects me. "I'll text you." He shoves his hands in his pockets and backs away, heading toward his car without turning to face it. "Let me know when you get home, okay?"

I nod. "Will do. Have a good night."

"You too, Slippers."

I spin on my heel, racing toward the subway station before I can change my mind and hop in that stupid car.

I need some space from Cord Donovan, and I need it now.

NINE

Cord

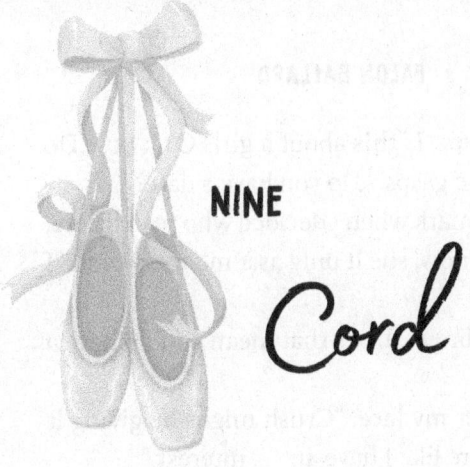

I barely sleep that night. Every time I close my eyes, all I see is the scooped neckline of the tight dress Allegra wore, the way her skirt flared around her hips as she twirled, the way she flushed and smiled when I dipped her. The way her waist fit perfectly in my hands.

The situation is drastic. So I do something unthinkable. I FaceTime my sister.

She answers on the first ring, eyes wide. "What happened? Is it Mom? Do I need to book flights home?"

"Jesus, Coco, relax. Can't I call my favorite sister without there being some kind of emergency?"

"Historically speaking, no, you cannot. Also, I'm your only sister."

I sigh. "Everyone is healthy and safe as far as I know."

"Good." She settles back on her lavender velvet couch. "Seriously though. Why are you calling me instead of texting like a normal human being?"

"Believe it or not, I wanted to get your advice, though I am already regretting that decision."

She visibly perks up. "Is this about a girl? Or a boy? Do you have a crush?" She gasps. "Do you have a date?"

Really missed the mark when I decided who to call here, but if I don't explain now, she'll only assume the worst. "I do not have a date."

She raises one eyebrow. "Does that mean you do have a crush?"

I scrub a hand over my face. "Crush might be giving it too much weight. More like I have an . . . interest."

She struggles to contain her glee and fails miserably. "Thank god. Go get laid, don't overthink it. Is that the permission you need?"

"I can't."

"That sounds like a conversation you should be having with your doctor and not your twin sister."

I flip her off. "I can't because I'm giving her lessons. I'm basically her teacher."

She wrinkles her nose. "Lessons? What kind of lessons could *you* possibly offer?"

I ignore that slight. "I'm helping her prepare for an audition." I take a deep breath and bite the bullet. "She's a ballerina. With BNY."

Any hint of glee fades from her face. "Oh. Shit."

"Yeah."

"Have you told her?"

"About my long and complicated hatred for the institution she has dedicated her life to? No, I have not."

Her eyes, the same bright blue as mine, soften. "Why did you agree to help her in the first place?"

I fidget with the hem of my shirt, avoiding her gaze. "She told me something her director said to her, and it pissed me off and I want to give her the chance to prove him wrong." It's frank and honest, even considering Chloe knows me better than anyone, and I need to balance out the emotions. "Also, she's really hot."

Chloe ignores me because she has known me since literal birth. "I guess you have two choices then: wait until these lessons are done and tell her you want a quick fuck or start getting comfortable with ballet being a part of your life again."

I grimace. "I don't think I can do that." I know Chloe will interpret that to mean I can't see myself accepting ballet into my existence, but it's equally true for the former.

I've thought a lot about what it would be like to fuck Allegra, and nothing about it would be quick.

I clear my throat and wipe those images from my mind. "Well, as usual, you have been no help."

This time she's the one flipping me off. "Leave me in peace then, I was just about to watch *Real Housewives*."

"Yeah, yeah." I hold up my hand to wave, but she doesn't wave back.

"Be careful, Cord. Think about the consequences of your actions for once."

It's not totally unwarranted advice, but as she ends the call and my screen fades to black, I can't help but think it might already be too late to heed it.

ON MONDAY, I HEAD TO THE STUDIO FOR REHEARSAL, EVEN though I don't really need to be there. I have plenty of paperwork and behind-the-scenes things that need my attention, but I know if I sit in my office alone all day, I'll do nothing but think about Allegra. And thinking about her will only lead me to start justifying all the reasons why it wouldn't be so bad to make my move.

So instead, I do something I haven't done in a long time. I line up in the back of the studio and rehearse.

I still remember the first time I walked into a ballet studio, even though I was only six years old. Chloe was so excited for her first ballet lesson, but there wasn't much of anything we did at that age without the other in tow. She pretty much refused to go to class if I didn't go with her. When we arrived, my mom and I sat in the corner with the other family members to watch. Ballet for six-year-olds is a lot of the basics and even more just spinning around the dance floor, trying to get as dizzy as possible without falling down.

Chloe was a natural, and when her teacher saw me sitting along the back wall, toes tapping in time with the beat of the music, she zeroed in on me like a lioness.

Boys are a rarity in ballet, and I'm not the only dancer I know who got their start because they accompanied their sister to class.

Turned out, I was a natural, too.

We danced together for our entire childhoods, well into our teenage years. Chloe always had the love for ballet, the ambition. I had the talent, and the desire to always be the star in the room. Even though I never loved ballet—even when I was dancing it, so much of it seemed trite—I loved performing.

And it didn't hurt that my ego was consistently stroked. As we got older, I learned that being a male ballet dancer wasn't without its perks.

Chloe often talked of us going pro and being a part of the same company. She got her wish, but life as a professional ballerina didn't go exactly as she had planned. Sometimes it's easy to forget everything that happened to lead us to where we are today, but working with Allegra has brought it all rushing back—the good, the bad, and the very, very ugly.

Creating Six Pact let me change the course of my dance life. Now I get to dance how I want to dance, with people who I respect and dancers who are treated like the talented artists they are.

Today, I let myself revel in that. Ballet be damned.

Rehearsal ends and Noah, as dance captain, releases the rest of the crew. I could have stepped in as director, but today I just wanted to dance, and Noah is very good at his job.

As the studio clears out, I grab a towel and a water bottle from my bag, wiping the sweat from my face and chest before chugging the contents of the bottle. I refill it at the water fountain.

Noah is waiting for me when I get back to my spot, arms crossed over his chest. "Didn't expect to see you here today."

I shrug, drinking another gulp of water. "Needed to get a workout in."

"Something got you stressed?"

"Nah. One of the Texas franchises is having some trouble, but nothing major."

Noah arches an eyebrow. "You know I'm from Texas. Happy to fly out and take a look if you need an ambassador."

I zip up my bag and sling it over my shoulder. "I don't think they're that far gone, but I'll keep it in mind." I clap him on the shoulder. "Nice work today."

"Thanks, boss." He hesitates for a second. "You know, I sent you an event that's happening tonight. You should have a DM."

I frown, pulling my phone from my pocket. "You know I never check my DMs. What's the event?"

"They're doing a movie-in-the-park showing of *Center Stage*."

I find the message but don't bother opening it. "Why would I care about that? You know how much I hate that movie."

Noah shrugs. "Oh, you know. Just thought if you knew someone who liked ballet that they might be interested and maybe you could also ask said person who hypothetically might want to go if you could hypothetically take them."

I shove my phone in the side pocket of my bag. "It's hard to tell because I'm not sure you're speaking English, but are you suggesting I ask Allegra to go with me to see *Center Stage*?"

He grins. "What a great idea, boss." This time he claps me on the shoulder. "You should definitely do that, I bet she would love it."

"I'm not into her, you know," I grumble. "I'm just her tutor."

"Right. Sure. Most definitely. You're certainly not attracted to her and she's definitely not attracted to you and it hasn't been months since you've been on a date. Well, will you look at the time." He checks his wrist though he wears no watch. "Gotta run, see you later, boss!"

It takes me a second to process. "You think she's attracted to me?"

The studio door thuds shut behind him and I realize I'm the last one left and I'm directing my question at no one. I head for the door myself, but my feet stutter to a stop before I can reach for the handle.

Should I ask Allegra to go with me to see the movie?

No. Absolutely not.

It wouldn't have to be a date, of course. Friends go to the movies together all the time.

Yeah, Chloe told me to get laid, and sure, Noah reminded me I haven't been on a date in months, but none of that matters. Allegra and I are certainly capable of going to a movie together without it being a whole thing.

I take out my phone before I can talk myself out of it.

ME: Hey, I know it's late notice but if you don't have plans tonight, they're showing *Center Stage* at Bryant Park.

The typing bubbles pop up right away and my stomach does a pirouette.

ALLEGRA: You don't strike me as a *Center Stage* guy.
ME: Excuse me, I am the original Cooper Nielson.
ALLEGRA: Too bad you were like five when that movie came out.
ALLEGRA: I was actually already planning on going. My friend was going to come but she bailed so I guess we could meet up if you want?

I grin like an idiot because there's no one here to witness it.

ME: Sounds good. I'll text you when I get there.
ALLEGRA: See you then.

I STAND IN FRONT OF BRYANT PARK THREE HOURS LATER LIKE

a total fucking chump. I've got a blanket tucked under one arm and a picnic basket in the other. I spent my monthly grocery budget on fancy cheeses and fruit and crackers and wine even though I know Allegra is on a strict diet. Hell, I'm on a strict diet, too, though I don't have to deal with anyone shaming me for my weight if I put on a few extra pounds. I know what the pressure is like for her to maintain her body and I'm putting her in a terrible position by tempting her with things she likely won't eat.

This whole thing was a mistake. A colossally terrible idea. I don't even like her, there's no reason for me to be so wrapped up in my head. I should just leave now and tell her something came up.

I spin on my heel, about to make my way to the subway station.

And I almost run directly into a stunning blonde.

"Cord!" She recovers from her surprise first, flashing me a warm smile. "Sorry I kept you waiting, subway was running behind."

I breathe through my mouth because when I say I almost ran directly into, I really almost ran directly into her and now we are very close and the floral scent that seems to emanate from her skin is filling my nose and doing bad things to me. "No problem. Should we find a seat?"

"Sure." She hoists her reusable grocery bag over her shoulder.

I take it from her, handing her my blanket in exchange.

"Is that an actual picnic basket you've got there?" She eyes me with a teasing smile.

"Oh, this old thing?" I bought it an hour ago, but she doesn't need to know that.

She laughs and I wonder if it's the first time I've heard the sound or if it just sounds special because it comes from her.

Holy shit.

I am losing my goddamned mind.

Allegra leads us to a small spot on the crowded green—it seems like half the city turned out for this event. I don't spend much time in Bryant Park, but even I can't deny that it's a beautiful night and the perfect setting, the New York Public Library standing proud behind us, the happy chatter of people who can finally spend time outdoors after a frigid winter.

We spread the blanket out on the grass, settling into opposite corners. Not that leaving an entire ocean between us would be enough space.

"Everything okay?" she asks me as we start to unpack our respective bags of food. As expected, Allegra has brought fresh-cut veggies with hummus and sparkling water.

"Yeah. Good. Great. Supergreat."

"You seem a little distracted." There's that teasing smile again.

"Just a lot going on with the show."

She nods, settling in and popping a carrot into her mouth. I stack some cheese and salami on a cracker and shove it in mine. For a minute, there's nothing but the sound of each of us crunching on our snacks. Which is not awkward at all.

"That's quite the spread you packed." Allegra points to my array of cheeses with her carrot stick.

"I'm a bit of a foodie." It's not a lie, but it sounds pretentious and douchey, even to my own ears. "How was rehearsal today?" I change the subject, though this one isn't much better.

"It was good." Her shoulders tense and the lines around her mouth tighten.

I know I should press her further, just as I also know I

don't really want to talk to her about ballet. Which is going to make the rest of the night interesting considering we're watching a whole damn movie about ballet.

Luckily, the lights around the park begin to dim and the screen brightens. Allegra flashes me a small smile and the pressure to make conversation disappears. We both visibly relax. I haven't felt this tongue-tied in front of her before and I don't know why my brain has decided to stop functioning.

I stretch out my legs in front of me and she tucks hers to the side. The movement leaves a mere inch of space between our thighs and I spend more time focusing on that tiny gap than I do on the movie playing out on the screen in front of us.

My eyes dart between that stupid gap and Allegra's face. Watching her watch the movie is far more entertaining than the film itself. She has to have seen it at least a hundred times—I know Chloe made me watch it at least that many—but she still smiles and laughs and gasps as if it's her first time, even as she mouths the words.

She catches me watching her and gives me a questioning look. I dart my eyes back to the screen. A second later, I shift my legs the tiniest bit so that our thighs press together. She doesn't move away.

TEN

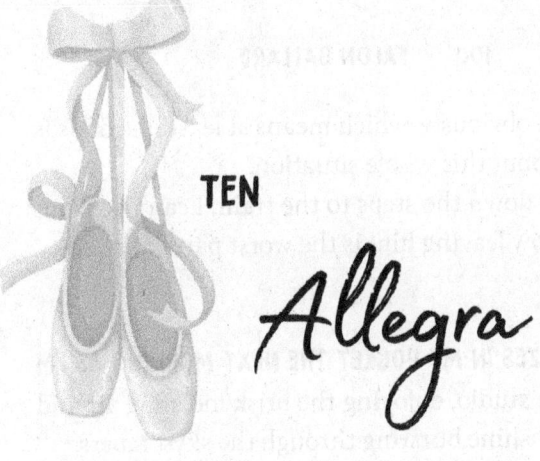
Allegra

Cord walks me to the subway when the movie ends and I wish it weren't right on the park's corner. We spent the last half of the movie with our legs pressed together, each of us pretending like we didn't notice. I swear, it's a good thing I have this movie memorized because I spent more time watching him than I did watching the film.

It's stupid to think Cord Donovan would be interested in someone like me. It's even more stupid to pretend like I have any extra time in my life for flirtation, especially now.

I don't have time for a fling with a stripper.

I also can't deny that seeing his name on my phone screen is the highlight of my day. That I look forward to our lessons, and even more so to these excursions that seem like lessons but feel more like dates. Of course, it's been a long time since I've been on a date so maybe I'm reading the whole situation totally wrong.

All I know is that when Cord leans in to give me a hug at the end of the night, I want him to be leaning in for a kiss.

He doesn't, obviously, which means at least one of us is being smart about this whole situation.

But as I jog down the steps to the train, I can't help but think about how leaving him is the worst part of my day.

MY PHONE BUZZES IN MY POCKET THE NEXT MORNING AS I'M walking to the studio, enjoying the brisk morning air and the peek of sunshine bursting through the skyscrapers.

CORD: Hey, Slippers. I hate to do this, but I have to head out of town for a little while.

I wish I could say my first instinct is to worry about my audition and the precious time we'll be losing.

I wish that was my first instinct.

ME: Okay. No problem.
CORD: I know how important our lessons are, and I know time isn't exactly on our side. I wouldn't leave if I didn't have to.
ME: It's fine, Cord. Really. I'll try to keep working on what we've already practiced until you get back.

I force myself to not ask when that will be because I don't truly need to know the intricate details of Cord's schedule.

CORD: You're not getting off that easy, Slippers. Be at this location on Wednesday night at 7:00 pm.

I click on the link, but all it shows me is an address, no other hints as to what surprises might be waiting to greet me there.

ME: Got it. I'll be there.
CORD: Try not to miss me too much 😉
ME: I'll do my very best.

Too bad I think I really will miss him, which is unfortunate because this time apart will be good for us. Good for me, mostly. Somehow I doubt Cord is going to be pining away for me, and I certainly don't plan to do that for him.

Of course, he makes it difficult for me to completely put him out of my mind. He texts me again the next morning, right as I'm finishing my workout and about to head to the studio for company class.

CORD: Today when you're dancing, I want you to look in the mirror and notice something positive.
ME: Ugh. That might be even worse than trying to find something about myself I consider attractive.
CORD: You hated that assignment when I first gave it to you, maybe this one will turn out to be not as painful as you think.
ME: I doubt it.
CORD: Obviously you're a good dancer, or you wouldn't be with one of the best companies in the world, Slippers. Is it so hard to fathom that you're talented?
ME: I know I'm talented.
CORD: Just not talented enough?

I really hate when he's able to get in my head like that.

ME: I'll try.
CORD: That's all I ever ask.

I take his words to heart, and during class, and later

during rehearsal, when I watch myself in the mirror, I don't focus only on the flaws.

I definitely notice the flaws because it's not like I've gained a whole new personality overnight, but I try to also notice the good qualities. My extension is long and graceful. My leaps are higher this year than they were last year. Even though I've been dancing my whole life, I still strive for improvement, and my hard work shows.

If only I could get David to notice it.

Wednesday is another long and grueling day in the studio. Our show is coming up in just over a week and David is hitting his crankiest heights. The next few days will be even worse, but he screamed at more people than usual today and I was lucky to escape mostly unscathed.

Of course, I want him noticing me, but not if it means catching his ire just a few weeks before auditions.

I almost cancel on Cord's mystery lesson, my muscles already aching by the time I make it back to my apartment with just a few minutes to change and grab a bite before I have to head out. My body would much rather enjoy a long, hot shower than whatever torture he has in store for me, but he went to the trouble to find me an alternative session when he couldn't be there, I don't think it would be fair to back out last minute.

I regret that decision the moment I push through the door of the address he sent. From the outside, the building is innocuous, the windows covered with pink curtains that block out any hint of what might be hiding inside.

But the second I step into the space, I have a sinking feeling that I know exactly what I'm in for.

It's a dance studio, the same scrubbed maple floor I'm

used to dancing on, the same wall of mirrors I'm used to staring into.

But this studio has one major addition.

Poles.

Shiny silver poles are anchored from the ceiling and into the floor.

I regret everything in that moment.

"You must be Allegra!"

I turn to find a drop-dead gorgeous woman entering the studio from a small office tucked off in the back corner. She's tall and curvy, with dark hair that flows down her back and bright blue eyes I can see from across the room.

Familiar blue eyes, I notice as she crosses to me and wraps me in a hug.

"I'm Chloe, it's so nice to meet you!" She lets me go, putting enough space between us that she can give me a full once-over. "I've heard so much about you. Cord was right, you are absolutely stunning."

My cheeks flush at the compliment, and at the thought of Cord telling anyone I'm stunning.

"I'm Allegra," I finally manage. "Though it seems like you already know that."

Chloe laughs, the sound bright and airy as it echoes around the room. "Not to sound like a total creeper, but I know everything about you."

"That's not creepy at all."

She smiles, slipping her arm through mine and tugging me into the center of the studio.

"I take it you're Cord's sister?"

"What gave it away, my sparkling personality?" She winks at me, leaning her hip against one of the poles.

"Has anyone ever described Cord's personality as sparkling?"

This time she throws her head back when she laughs, like she can't contain the joy. "Oh, I like you already. We are going to be great friends, I can tell."

"I think most of that depends on what exactly you are planning to make me do here tonight." I eye the pole warily. I don't like where this is going.

"Have you ever taken a pole dancing class before?" She asks the question so seriously, like I would have often had occasion to do so.

"I can't say that I have."

Chloe studies me, her eyes boring into me much like her brother's tend to do. "Don't judge it 'til you've tried it, you're going to be sore in places tomorrow I don't even want to mention."

Like my vagina? I want to ask, but refrain.

"I imagine you've done plenty of stretching already today, but let's do a quick warmup before we get started." Chloe gestures to the space in front of the pole.

We stand and face the mirror, and I follow Chloe's lead as we stretch our muscles. I try to keep my eyes on myself in the reflection, but it's hard. Chloe's body is a knockout. She's all curved muscle tone, and with her sports bra and tiny shorts, so much of her skin is on display. She's gorgeous, no one could dispute that, but it's more than just her looks, it's the way she carries herself. With confidence, and with a sense of inner peace.

"Cord told me about your audition. You dance for BNY?" Chloe asks as we both sink to the floor in a center split, legs stretched out to either side.

"Yeah. I've been with them since I was a kid at the feeder

school. I'm hoping this audition will be my chance to get a leading role and make principal."

She whistles. "Principal at BNY? You really are a big deal."

My cheeks flush once again and I hope the color doesn't spread to my chest. "I don't think I would go that far."

"Don't downplay your accomplishments. Do you know how many people work their whole lives to be a ballerina and never even make a company?"

"Did you take ballet as a kid?"

This time it's her cheeks that color. "For a few years." She clears her throat and hops to her feet, striding to the pole in the center of the room. "Let's get started." She wraps her leg around the pole, her hands gripping the metal as she effortlessly spins around. "Now, I doubt you will have much trouble with the mechanics of all of these moves I'm going to demonstrate." She lets go of the pole with one hand, her arm floating gracefully over her head. "But the real challenge is going to be in selling it."

I grimace, my eyes latched on to her movements, the ease with which she spins. I don't think I'm equipped for this.

Chloe's legs unfurl from the post and she lands back on both feet. "Come on over and give it a try."

"Already? Don't you think I need to see a few more demonstrations?"

Her smile is kind and encouraging. "The best way to learn is by doing, I'm afraid."

I trudge over to the pole. Chloe positions my leg around the cool metal, instructing me as she goes. "Now, the key is to concentrate on the grip of your leg. That's what's holding you up. The stronger your grip, the more freedom you'll have to move your arms, and the faster you'll be able to spin."

I squeeze, the pole captured between the back of my thigh and calf.

"Hands go here."

I hold on for dear life.

"Now, just let go and let yourself spin."

I look at Chloe like she has suddenly sprouted an extra head. "Just let go?"

She nods. "Let the force of your weight swing you around."

I pull in a deep breath, wondering why I'm more anxious for this than I've ever been trying new lifts. Surely being thrown in the air is way more dangerous than swinging around a pole, and yet I can't seem to make my other foot leave the ground. That foot is all that stands between me and the unknown, and there are few things in this world I like less than the unknown.

"I'll be right here," Chloe says softly. "I promise I won't let you fall."

I nod, swallowing the lump in my throat. Closing my eyes, I lift my foot and let myself spin. For a second, I feel almost weightless, but my hands and one leg are still gripped tightly to the pole, keeping me from faceplanting on the ground.

"Good! That was great for your first try!" Chloe's enthusiasm sounds completely genuine.

I don't fight the small smile that curls my lips. Dare I say, that might have been a little bit fun.

"Try it again, and this time try to make two rotations before you stop."

I follow her instructions, inordinately pleased with myself when I make it around the pole two and a half times before my momentum slows me down.

Chloe claps her hands as I come back to the ground. "Amazing! You're a natural!"

My cheeks flush at her praise and it makes me want to keep going, keep pushing to work my way up to more spins. Just the simple act of her positive reinforcement makes me feel like I want to do more.

Hmmm. Perhaps this is what has been missing from my studio classes and rehearsals lately. When David gets into show mode, it's all corrections and critiques, and by the end of the day, I leave feeling exhausted and practically brain dead. How might a compliment or two act as a recharge in the situations when we need them most?

"Thanks," I tell Chloe. "This is actually kind of fun."

She grins. "Just wait until we work our way up to some of the bigger tricks. Want to try something else?"

I nod, letting Chloe take to the pole as she demonstrates the next move.

I don't even notice the time, it flies by so quickly. Chloe and I are deep into practicing some more advanced moves when the trill of her phone breaks us out of the zone.

She hops down from her pole and grabs her phone, answering and holding it up in front of her face. "I think it's safe to say our dear Allegra has a new favorite Donovan twin and spoiler alert, it isn't you."

Cord's voice booms through the room. "You wish, Coco."

My stomach swoops, and it has nothing to do with the way I'm wrapped around the pole a solid six feet off the ground.

"Calling to check up on me or your star pupil here?"

"Why can't it be both?"

I look down just in time to see Chloe spinning the phone so it's facing me.

"Not to take all the credit, because Allegra here has been killing it, but pretty sure it's mostly my stellar teaching skills." She nods at me, gesturing for me to show off what we've been practicing.

And I should feel nervous. There should be butterflies beating their wings in my tummy as I think about performing this new trick where I flip upside down and spin around the pole, one that could make me look like a complete idiot in front of both Chloe and Cord if I can't do it.

But those aren't anxious butterflies flapping around in my stomach. They're excited.

The idea of Cord watching me perform these moves is exciting.

I don't shy away from the anticipation, I let it fuel me. I arch my back and kick out my leg, letting my body lead me in the moves. Spinning around the pole is exhilarating and the smile on my face is genuine.

This is fun.

And knowing Cord is on the other side of that screen watching me, it does something to me.

I work my way back down to the ground, my feet hitting the floor with a graceful sweep. Remembering Chloe's number one tip, I toss my hair as I straighten and stand, letting the mass of it trail down my back. Chloe's grin is wide, her eyes bright with pride, but all I can really see is Cord. Even through the grainy screen and slow connection, his eyes are wide, the blue somehow darker, though it could be a trick of the light.

Chloe pulls me to her side so both of us are in the picture. "Isn't she amazing?"

"Incredible," he says, his voice sounding a little strained. "That was incredible, Slippers."

Instead of brushing off the compliment, I accept it. "Thank you. And thanks for setting this up. I was hesitant at first, but this turned out to be a lot of fun."

Chloe presses her cheek to mine. "Anyway, thanks for introducing me to my new best friend, we're off to have fun without you! Bye!" She doesn't wait for Cord to respond before ending the call.

I see the time on her phone and reality sinks back in. "It's late. I should go, I've got early class tomorrow."

"Of course!" She pulls me into a side hug. "Make sure you stretch really well in the morning, I wasn't kidding about the sore muscles."

I nod. "Got it. And thank you, for tonight. This was awesome."

"You're welcome anytime. I have the class schedule listed on my website, but you're also welcome to come after hours for a private session anytime you want."

"That would be amazing. Thank you, Chloe."

On the subway ride home, I start to think that Cord might know what he's doing after all. When he was watching me, even through that tiny phone screen, I've never felt sexier.

ELEVEN

Cord

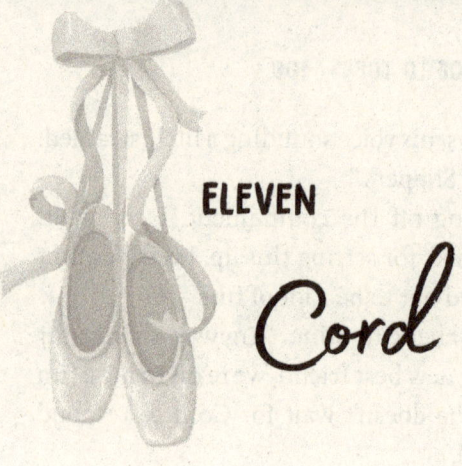

My eyes fall closed the moment the screen goes dark and the FaceTime ends. But the darkness doesn't help. All I see in my mind is Allegra, her leg wrapped around that pole, spinning like it was effortless. Like she was having fun. I toss aside the choreography notes I've been working on, knowing there's no hope for my focus now.

I envy my sister for the ease she has with people, even after everything she went through. She never lost her ability to trust and open up. I don't know that I had that ability to begin with. But watching her and Allegra together, it hits me harder than it ever has before.

My phone buzzes in my hand, where my fingers are still clenched tightly around it.

CHLOE: Mind if I ask Allegra out?
ME: Seriously Coco? I've been gone for like three days.
CHLOE: What does that have to do with anything?
You aren't going to ask her out, so why can't I?

I rub a hand over my face.

ME: I don't even know if she likes girls.
CHLOE: She's bi. I asked. All the best of us are 😉

I fall back on the too-firm hotel bed. I've been in Texas trying to work with this struggling franchise, which is normally a part of the job that I love. But I do not love living in hotel rooms.

I probably should have sent Noah in my place. He's capable and from the area, and I do want to train him to take on a bigger role in the company. And yet, when it became clear someone needed to come here in person, I jumped at the chance to put some space between me and Allegra.

Which probably means I shouldn't care that my sister wants to ask her out.

ME: Yeah. Okay. I guess if you really like her and you think you can handle the ballet of it all.

I watch the typing bubbles dance across the bottom of my screen.

CHLOE: Wow. I honestly wasn't expecting you to agree.
CHLOE: I thought you really liked her.
ME: I do. We both know I can't be any good for her. But maybe you can be.
ME: I think she could probably use someone like you.
CHLOE: Shit. You do really like her.
CHLOE: I have no intentions of asking her out, btw.

Relief washes over me but I swipe it aside.

ME: Then why are you torturing me?
CHLOE: I wanted to see how much you like her, and it's even more than I thought.

ME: Me telling you to ask her out means I like her more than you thought?
CHLOE: You want her to be happy.
CHLOE: That says a lot, Cord.
CHLOE: And for what it's worth, I think you should go for it.
ME: Not going to happen. Take your little rom-com dreams elsewhere.
CHLOE: Yeah yeah. Love you.
ME: Love you too.

No sooner have I tossed my phone to the side than it buzzes again. I sigh, about to swipe open and call Chloe rather than deal with another barrage of texts.

But it isn't her name on the screen.

ALLEGRA: Thanks for setting up the class. That was a lot of fun.
ME: Yes, Chloe is the fun twin, I'm well aware ☺
ALLEGRA: You're not wrong, but I appreciate you connecting us.

My stomach spins. Is Allegra hoping for more of a connection between her and Chloe? Damn, it's not often I have to compete with my sister over potential partners. Not that that's what Allegra is, obviously.

ALLEGRA: Any chance you're going to be home by Friday?

I'm scheduled to be in Texas until Monday morning, but my curiosity is piqued.

ME: Why, what's going on?
ALLEGRA: One of the guys in the company was asking if anyone wanted his two tickets to the Brooklyn Food Festival and that sort of went over like a lead balloon with our

crowd, but if you were going to be home, I wondered if maybe you would want to go?
ALLEGRA: You being a foodie and all 😊

I actually already had tickets to the food festival, but I'd passed them along to one of my guys when I realized I was going to be out of town. I'd been looking forward to going, and it doesn't escape me how a food festival is likely not how Allegra wants to spend her typical Friday afternoon.

ME: I'm coming home Friday morning, actually.
ME: And I would love to go with you.
ALLEGRA: Great! I'll send you the info. Have a good night!
ME: You too.

I close my messages and swipe over to my airline app. Booking a last-minute flight isn't cheap, and I'll have to turn around and come back to Texas Saturday morning.

But something tells me the cost will be worth it.

I'M JET-LAGGED AND EXHAUSTED WHEN MY LYFT ARRIVES IN Park Slope. My flight was delayed so I barely had time to drop off my suitcase at my place before I had to grab a ride over the bridge.

But all that seems to fade away when I see Allegra waiting out in front of the check-in tent for me. She's wearing jeans and a plain gray T-shirt, white sneakers on her feet and a gold necklace around her neck. Her hair is down, the long blond waves hanging over her shoulders and highlighting the gorgeous angles of her face.

I don't know that she's ever looked more beautiful.

I take a chance, leaning in for a hug and pressing a quick

kiss to her cheek when I greet her. She leans into me and I think it must be lavender, that floral scent that always seems to tease me.

A bright pink flush colors her cheeks when we part.

She hands me a lanyard with our plastic badges on them. "Shall we?"

I slip the badge over my neck and let her guide me, my hand falling to the delicate small of her back as we make our way through the narrow entrance.

The food festival is set up along one main street, traffic blocked off on either end. There are booths lining the sidewalks on each side, offering everything from homemade bagels to gourmet mac and cheese. The smells are mouthwatering and my stomach rumbles. I haven't eaten all day, wanting to leave room to sample as much as I can.

"Where should we start?" Allegra turns to me, her eyes a little wide.

"How about we start on the right and make our way down? We can loop around and end up back where we started?"

She nods, her teeth digging into her lower lip.

I reach for her hand as if it's the most normal thing in the world. "I'm normally on a pretty strict diet, but I might splurge a little today. I'm going to be mindful of my portions, though, and probably just try a small sample from each booth."

Her shoulders soften a little and she flashes me a small smile. "That sounds good."

The first booth features a local Italian restaurant and I select gnocchi with pesto sauce and burrata with fresh tomatoes and olive oil. Both are served in tiny disposable bamboo boats. I hand the burrata to Allegra and try the gnocchi first. The sauce is creamy and fresh, the gnocchi perfectly cooked.

I make a happy humming sound. "This is amazing."

Allegra cuts off a small piece of the burrata and spears it on her fork along with a tomato slice. I pay way too close attention to the way her lips part. Her eyes close for a half second and she sighs in pleasure. "It really is."

We stop for a second at a high-top table set up in the middle of the street.

"Have you ever been to Italy before?" I ask her as I shovel another bite of gnocchi in my mouth.

She shakes her head, taking one more bite of the creamy cheese before pushing it over to my side of the table. "I really only travel when I'm dancing for other companies. Otherwise, I don't want to be away from class for too long."

I nod, all too familiar with that line of thinking. "It's beautiful. Highly recommend if you get the chance to go."

She stabs one piece of gnocchi and nibbles off a bite. "Have you done a lot of traveling?"

"Not as much as I would like, but it's one of my favorite things to do."

"Where's your favorite place you've been?"

I scoop the remainder of the burrata on my fork. "Probably Scotland. Edinburgh is one of my favorite cities, but the Highlands are absolutely incredible. It's like being in a fantasy novel."

"Sounds amazing." She watches me as I finish the last of the two dishes and I don't miss how her eyes linger on my lips.

Gathering our trash, I sweep out my arm in the direction of the next booth. "Ready?"

She nods. Neither of us reaches for the other this time,

but we walk with our shoulders close enough that they brush with each step. She doesn't move away, so I don't either.

The next booth features Indian food, which is one of my favorites. I ask for a samosa and butter chicken. Allegra tries a bite of each and when the flavorful foods hit her tongue, pleasure dances over her face.

If her diet is anything like I expect, coming to a festival like this probably isn't easy for her. And yet, she went out of her way to ask for these tickets, because she knew I would like it.

Something warm spreads through my chest.

"Everything okay?" she asks me as I toss the wrapper of our latest treat—a homemade bagel with thick lox—in the trash. "You're looking at me funny."

I nudge her with my elbow. "Am not."

She laughs, and more than one person in the vicinity turns to look at her. Not because she's loud and obnoxious, but because she sounds like a fairy or a nymph or some otherworldly creature. I don't miss how some of those looks linger. I press myself closer to her side as we come to the next booth.

"So you had fun with Chloe?" I ask as we wait for a freshly made sushi roll to be prepared.

"I think it's impossible to not have fun with Chloe."

"Oh trust me, it's possible."

She rolls her eyes. "I have a sister, I'm aware. But Chloe is pretty great."

I take the proffered roll and we find a spot at another table. "She is."

"You two are close?"

I nod. "We've been through a lot together."

Allegra gives me time to expand, but I don't, even though

I'm tempted to. That's a conversation I don't ever *want* to have with her. Instead, I dip the sushi in eel sauce and shove it in my mouth. "Want a piece?"

She nods and reaches for a set of chopsticks, but I scoop up a piece, swirl it in the sauce, and offer it to her.

She lifts her eyebrow at me before leaning in, opening her mouth so I can feed her the sushi.

Strangely, it's the most erotic thing I've witnessed in a long time.

Allegra covers her mouth as she chews, but she doesn't drop my eye contact. "That's really good," she says once she's swallowed.

I nod because my brain seems to have stopped functioning. I eat the last piece of sushi and then guide her to the next booth. We've almost made our way back to the beginning, but I'm not quite ready for our time together to end.

Instead of eating our last finds at the festival—pastries from a Japanese bakery—we take them in bags to go, some unspoken agreement between us that this won't be our last stop.

We find a coffee shop and since the sun is just setting and it's not too cool yet, we take seats at an outdoor table, a mug of coffee for me and of tea for her, plus our pastries to share.

"Thank you for bringing me to this tonight."

Allegra wraps her hand around her mug, bringing it to her lips to blow on the steaming beverage. "You're welcome. I figure it's the least I can do with everything you've set up for me lately."

"I've been enjoying spending time with you." The words are out of my mouth before I can fully think them through. Not that I don't mean them, but I don't know if I should be saying them out loud.

She looks at me over the rim of her mug. "Me too."

It would be so easy right now to close the small gap of space between us and press my lips to hers. There's something here, something between us that I haven't felt in a long time, and my chest physically aches with the longing.

But I don't close the gap. Instead, I sit back farther in my seat. "But I think you should know I'm not really a relationship guy."

Something in her hazel eyes darkens, her face falling without moving a muscle, though she tries to hide it. "Oh. Yeah, of course. I didn't mean to imply . . . I just meant . . . the lessons have been helpful. That's all."

I nod, as if it doesn't stab me in the heart to see the hurt in her eyes. "Yeah, I know. I know you probably don't do relationships either. What with your schedule and all."

"Totally. Yeah. Relationships are not really my thing." She sips her tea and I don't know if the wince is from the sting of a too-hot drink or the awkwardness of this conversation.

I mentally kick myself for ruining what had been a perfect night. Why couldn't I just shut the hell up and text her later if I thought she was getting too close?

Because she's not the one getting too close, idiot, I think.

"Ready to head home?" I ask, even though I still have half a mug of coffee and Allegra's barely touched her tea.

She nods, abandoning her cup and pushing back her chair. "I'm just gonna catch the subway. You getting a ride?"

For a second I consider telling her I'll ride the train with her, but right now she looks like she'd rather be anywhere but here. "Yeah. I'll just catch a Lyft." I follow her out to the sidewalk.

She hesitates, like she might just want to walk away

without saying goodbye. "Are we on for our regularly scheduled lesson tomorrow then?"

Fuck. I've backed myself into a corner now. Of course she would assume I'm back in town for good. "Um, I'm not going to be around tomorrow, actually."

Her brow furrows and I immediately sense that she's jumping to the wrong conclusion.

"I have something else planned for you, promise," I jump in. "But I actually have to go back to Texas tomorrow morning."

The lines on her forehead deepen. "You're going back tomorrow morning? You just got in this afternoon. Why did you come back for less than twenty-four hours?"

I drag my eyes away from hers and lock them on the sidewalk between us. "I had some work to do. And I didn't want to miss the food festival."

She takes a step closer to me, her shoes the only thing I can see. She waits for me to look at her, and when I do, all traces of ire have faded. "You flew here from Texas just to go to the food festival with me?"

I shrug, shoving my hands in my pockets so I don't reach for her. "It wasn't a big deal. I needed to come back to the office anyway." It's a lie and we both know it.

Allegra rises on her toes and presses a kiss to my cheek. "You didn't have to do that. But I'm glad you did. Safe travels, Cord."

"Have a good night," I finally manage to choke out when my heart has stopped spinning from the feel of her lips on my skin.

I wait until she's disappeared down the stairs of the subway before I force my suddenly leaden feet to move, my body just as mesmerized by her as my heart is.

TWELVE
Allegra

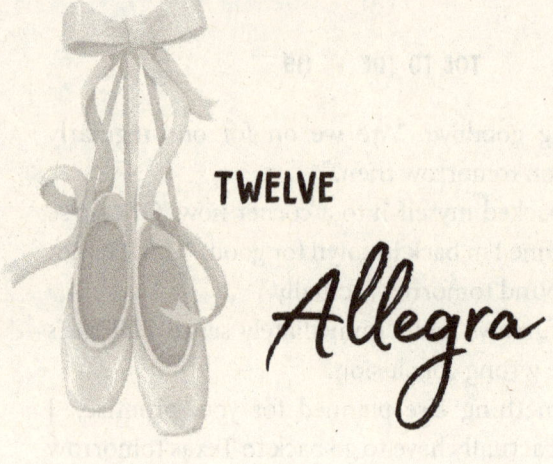

I barely sleep the night of the food festival, which means I wake up the next morning cranky and sore—my muscles still haven't fully recovered from pole dancing. But I think my brain hurts more than my body. Cord Donovan is giving me emotional whiplash.

It's not like I want the guy to fall in love with me or anything, but the way he came out with that whole I'm not a relationship guy bit last night makes it seem like he thinks I'm falling for him. Which I'm not. Obviously.

And yet. When I see his name flash on my phone, I can't deny the flutter in my stomach.

CORD: I'm sorry about how things ended last night. I had a really great time with you and I hate that I ruined it.
ME: You didn't ruin it. I had fun with you too.

I bite my lip, typing and retyping my next text before I finally bite the bullet and send it.

ME: Look, maybe we should just admit that we are two attractive people who are attracted to each other but aren't looking for anything serious. Maybe if we stop denying it, we can just let it be.

CORD: Damn, Slippers. Are you telling me you're attracted to me?

ME: Are you going to pretend like you're not attracted to me?

CORD: No.

CORD: Also, is this Chloe's influence? Where did this boldness come from?

He's not far off, assuming it came from my lesson with Chloe. But he is equally responsible.

ME: Actually, I think this is just coming from me.

CORD: I'm impressed.

CORD: I'll see you next week, okay?

ME: Sounds good.

Cord is impressed with me. Bolstered by the thrill, I dance better than I have in a long time.

At the end of rehearsal that day, as everyone is packing up their bags and shuffling toward the door, David pulls me aside. "Nice work today, Allegra. I couldn't take my eyes off you up there."

A couple of the other dancers slow down as they pass us, their ears perked to hear what kind of comments David felt the need to tell me in private.

The ickiness of the sentiment is outweighed by the power of a compliment from David Morgan. He didn't say anything nearly as nice to any of the principals, instead he was focused on me. It's exactly the kind of attention I need from him as we close in on auditions.

I flash him a small but polite smile. "Thank you. Any

improvements you've seen from me are credit to your instruction." It's a flat-out lie, but from the smirk on his face, he believes it.

"What was that all about?" Lucy asks as we duck out of the rehearsal room and into the hallway.

"Nothing," I lie again, though this time I take no pleasure in it. "Any fun plans for the weekend?" I throw the question at her in hopes of distracting her.

The look in her eyes tells me she isn't buying what I'm selling, but she doesn't push me. "I've got a date tonight, actually."

"Oooh, that's exciting. Who with?"

Lucy rambles on about her upcoming date as we make our way out of the building and onto the bustling streets. It's late in the evening, but it's Saturday and this is New York and therefore people still crowd the sidewalks.

"What about you? Any interesting plans? How are things going with your sexy stripper?" Lucy waggles her eyebrows at me as we wait to cross the street.

I roll my eyes. "First of all, he's not a stripper. Second of all, he's out of town for the week so the only exciting plans I have are dinner with my family tomorrow."

Lucy flashes me a sympathetic smile. "How are things with your mom?"

Though Lucy and I both have similar histories with our moms—moms who long for us to achieve the ballet dreams they never got to realize—Lucy has established firm boundaries with hers. Honestly, she could probably teach a class on mother/daughter boundaries and I bet a lot of us in the company would pay good money to learn her secrets.

"They are what they are." I haven't actually spoken with

my mother since that phone call in Times Square two weeks ago. I probably have a few missed calls, if I were to check my recent call list, but she didn't bother leaving voicemails or sending follow-up texts. Which means I will be on the receiving end of a passive-aggressive lecture or two at dinner tomorrow.

Maybe with Bethany's wedding right around the corner, her motherly attentions will be so focused on that, she won't have time to guilt me.

I SHOULD HAVE REALIZED THERE'S ONE THING MY MOTHER ALways has time for, and that's guilting me.

"It's been so long since I've gotten to speak to you, dear," she says, air-kissing my cheek the moment I walk through the front door of my childhood home, an Upper West Side apartment that not only could be but has been featured in *Architectural Digest*. "You must be so busy with work, you don't have time to check in with your mother. Did you get the Venmo I sent the other day? I assume it went through, but I didn't hear from you, so I wasn't sure."

I don't have to roll my eyes because Bethany does it for me. "Sorry, Mom, between *Swan Lake* and preparing for the audition coming up, I haven't had a ton of free time. But thank you for the money, I appreciate it," I add as an afterthought. I do appreciate it, of course, I just hate that I need it in the first place.

Her eyes light up at the mention of the audition. "That's right! Your audition. How is it coming along? Are you feeling confident? Should we have skipped dinner so you have more time to practice?"

Bethany loops her arm through mine and drags me into

the living room to the pristine cream sofas we were never allowed to sit on as kids. "She doesn't need to practice, Mom. Allegra knows exactly how to nail this audition."

"Aw thanks, little sis. I'm so flattered by your faith in me."

She shoves me, mostly gently, into the seat next to her fiancée Cassidy, a Black woman with buzzed hair and impeccable style. "You're not escaping this dinner because we have wedding things to discuss."

"I should have known you had ulterior motives." I lean over and give Cassidy a hug. "It's not too late to back out you know. No one would blame you for wanting to escape the Hart women."

Cassidy laughs. "Unfortunately, I think you're as stuck with me as I am with you."

Bethany plops down next to me, grabbing a large binder from the coffee table and pushing it into my hands. "Okay, so I, of course, have most of the important details figured out. But I'm putting together the seating chart and I need to know who you're bringing as your plus-one."

I flip aimlessly through the pages, appreciating Bethany's color-coded spreadsheets. "I don't have a plus-one, B."

She lowers her voice. "Well, you might want to get one. Mom hinted she would be happy to find you a date if you didn't have someone in mind already."

I groan. As if my mother's meddling in my career isn't bad enough, I certainly don't need her butting her nose into my nonexistent love life, too. "Maybe I could ask Lucy?"

My phone vibrates right as I'm pulling it out of my pocket to text Lucy and see if I can bribe her with an open bar.

CORD: Just checking in and making sure you're still up for Tuesday?

"Oooh!" Bethany reaches for my phone. "Who is Cord Donovan?"

"Cord Donovan?" My mother chooses this incredibly inopportune moment to enter the room with a tray of appetizers like this is the 1950s or we're some royal family—she's even wearing a retro-style cocktail dress, her hair and makeup impeccably done even though the rest of us are in leisure wear. She sets down the tray on the coffee table and rises, her hands finding their normal resting place on her hips as her brow furrows, though her forehead barely moves and remains wrinkle-free. "That name sounds familiar. Do I know him?"

My cheeks flush at the thought of my mom knowing anything about Cord. "I don't think so."

"Allegra's going to bring him to the wedding!"

I pinch Bethany on the arm, hard. "I am absolutely not bringing him to the wedding."

She looks at me with wide, fake innocent eyes. "Why not? You guys are going out this week, right? Didn't he just text you to confirm?"

"You're going out during the week? Is that wise when you have so much on your schedule for work?" My mom sits primly in an armchair, crossing her ankles and pulling her pencil skirt down.

"I don't have a date this week or any week. I am not bringing Cord to the wedding. And I'm perfectly capable of budgeting my time all by myself." I reach forward, grabbing a deviled egg from the appetizer platter and shoving the whole thing in my mouth.

"Allegra, you know I use full-fat mayonnaise in those."

Cassidy takes one of her own, chomping a big bite. "And they're delicious, Mrs. Hart!"

Mom flicks invisible lint from her skirt. "Cassidy, dear, I have told you, you must call me Julie. You're about to be my daughter-in-law."

I shoot Cassidy a grateful look. "How are wedding plans coming? You must be so busy focusing on throwing the perfect event."

My mom takes that as her cue to launch into a tirade about the caterers, which quickly turns to how incompetent the florist is and how much the photographer is overcharging.

Bethany glares at me, but it's her own damn fault for mentioning Cord.

I snatch my phone back from my sister while my mom is distracted. I have to cough to cover the gasp that flies from my mouth when I see the texts she's sent.

ME: Would you want to come with me to my sister's wedding?
CORD: That depends. Is there an open bar?
ME: Of course.
CORD: Then count me in, Slippers.

"I am going to murder you," I mutter under my breath to my former sister.

Bethany smiles at me sweetly. "Don't pretend like you don't want him there, I know you do. We will be talking about this later. I want all the details, or I'll make sure to let Mom know how much you would love for her to set you up with one of her friends' sons."

Scratch that. Murder is too good for her. I will be sneaking into her room the night before her wedding and shaving her eyebrows.

I DON'T GET A CHANCE TO TEXT CORD BACK FOR THE REST OF the night, but I fully plan to tell him there's no need for him to come with me to my sister's wedding.

Then I imagine what he must look like in a tux and I sort of forget to send the text at all.

Tuesday afternoon after rehearsal and class, I show up to another random address, and for the first time wonder if Cord has really steered me wrong. It's a brick building on the West Side Highway, and if it weren't for the fact that I don't think he would put me in danger, I might not go in because it has sketchy warehouse vibes written all over it.

But eventually I make my way inside and up to the third floor, to the suite number Cord directed me to. I open the heavy black door and find myself in a large studio. Not one for dancing, as I expected, but one for photography.

Golden afternoon light streams in through the windows that line an entire wall, and assorted cameras and photography equipment are scattered throughout.

The door slams shut behind me with a thud so loud that I jump.

A white person with a bright pink pixie cut emerges from what could be some kind of darkroom, and a wide smile spreads across their face when they see me standing there. "You must be Allegra."

Yet another person who knows me, and I have no clue who they might be. At least I'm fairly certain this person isn't related to Cord.

"That's me." I stick out my hand.

They slide their palm into mine and give me a firm shake. "Ava. They/them. I'll be your photographer today."

My eyebrows rise, because even though it's fairly obvious what this place is, I still don't know what I'm here for.

Ava laughs, tucking their arm in mine and leading me farther into the space. "I take it Cord didn't give you many details?"

"It seems to be a pattern with him."

"Well, I'm a photographer, obviously." They pull me into the far corner of the room, where sunlight highlights one of the only pieces of furniture: a bed. "And I specialize in boudoir shoots."

I suck in a breath. Of all the things I could have expected, this was not on the list. "To be clear, what that means is . . . ?"

"You're going to put on some killer lingerie I picked out just for you." Ava turns my gaze to a rack holding several scraps of lace and not much else. "And I'm going to take a bunch of pictures of you in it."

"Right." I nod my head, repeatedly, as if that will make this all make sense.

"I hope you don't mind, but Cord told me a little bit about what the two of you are doing, and why, and I know the thought of this can be a little overwhelming and intimidating, but I think if you give it an honest shot, you might find that it really helps." They lead me over to the rack of lingerie. "I work with a lot of people and one of my goals is to make everyone feel powerful and sexy in their own skin. And this is a one hundred percent judgment-free zone."

"Do you share the photos with anyone?"

"Not without your permission."

"Not even Cord?" I have to imagine he's paying Ava for this session, and I have to clarify if that entitles him to see the finished product. For some reason, the thought of him seeing me half naked and posed on a bed doesn't terrify me in the way it probably should, but I still need the reassurance that he won't have access to the photos without my permission.

"Not even Cord."

I half-heartedly flip through the pieces of fancy underwear Ava has chosen for me. "I don't think I'm going to be any good at this."

They squeeze my shoulder. "There's no way to be good or bad at it. This is just a chance for you to express yourself." They rifle through the rack and hand me one of the pieces that has a bit more coverage. "Plus, you get to keep any of the pieces we end up using."

That's not the selling point Ava thinks it is, but I take the lacy bodysuit from them anyway. "All right. Let's do this, I guess."

As much as I hate to admit it, Cord has yet to steer me wrong in this whole "make Allegra appear to be sexy" endeavor, so if he thinks this is a good idea, then I'm willing to give it a shot. The worst thing that can happen is I embarrass myself in front of Ava, and at least I never have to see them again.

Ava directs me to the bathroom, where I change into the lingerie and slip into the soft cotton robe they provided. When I emerge from the bathroom, we've been joined by a hair and makeup person, who does quick work in making me look glamorous but not overly done. They take off as soon as they're finished, so it's just me and Ava left in the studio.

They direct me over to the bed, and for a minute, just have me sit while they position the lighting and check angles and do a bunch of other technical things. Then they come over to the bed and instruct me to lie down in the center. Ava musses up the sheets, making them look as if I've just rolled around in the bed. "Okay, this looks great. Let's work on your pose."

"What, you mean me lying here like a dead fish isn't sexy?"

Ava laughs. "I promise, Allegra, by the end of the next hour, you're going to feel hotter than you ever have in your life. Is it okay if I touch you?" When I nod, they bring up one of my legs so the foot of one leg is tucked near my knee on the other. They raise both arms over my head and bend my arms at the elbows. "Now arch your back and look off to the left. And hold that pose."

Ava grabs their camera and the room is filled with the clicks of shots. They move all around me, shooting me from every angle, even climbing onto the edge of the bed and shooting me from above.

I try to follow Ava's direction to relax and breathe normally, but my muscles feel stiff and awkward.

"So Cord tells me you're a ballerina?"

I nod, still holding tight to the pose they arranged me in.

Ava smiles. "You can talk, in fact it sometimes helps relax your facial muscles. What made you want to be a dancer?"

"I don't remember a time when I didn't want to be a dancer, honestly. My mom put me in my first class when I was three and I never looked back."

Ava checks the screen of the camera before directing

me into a new pose. "Wow. That's impressive. Sounds like you've been very dedicated to your craft."

"I didn't have a choice, in the beginning at least." I shift my head so I'm not looking directly at the camera, waiting for Ava to scold me back into position. But they don't say anything, so I keep my gaze focused on the brick wall to my left. "My mom made it pretty clear that ballet was going to be my thing, whether I liked it or not." I shrug. "I guess it's good I liked it."

Ava moves the camera away from their face. "Do you think you would have stuck with it this long without her influence?"

I note their careful choice of words and wonder how many of these photo shoots turn into therapy sessions. "I'd like to think so, but I don't really know."

They snap a few more photos. "These look perfect." Ava hops off the edge of the bed and looks at the screen of the camera. "Look how fantastic you look." They show me the tiny screen.

I'm in a slight state of shock as they flip through the images they just captured. If I didn't know that was me, I would have easily breezed right by those photos, assuming it was some gorgeous, self-confident model. "Holy shit."

"And we're just getting started. Once you learn these poses and the best angles, we're going to be unstoppable."

Ava directs me into the next pose, on my stomach with my feet kicked up behind me. After that I do a wardrobe change, and after looking at another incredible round of photos, I start to feel like I might be getting the hang of this. I pick a skimpier set of lingerie this time and follow Ava's instructions when they tell me to get on my knees.

"Good. Now move around a bit while I'm shooting you, play with your hair, brush your fingers along your skin."

I follow their instructions, amazed with how much more comfortable I feel after just twenty minutes of posing.

Ava pauses again, checking their camera, this time without showing me the results. "Do you happen to have your pointe shoes with you?"

I nod, digging them out of my bag. "Should I put them on?"

Their eyes light up and they rush over to the wardrobe rack, handing me a pale pink bra and panties. Even with my newfound disdain for the color pink, I can't help but love this set. I dash into the bathroom to change before slipping into my pointe shoes.

"Is there any way to wrap the ribbon higher on your leg?" Ava asks.

I search my bag for extra ribbon. "I can sew on some longer strips. It'll just take a minute."

They watch me with interest as I work on the shoes. "Do you have to do that every time?"

I laugh. "Yup. You should see what we all do to prepare our shoes. Everyone has their own method." I quickly sew on the ribbons and lace them halfway up my calf.

"Perfect," Ava declares, leading me over to the window. "All right. Give me some moves."

"Any moves in particular?"

"Try to keep it sexy of course, but really, just whatever comes to you."

I take a minute to stretch out my ankles before going up on pointe. I hear the camera clicking, but I tune Ava out and focus on my body. I extend my arms and kick up my leg, giving her long lines and graceful movement. Then I take the lessons she's just taught me, bracing my hands on the window frame so I can arch my back.

"Fuck me these are fucking perfect!" Ava's excitement pulls me back into the present.

I come down onto flat feet, breathing heavily even though I haven't really exerted myself.

"Can I push you to do one more thing?"

I nod, at this point ready to give Ava my firstborn if that's what they want. Ava works miracles, never before have I felt this good about myself, and the confidence feels like a drug. I want more.

Ava asks me to strip out of the bra and panties I'm wearing, and I do so without a hint of hesitation. They angle me in front of the window once again, and it never occurs to me to be shy about the fact that I'm standing naked in front of a window overlooking the streets of New York. They position my arm in a traditional ballet arch, making sure it covers my breasts.

I go up on pointe and the camera clicks into action once again. I know my butt will be fully visible in these shots, but I don't even care. I worked hard for that butt.

"One more pose," they tell me, guiding me back to the bed.

I lay down with my head pointing toward the foot of the bed, using the sheet to cover the lower bits, and kick my legs, pointe shoes and all, up against the headboard.

"Do you want to cover your breasts too?" Ava asks.

"No, let's show them off."

"Yes, love it. Your fifty-year-old self will thank you for capturing them in their naturally perky state."

I laugh, hoping they're right.

Five minutes later, Ava tells me we're all done.

It's been a little over an hour since I first set foot in the studio and yet, I feel like a different person. I change back into my regular clothes and when I exit the bathroom, Ava hands me a gift bag with the pieces of lingerie I wore inside. When they open their arms for a hug, I don't hesitate to step into their embrace.

I don't know where the tears come from, but Ava doesn't seem thrown off by them. They reach for a tissue, and the box's accessibility tells me I'm not the first one to cry in this room.

"Thank you, truly, Ava. That felt life-changing."

"Just wait until you see the final results." They give me a warm, wide smile. "I'll do some light editing, pick the best shots, and send you the files within a couple of weeks."

"I can't wait to see them." The surprising part is that it's the truth. I thank them again, hug them again, and head out of the studio, with my sexy new pieces in tow. I might actually find an occasion to wear them, too.

I take out my phone and find Cord has already texted.

CORD: How did it go?
ME: That was incredible. Thank you so much for setting that up.
CORD: You're welcome. I hope it helped.
ME: It did. I honestly have never felt sexier.

I can't believe I just typed those words to him, but I don't let myself linger in the self-doubt.

CORD: Good. You deserve to feel the way you look, Slippers.
ME: Did you just call me sexy?
CORD: Yes.

CORD: Unless that makes you uncomfortable, in which case I was just commenting on the task at hand.

I bite my lip to tamp down on the grin threatening to overtake my face.

ME: It doesn't make me uncomfortable.
CORD: Good. Sweet dreams, Slippers.
ME: You too.

THIRTEEN

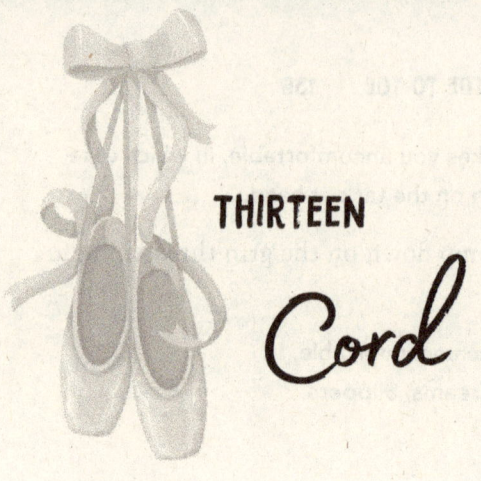

Cord

I don't text Allegra for the rest of my trip. It's harder than I would like to admit. I reach for my phone often, when I'm bored, when I'm tired, when I'm missing home.

It's ridiculous. And dangerous. I know I'm playing with fire, but I can't seem to stop.

I almost suggest we skip our session the Saturday after I get home, telling myself Allegra is prepping for a show and it would be better for her to have the night off. But we need to start working on the choreography for the piece she promised me.

And the way the first glimpse of her pushing through the studio sends a wave of excitement through me surely only has to do with my excitement for the piece.

"Hey, Slippers. How was rehearsal?" I modulate my voice, so it sounds almost bored.

She tosses her bag onto one of the couches before sinking down to the floor next to it and leaning into a stretch. "We open in four days."

I laugh, appreciating the length of her legs as they swing

out to the side and she folds herself in half. "What ballet are you doing again?"

"*Swan Lake*."

I don't bother to hide my disdain, my nose wrinkling at the image of the staid and stodgy work.

"What's wrong with *Swan Lake*?"

"Nothing, I guess. If you're into boring music and outdated choreography."

She pushes herself off the floor. "Not all of us can be as innovative as Cord Donovan. Where did you come up with the completely original idea for hot male strippers, again?"

I roll my eyes. "We are so much more than strippers."

"And *Swan Lake* is so much more than a classic ballet. It's history. And it's art."

"It's boring as fuck."

Her mouth drops open in indignation. "Reisinger would never."

"Who?" I grin, though I know damn well who the choreographer of the famed ballet is.

She reaches into her bag, pulling out a beat-up pair of ballet slippers that promptly get launched directly toward my head.

I catch them easily and toss them right back. "You're going to need those."

She takes them and slips them on. "You don't want me on pointe for this?"

I shake my head, gesturing for her to join me in the center of the studio. "We're not going to go strictly ballet here, I want to experiment with some more modern movements, too."

"How innovative."

"I don't remember you being this sarcastic last week." I smirk at her sass and she gives me one of her own in return.

"That was before you introduced me to Chloe and Ava." She shrugs, shaking out her arms and stretching them across her chest. "You brought this on yourself."

"I've created a monster," I mutter, even though I secretly love it. It's good to see a little fire in her. I step behind her, both of us facing the mirror. "All right. So I'm thinking we'll start on opposite sides of the stage. I want the beginning of this piece to be a little combative, like these two don't like each other, but they can't help coming back together."

She nods. "So they have some kind of history?"

"Maybe. Or maybe there's just something fundamentally different about them. They have different ways of looking at life and its priorities."

"Is that enough to keep two people apart?"

I cross to the other side of the room. "The whole point is that it's not."

She turns to face me, both of us lined up on opposite sides of the studio. "So how do they come together? How do they bridge this gap?"

"That's what we're going to figure out." I begin walking toward her, slowly, like a jungle cat stalking its prey.

Allegra matches my pace, the two of us meeting in the center of the studio, so little distance left between us that I can see the circle of light green around her pupils. Her breath hitches and I take the opportunity to breathe in the lavender dancing in the air.

"Is it okay if I touch you?" I ask.

She nods, eyes on me.

My hand cups the nape of her neck. Without me instructing her, her hand grips the side of my throat, mirroring the pose. "How did you know I was going to ask you to do that?"

She shrugs. "Intuition, I suppose."

I swallow, ignoring how good it feels to have her skin pressed to mine. "Good. With your other hand, grab my wrist, the one that's on your neck."

She does as I ask, easily falling into the spin that comes naturally afterward.

"Did you sneak a look at my choreography notes, Slippers?" I come up behind her, my hand sliding across her stomach.

"I wouldn't think you would bother with notes."

I raise my eyebrows. "Is that an insult?"

"Only if you take it as one. I was thinking you were more of an on the fly, wherever the movement takes you kind of a choreographer."

"I can be." My hand tightens on her waist. "What should come next?"

She leans back into me, letting her hand latch on to my forearm. I lower my head, my nose running up the side of her throat. She spins in my arms, her hands coming to rest on my chest. Then she pushes me away.

"I like that." Rounding my shoulders, I slide even farther away from her, putting more space in between us. "We'll put some kind of solo in here. Do you have any thoughts?"

Her head tilts to the side. "Do you have a song picked out?"

"I'm still looking for the perfect one. But it will be pretty slow. Probably something R and B."

"Let me think on it."

"Sure. Let's plan on an eight count and then we come back together." I cross back to the center of the floor and crook my finger in her direction.

"Did you just summon me?" A pink flush spreads over her chest. I can't tell if she's embarrassed or turned on, but I know which I would prefer.

My hand finds the back of her neck again, but this time I cup her gently, cradling her head in my hands. "Dip," I warn a second before lowering her almost to the floor. I bring her back to standing, my hands trailing down her arms to settle on her hips. "Hands on my shoulders," I instruct.

She doesn't say anything, but she follows my directives, our movements flowing seamlessly from one to the next. She's looser than I expected, open to my choreography and bringing her own flair to it.

I lift her, spinning in a slow circle. When I lower her back to the ground, her body drags against mine. I don't let her feet find purchase. "Wrap your thigh around my hip." My voice comes out huskier than it should.

She positions her leg and I step into a deep lunge. The move presses our cores together and we take in a collective breath. We rise once again and my hands move to her elbows.

"Drop into a split." I lower her and raise her again with ease, spinning her around so her back is pressed to my front. "Now let's put those salsa lessons to good use." My hands brace her hips and she leans back into my chest.

I lead her in a slowed-down version of the salsa steps we practiced in the club. Her hips move easily now, curving and swaying right along with mine.

I add a few more steps and then we go back to our beginning positions and run through everything. I pause to ask for her thoughts, her ideas, the piece becoming more of a collaboration than one I've choreographed on my own. It's a give-and-take, and I find myself enjoying the process.

I check my watch after our second run-through. "We should probably stop here. I want to work on some lifts, but I want Noah to be here so we have an extra spotter, and I know how packed the rest of your week is."

She shrugs. When we finished with the choreography, she dropped her hands from around my neck, so I dropped mine from her waist, but we still stand close enough together that I can read the reluctance in her eyes. "We don't need a spotter, I know how to fall."

I raise both eyebrows. "You think I'm going to chance you getting injured right before you open a show?"

"I thought you hated *Swan Lake*."

"Just because I think classical ballet is boring doesn't mean I don't understand what it means to you."

She opens her mouth and I expect one of her fiery comebacks, but instead all she says is "Thank you."

I mask my surprise at her genuine thanks. "For what?"

"For respecting me and my career."

My jaw clenches. "You don't have to thank me for the bare minimum, Allegra."

She shuffles a step away as if the small distance between us can keep me from seeing too much.

I clear my throat, needing this lesson to come to an end even more than she does. "Anyway. It's getting late. Do you need a ride home?"

She shakes her head. "Subway is fine." She crosses the studio to the sitting area and gathers her things. "I have a dress rehearsal Tuesday evening and a show on Saturday, so I won't be around for another lesson."

I nod. "I figured as much. We can finish working on the piece next week. Tuesday?" I make my voice casual but can't deny that I want to know when I'll see her again.

"Sounds good." She takes her time slipping into her sweatshirt and stepping into her joggers and Uggs.

I watch her the entire time, my eyes unable to pull away. "Next week is our last week before auditions, right?" She's ready, I know she is. But the real question is whether or not she knows she is.

Her face falls slightly. "Yeah, that's right."

"And the weekend after auditions is your sister's wedding?" It's a cursory question because I know exactly when the wedding is. "How is planning going?"

"You are not actually coming with me to my sister's wedding."

"You think I'm going to disappoint Bethany on her big day?"

"How do you know my sister's—you know what? I don't want to know." She throws her bag over her shoulder and heads toward the door. "See you next week, Cord."

"Merde, Slippers."

It isn't until she's already out the door that I realize I might have fucked up, bestowing her with the traditional send-off ballet dancers give to one another before a show.

Oh well. There's no way she hasn't figured out something about my training by now. But she clearly doesn't know the whole story, at least not yet. Or she wouldn't keep coming back here.

FOURTEEN

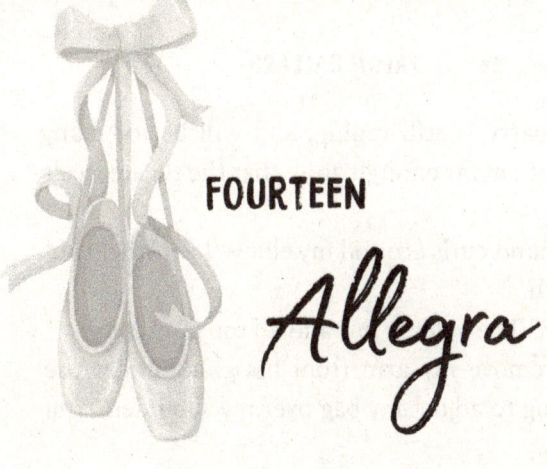

Swan Lake opens to three nights of sold-out crowds and standing ovations. Even though part of my job as one of the Little Swans is to blend in, it doesn't keep me from blushing each time someone tells me I was the standout performer in our foursome. We have an opening-night gala for our patrons after our first show and I catch David watching me as guest after guest compliments me. I meet his eyes, arching one eyebrow, because I hope he is noticing the reactions my performance has been garnering.

He raises his glass, offering me a silent toast.

It should bolster me even further, but instead, his simple gesture turns my stomach. I adjust the hem of my black sheath dress, tugging it down as if I can hide behind it.

Auditions are in a week, I silently remind myself. If ever there was a time to indulge David, now would be it.

The moment it's safe to leave the party without being rude, I slip away from the lobby of the theater and head back to the dressing rooms to grab my stuff. I gather my dance bag and my purse and head back out into the dim hallway. The party is still raging, and will be for many more hours, but I'm far enough away that the theater feels empty.

So when a hand curls around my elbow, I can't help but let out a screech.

"It's just me." The voice is low and all too familiar.

"David." I remove my arm from his grasp under the guise of needing to adjust my bag over my shoulder. "You scared me."

He chuckles and doesn't apologize. "I saw you sneaking out and wanted to make sure I had a chance to tell you how magnificent you were tonight."

We both know he could have very well saved his comments for our next company class, but I force a smile. "Thank you. That means a lot."

He leans against the wall, one hand in his pocket, the other wrapped around a glass of whiskey. "Are you still planning on auditioning for the role of the courtesan?"

My throat closes and I subtly move another step away. "I am."

He leans forward, erasing the distance I just put between us. "I can't wait to see what you can do." He removes his hand from his pocket, drawing a single finger down the length of my bare arm.

I wish I'd put on my coat in the dressing room. "Hopefully I won't let you down."

"Perhaps we could think of tonight as a little preaudition session?" He pushes off the wall, closing the distance between us. There might be little light in the hallway, but there's enough to make out the glaze in his eyes. Who knows how much he's had to drink at this point?

My phone vibrates inside my purse, the rattle loud

enough to startle both of us. I welcome the distraction, moving out of David's orbit as I pull it from my bag.

Cord Donovan flashes across my screen and never have I been more grateful for an unexpected phone call.

"I have to take this, have a good night, David," I say with a smile, striding quickly down the hallway toward the doors, my footsteps echoing on the linoleum tile, swiping to answer the call as I walk. "Hello?"

"Hey Slippers." His voice is soft and hesitant.

"Oh hi, thank you so much for taking the time to call me back at such a late hour. I've been waiting for your call." I raise my volume, hoping it's enough to deter David and keep him from following me.

"Allegra? Everything okay?" Concern laces his words.

I grip the phone so tightly I'm afraid it will leave a mark. I finally reach the doors, pushing out into nighttime air that has grown a little chilly. I never put my jacket on, but the rush of cool air soothes my skin.

"Allegra?"

"I'm okay." I check behind me, relieved when I don't see anyone following in my rushed steps.

"What's going on? Do I need to come get you? Where are you?"

The frantic concern all too apparent in his voice calms my racing heart. I pause on the sidewalk, taking in a few deep breaths before shrugging into my coat and continuing to make my way home.

"I just left the theater, and I'm fine."

"What happened?" His voice has gone quiet, laced with something bordering on dangerous.

"David cornered me in the hallway on my way out, but you called just in time."

"Did he hurt you?"

"I'm fine," I repeat, more firmly this time. "Promise."

He lets out a long sigh. "Okay."

"So how can I help you?"

"What do you mean?"

I laugh, and it sounds strained even in my own ears. "You called me, remember?"

"Oh. Right. I was just calling to see how the show went."

I bite my lip to keep a grin from spreading across my face. We aren't really pick up the phone and call to see how the show went kind of friends. "It was good. I felt really good about it, actually."

"Good." He clears his throat. "Um, are you walking home?"

"Yes. Just a couple blocks away." The one good thing my studio has going for it is its proximity to the BNY building.

"Mind if we stay on the phone until you get home?"

I roll my eyes. "I make this walk late at night all the time, Cord. When did you get so protective?"

"Just guarding my investment. I provided your lessons, just want to make sure I get to cash in on my performance."

"Right." Whatever the reason, it warms something in me.

I reach my building a couple of minutes of small talk later. "I'm opening the front door of my building. I just pressed the button for the elevator. I am now on the elevator."

"Haha. Your wit knows no bounds."

"I know." I step from the elevator and walk down the hall to my door. Where a huge bouquet of pink and purple flowers sits on my doormat. "Huh."

"Everything okay?"

"Yeah. Someone sent me flowers, which is odd because my parents are coming to the show tomorrow so they could have just brought them then." I scoop up the heavy vase after I unlock and open my front door. Setting the blooms down on my kitchen counter, I search for a card, finally locating one of those small rectangular ones that come standard from the florist.

Congrats on your opening. I'm sure you were wonderful, even if Swan Lake is vastly overrated.

I run my thumb over the words, a grin breaking across my face. "Are these from you?"

There's an awkwardly long pause. "Yeah, they are. Congrats on opening night, Slippers."

"They're beautiful. Thank you."

"You're welcome. You should get some sleep. I'll talk to you later."

"Sure. Thanks for calling."

He clears his throat. "Of course. I'm glad the show went well. I'm sure you danced beautifully. You always do."

THE SUNDAY OF OPENING WEEKEND IS THE FIRST DAY OFF I'VE had in months, and I start it with an optional class. When I was twelve, I got strep throat and had to miss three days of ballet. Upon my return, my instructor told me how much I had lost after just three days away, that even one day away from the barre is enough to show.

I don't think I've missed a day since, unless I've been injured, and even then, I would typically push the boundaries and be back in class before it was advisable.

So despite having just finished my third performance of

the week the night before, I still wake up early on Sunday. Still slide on my leotard and tights and joggers, still step into my pointe shoes. A day without ballet would be like a day without breathing.

I haven't spoken with Cord since our conversation on opening night. Every time I walk by the flowers sitting on my table, I can't help but smile.

Both Bethany and my parents asked about him when they came to see the show, neither fully accepting that the two of us are just friends.

It's getting harder and harder for me to accept we're just friends.

But I can't let myself go there. Auditions are in a week, and one hundred percent of my attention needs to be focused on securing this role, and hoping the role translates into the promotion I've been working for since the moment I first twirled around in a tutu.

When I walk into the Six Pact studio on Tuesday evening, I'm somewhat relieved to see both Noah and Cord waiting for me. I've been rehearsing what to say to Cord, and my attempts to sound cool and casual have come out as stilted as any rehearsed conversation might. Having Noah here means we have a buffer, and it feels like a much-needed one.

"Hey Allegra," Noah greets me warmly, wrapping me in an unexpected hug. His dark black hair is pulled back into a man bun and though it's a look I normally hate, it works on him. "How were your shows?"

I toss my bag onto one of the chairs, rifling around before finding my ballet slippers. "They were good, thanks for asking."

"I was hoping to make it over to one, but we have performances at the same time."

I pull on the slippers and do a couple of quick stretches. "Do you go to the ballet often?" I know Noah is classically trained, but I would have assumed Cord's general disdain for traditional ballet was a shared sentiment.

Noah shrugs, reaching an arm across his chest to stretch. I don't miss how the cotton of his T-shirt pulls tight against his rippling arm muscles. "I like to when I can. I still have an appreciation for the art of it, even if I'm not in it anymore."

"Hmm." I raise the volume of my voice since Cord remains on the other side of the room, fiddling with his phone. "So what you're saying is that ballet is highly entertaining and a totally valid form of art?"

Cord's eyes roll so hard, I can see it from across the room. "I never said ballet wasn't a valid art form."

"Just that it's boring?" I cross to the center of the studio.

Cord meets me in the middle. "It is boring."

Noah's eyes drift back and forth between us. "Perhaps we could focus less on the merits of ballet and more on the lifts you need me for?"

Cord's eyes meet mine. "Ready?"

"Always."

"I'll only be touching you if you need a catch, but is it okay if I put my hands on you?" Noah asks.

"Of course. Thank you for spotting." Even though it doesn't feel needed, I know the last thing I need a week before an audition is an injury. I turn to Cord before he can ask. "And yes, you can also put your hands on me." It's not the first time I've given him permission to touch me, but it is the first time my cheeks have heated as I've said it. I clear my throat and turn my attention to the mirror so I don't have to make eye contact.

Unfortunately, Cord's eyes in the reflection are only slightly less potent than his eyes directly gazing into mine.

Noah moves off to the side as Cord steps up behind me. "Okay, so first I want to try this one where you'll end up upside down. Your hand will wrap around my thigh and then I'll transition you into a cradle." His hands land on my lower back and he counts us off.

I jump as he lifts, his hands rotating me into position. He holds me up in the air for longer than needed so he can guide my hand movements, then he spins me around and I end up cradled in his arms before he sets my feet back on the ground.

I didn't really know what to expect, because you never know what to expect when partnering someone new, but Cord's hands are strong yet gentle, his grip firm enough to make me feel safe, but not so tight as to be bruising. Even though we've never done anything like this together before, we immediately have a balance, like we've been partners for years.

We do the lift a couple of times, until it's smooth and seamless. Noah only needs to step in once, and even then, his assistance is barely needed.

"Cool," Cord says. "Let's try one that's a little tougher." He takes a few large strides away from me, putting a decent amount of space between us. "I want you to run, jump into my arms, and then I'm going to push you up. Your hands can balance on my shoulders, I'll keep a grip on your hips."

Noah whistles, reminding me that it isn't just me and

Cord alone in the studio this time. He moves so he's standing behind Cord, ready to be an extra set of hands in case something goes wrong.

"Need a minute?" Cord asks, giving me space to freak out about launching myself at him and expecting him to catch me.

"No, I'm good." And I am. I know he won't drop me. "Ready?"

Cord nods and I take off, running just a couple of steps before leaping. Cord catches me by the hips easily, using my momentum to swing me up into the air. My hands find purchase on his shoulders and he steadies me, first with two hands. Once I'm stable and balanced, he drops one hand.

We hold the pose for a few seconds before he lowers me to the ground.

"That feel okay for you?"

I nod. "Do you want to try it with me going hands-free? It felt pretty steady on my end."

Cord nods his agreement and we take our starting position once again.

I don't miss how Noah moves closer to Cord, but I put all my focus on launching myself into Cord's arms. He swings me up in the air just as effortlessly this time. Once I'm steadily balanced on his one hand, I remove my hands from his shoulders, inching them away from the strength of his arms in case I need to grab on again. But Cord doesn't even flinch under the added weight and I don't so much as wobble.

"Why don't you toss and catch her for the dismount?" Noah suggests, coming around in front of Cord. "You feel okay with that, Allegra?"

"Yup." I say as little as possible, not wanting to take focus away from controlling my breathing and keeping my abs tight.

Cord bends his knees a bit before tossing me up in the air. I spin once and land perfectly in the cradle of his arms. It's warm and safe and our faces are so close together, I can see the stubble dotting his chin and the fleck of green swimming among the blue in his right eye. He shifts me in his arms, holding me tighter rather than putting me down. My hands are around his neck and my fingers brush the long strands of hair at his nape. His breath catches and I'm pretty sure the gap between our mouths shifts closer.

"You two are making this look ridiculously easy." Noah claps Cord on the back, breaking the spell.

Cord sets me back down on the ground, his hands lingering for just a second too long. He clears his throat. "I have just a couple more, if you're up for it."

"Sure." My stomach is flipping, but I don't think it has anything to do with the lifts, or the literal flips.

Cord runs us through two more lifts, each one smoother than the last. Noah continues to not be needed for much beyond color commentary and the occasional reminder that we're not alone here in the studio. Neither Cord nor I say much beyond his concise instructions and my tacit acknowledgment of the steps. We work quickly and efficiently, and I don't let myself linger in his embrace for longer than is absolutely necessary.

When Cord declares the session complete, Noah offers to walk me to the subway. Cord's jaw tenses when I agree, but he doesn't say anything beyond a simple goodbye. And neither do I.

I don't hear from him again until the weekend rolls around, when he texts to wish me luck for my upcoming shows.

CORD: Auditions are Tuesday, right?
ME: Yes.
CORD: Can you come to the studio Monday night? It will give us a chance for one more lesson.
ME: Sure. I'll see you then.
CORD: Merde, Slippers.
ME: Thanks. Good night, Cord.
CORD: Good night.

ON SATURDAY AFTERNOON, JUST AS I'M GETTING READY TO leave for the theater, my email pings with an incoming message. I check my phone and see it's from Ava. They've sent me the final proofs from my boudoir shoot, and even though I need to be on my way, I drop my ballet bag near my front door and swipe the message open. I can't wait to see the photos and I'm not going to risk opening them in the dressing room where anyone could be looking over my shoulder.

My breath catches as I scroll through the photos. If I didn't know better, I would think the person in these photos was a stranger. Someone sexy and confident, who knows just how beautiful she is. I flip through picture after picture, each one more captivating than the last. It's not just my body, which even I can admit looks phenomenal, there's a spark in my eyes, a fire I don't always see. A fire I don't usually feel.

I can't put into words what it feels like to see myself like this. I look beautiful. I look fucking hot.

I look like someone who is comfortable in her own skin. No, not just comfortable, someone who relishes and revels in her skin.

I look like someone I haven't felt like in a really long time. Maybe ever.

I don't realize that tears have pooled in my eyes until they're spilling down my cheeks.

"Shit," I mutter, wiping under my eyes. The last thing I need is to be puffy before a performance. I click off my phone and pick up my bag. I need to head out or I'm going to be late for my self-imposed call time.

But I don't open the front door, my fingers drawn instead back to my phone. I punch in my passcode and open my messages.

ME: I got the photos from my shoot with Ava back.
CORD: Awesome! Are you happy with how they came out?
ME: Beyond happy.
ME: I don't know what to say, Cord. I never would have thought to do something like that for myself, and I never would have thought it would make me feel so . . .
CORD: So sexy?
ME: So confident.
ME: But also sexy, I suppose.
CORD: Good. That was the goal.

I bite my lip, typing and erasing the next message three times before I finally decide, fuck it, and hit send.

ME: Do you want to see some of the shots?

I watch the typing bubbles dance along the bottom of my screen for what feels like an hour.

CORD: Do you want me to see them?
ME: I wouldn't have asked if I didn't.
CORD: Then I would love to, Slippers.

I suck in a breath, suddenly doubting myself. Why the fuck did I ask him that?

CORD: It's okay if you change your mind and don't want to send them.

I smile, because of course he's going to give me an out. I flick through the photos again, picking out my four favorites; in one of them I'm wearing the pink lingerie set and I almost laugh at the juxtaposition of the skimpy lace and the basic pink leotard I'm currently wearing. Before I can think about it further, I send them to Cord.

FIFTEEN
Cord

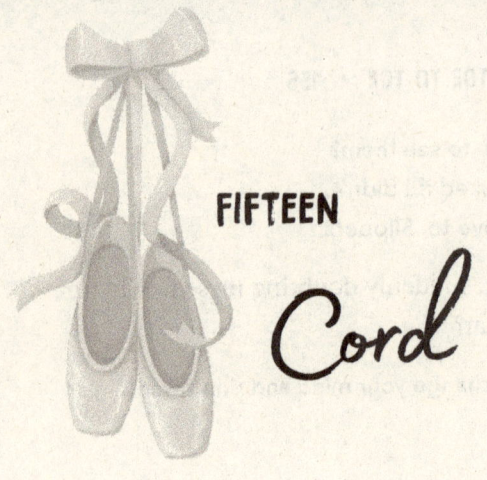

My phone buzzes in my hand, but I hesitate to look at the screen. Either Allegra has sent me the photos or she decided she didn't want me to see them after all. Either way, everything between us is about to change.

I take in a long breath and then glance at the screen. A thumbnail of an image pops up, then another, then another, then another.

I close my eyes, punching in my passcode by rote. When I open them, the first of the photos is there, enlarged on the screen.

Allegra, wrapped up in pretty pink lingerie, a sexy smirk on her face.

Allegra in a different set of lingerie, in an arabesque in front of a window. The light hits her face, making it look like a glow emanates from her skin.

Allegra, wearing nothing but her pointe shoes. Her body is angled and posed so the only thing I can really see is the perfect curve of her ass, but I stare at it for so long, I can almost feel the smooth skin under my palm as I imagine my hands skating over her bare flesh. The breath in my lungs catches there.

She's sent me one more. This one almost knocks me over, my hand blindly grasping for the wall.

Allegra, on a bed, her long legs resting against the headboard. A white sheet covers her lower half, but her breasts are bared, fully visible. Round and perfect and seemingly just waiting for my tongue to trace the peaked buds of her nipples.

I've been silent for way too long, but I don't know how I'm supposed to form coherent thoughts right now. Still, I don't want her to get the wrong impression—that I'm not responding because I'm not interested. Nothing could be further from the truth.

ME: Holy shit, Slippers.
ME: These are fucking stunning.
ME: I don't even have words. Seriously.
ME: Thank you for letting me see them.

I swipe back through each of the photos again, reaching down to adjust myself, my dick gone half hard in my jeans.

ALLEGRA: I'm glad you like them.
ME: I don't just like them.
ME: Fuck. These are going to be burned in my brain for a long time.

I don't know how I'm going to get them out of my brain. I don't know how I can expect my brain to regain function at this point.

ALLEGRA: Well, they live on your phone now so you can look at them any time.

ME: Is that so?
ALLEGRA: It is.

Is that an invitation? Do I want it to be one?

ME: Do you want me to save them for later, Allegra? Do you want me to look at them again later tonight, when I'm home alone?

I shouldn't want to, especially not after what I heard on opening night. It should have been a stark reminder of why this is a terrible idea. Why I need to stay the hell away from Allegra Hart and any association with Ballet New York.

But that doesn't stop me from pushing her.

ALLEGRA: What if I do?
ME: If you do, then I will.
ALLEGRA: I want you to look at the photos of me when you get home tonight, Cord.

My cock twitches in my pants. I'm seconds away from jerking myself off right now. But then my eyes catch on the time.

ME: Fuck.
ME: I have to go. We have a preshow meeting I'm supposed to be leading.
ME: And I'm not really in any condition to be standing up before a group of my employees at the moment.

There's a long pause, the typing dots dancing along the bottom of my screen. I keep my eyes trained on them, running banal images through my mind in the hopes of calming down my erection.

ALLEGRA: Okay. Have a good show tonight.
ME: Can I text you later?

I send the message before I truly consider all the reasons why I shouldn't. Am I going to get home tonight and spend my evening sexting with Allegra Hart? Am I going to stroke my cock while I look at her gorgeous body and think about all the things I would do to her if I had her in my bed?

I'm about to retract the offer when she responds.

ALLEGRA: Of course.

Fuck. I don't respond, shoving my phone in my back pocket and grabbing my bag. I'm already running late, so I jog to the theater, using the brief time and sharp air to clear my mind.

When I arrive at the Six Pact theater, the guys are already gathered in the audience, Noah onstage leading the preshow meeting.

I'm pissed at myself, but at least I know Noah is always here to cover for me when I fuck up. I give him a wave to let him know I'm here, then head backstage to my dressing room.

I try not to be a diva when it comes to the show, but the one thing I insisted on was a private dressing room, and tonight I'm grateful for it. I never drink before shows—I rarely drink at all—but I find the emergency stash of whiskey I keep in my cupboard and pour myself a shot. The liquor blazes a trail of fire down my throat and I let the burn center me.

Getting involved with Allegra would be a colossal mistake.

My brain knows this. Even my heart knows this, despite it protesting more and more lately.

It's my dick that's the real problem here.

Maybe the solution is to finally get laid for the first time in forever. God knows all I have to do is find a willing partner after the show. It wouldn't even be that hard.

But I've never been into casual sex, despite what people might assume about me and my job.

Something tells me casual sex is not the way to get Allegra out of my head anyway.

There's a knock on my door just as I'm pouring myself a second shot.

"Come in." I know it's Noah even before he opens the door, letting himself into the room and closing it behind him.

"Everything okay?"

Of course he's not mad at me for shirking my responsibilities and leaving him to pick up the slack.

"Is that whiskey? Jesus, Cord, is the club in trouble? What the fuck is going on?"

I hand him the shot instead of drinking it myself, sinking into the chair in front of the dressing table I don't actually use. Some of the guys wear makeup, both on their face and body—to enhance their muscles—but I've had enough stage makeup plastered on my skin to last a lifetime.

Noah perches on the table, downing the shot. "Never one to turn down free booze, but don't think you're getting rid of me that easily."

"I fucked up."

"This is about Allegra, isn't it?"

Fuck the people in my life for being so damn intuitive. Can't a guy get a little privacy? I don't confirm or deny, which Noah takes for the confirmation it is.

He sighs, leaning back against the mirror. "I don't really see what the big problem is, bro."

I shoot him a look. I haven't told the full story to many people, but Noah is one of them. If anyone should understand why getting involved with Allegra would be a terrible decision, it's him.

He shrugs. "Not sorry. I don't think it's fair to impose your personal history on another person who had nothing to do with the situation."

I take the shot glass back from him, refilling it. "I called her the other night, after her show opened."

He arches his dark eyebrows but doesn't say anything.

"She was in a panic, totally freaked out, couldn't catch her breath. Used me as a diversion."

"Shit. What happened to her?"

"I didn't get the full story, but from what I gathered, her director put her in some kind of uncomfortable position. I don't know the extent of it."

"But you can imagine," he mumbles, running a hand through his thick black hair.

"Yeah. I can imagine." I toss back another shot, securing the cap on the bottle and putting it back in the cupboard because I sure as hell don't need any more.

"How did it make you feel, hearing that?" It's the kind of insightful question I've come to expect from Noah, whose parents are both therapists.

"I think it's what the kids these days might call 'triggering.'" I don't mean to sound sarcastic, but it comes out harsher than I intend.

Noah nods. "I could see how that would be extremely triggering for you. How did you react in the moment?"

"I stayed on the phone with her until she got home." I sigh, leaning back in my chair. "But what I wanted to do was drive my ass uptown and deck the motherfucker. I knew he was toxic based on what he said to Allegra about her auditioning for the role she wants, but being so close to it was a rude awakening."

Noah crosses his arms over his chest, his eyes never leaving my face. "Given what you and Chloe went through, I understand why your boundary has always been no contact with ballet."

"But?"

"But it's been years, Cord. Look at what you've done, what Chloe has done, in the meantime. And if you let the actions of the past keep you from something you want in the future, isn't that just letting them win?" Noah checks the time on his phone. "I gotta go get ready."

The intercom in the room buzzes. "House is now open. Places in thirty."

"Yeah, me too."

Noah hops down from the table, clapping me on the shoulder. "Happy to talk more later if you need to."

I shake my head, knowing he's going to tell me more of the same, just as firmly as I know I'm not ready to hear it. "I appreciate it, man, but I think I'm good."

He levels me with a glare in the mirror. "You're still not going to let yourself have feelings for her, are you?"

I try to force a grin, but it doesn't work. Even if it did, he would know it's a lie. "I can't."

He nods. "Okay. You gotta do what feels right for you."

With another clap on the shoulder, this one maybe a little more forceful than the last one, he lets himself out of my dressing room.

The door thuds shut behind him and I let my head fall

into my hands. A second later, I reach for my phone, pulling up the images Allegra sent me. I know I don't have the strength to fully delete them, but I send them to a password-protected folder and vow not to look at them again.

At least, not until I've figured out my shit.

SIXTEEN

Allegra

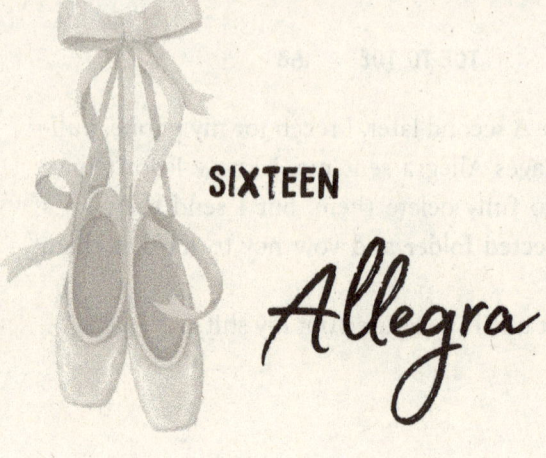

Cord doesn't text that night.

I wake up the following morning with a pit in my stomach and it takes me a second to remember why.

The texting, and the flirting. The ghosting.

I know there are a million practical reasons why he might not have been able to text me last night like he said he would, but there's only one that keeps playing on repeat in my brain.

He doesn't find me all that attractive after all.

Or, maybe worse, he does find me attractive, but just not attractive enough.

He probably went and did his show, saw the crowd full of perfect women, and decided to take one of them home instead. Why would he settle for a few slightly suggestive texts with me when he could have a real live woman in his bed, one who's had confidence in herself for more than a few days?

I get in my head during the show that day and I hate myself for letting him affect my performance. I vow never to let that happen again.

When I arrive at the Six Pact studio on Monday, the night before my big audition, I'm a few minutes late, which for me might as well be hours late. I almost didn't come. But I owe it to Cord to see my end of the bargain through. And with my audition tomorrow, I know I can't turn down the chance for this final lesson.

"Hey," Cord says when I enter the studio. He's standing near the sound system, in the far corner of the room. Like he wants to keep the distance between us.

"Hi." I toss my bag on one of the chairs, sinking to the floor to change my shoes and stretch.

"How were your shows this weekend?"

"Fine." If he wants to play the avoidance game, I certainly am not going to be the one to make things awkward and ask what happened. "Yours?"

"Good." He fiddles with his phone for a minute, not bothering to even look in my direction.

"Did you pick a song?" I finish my final stretch and hop to my feet. The stilted silence is killing me, and I long for him to hit play and fill the studio with the sound of literally anything.

"Yeah." He punches something on his phone screen and the sound of Alicia Keys's "If I Ain't Got You" blares from the speakers.

He adjusts the volume, and I take a minute to really listen to the song. I've heard it before, of course, but I focus on the beats and the lyrics as more than a casual listener. It's a love song, about how what's on the outside, the superficial things in life, don't really matter if you don't have someone to share it all with.

"I, uh, thought the beat was good." Cord abandons the corner of the room and crosses to the center of the studio.

I nod. "I like it. Is the plan for today to run everything with the music?"

We've yet to put the entire piece together, with full choreography and lifts.

"Yeah. I thought we could run it a couple of times and then I have one final thing for you, a sort of test if you will."

I arch an eyebrow, not that he can see it because he still hasn't looked at me. "A test? What kind of test?"

"You'll see when we get there." Finally, he deigns to look my way. He's far enough away from me that I can't get a good read on his expression, but not so far that I can't see that there's something brimming in the depths of those stupid blue eyes of his.

"Okay. Shall we get started then?" The sooner we do, the sooner I can be out of here. The sooner I can turn my attention to the biggest audition of my life instead of thinking about Cord Donovan's eyes and the emotions they may or may not hold.

We move to our opening positions.

"Let's mark it once without the music, just to get the flow of things," he suggests.

I nod, waiting for his counts before beginning the slow walk to meet him at the center of the stage.

There are maybe three beats in the whole piece where our bodies aren't touching in some manner, and I'm dreading it, that first physical contact with him. But we're marking the moves, not doing everything full out, and it allows us to get close without being fully intertwined with each other.

I appreciate the chance to reacclimate myself to him, to being in his space. Now he has no choice but to look at me, and I forget every time what it feels like to be caught in his gaze.

We make it through the first run-through, and I know that was as easy as tonight is going to get.

"With music?" Cord asks.

I nod, moving back to my starting point.

Cord hits play on his phone, then slides it across the floor.

We meet in the middle and his hand reaches up to cup the nape of my neck. It's the first move of the dance, but it feels like something else entirely. I don't know if it's the addition of the music, or the combination of the choreographed moves all coming together, but I fall into him. Our eyes stay locked throughout the entire dance, our bodies connecting, each touch more electrifying than the last. In the few moments when we separate, our hands reach for each other, like even the tiniest distance between us is too great. Whatever it was between us, whether the silence from the other night, or the realization it can never work, it melts away with the notes of the song, until there is nothing left separating us.

The moves are choreographed, and yes, we each know what step comes next, but there's also an underlying understanding, a connection between us that makes it feel like we've been dancing together long enough to anticipate each other's every move, every twitch.

Cord picks me up for the final lift, our final pose, my legs wrapped around his waist, my face buried in the crook of his neck. One of his arms wraps around my lower back, keeping me steady. The other plunges into my hair.

The song ends.

I'm breathing heavily, because of the exertion of the

number. The hand of mine splayed across Cord's chest rises and falls with his own heaving breaths.

We hold the pose for so long that by the time Cord sets me back on my feet, my breathing has regulated.

He keeps his arms locked in place around me. Our faces are so close together, all I would have to do is tilt my head and my lips would graze his. I wonder if they feel as soft as they look. My fingers tighten in the fabric of his shirt without me realizing what I'm doing.

Cord drops his hand from my hair, then from my back. He takes a step away from me. "Should we run it a couple more times, just to be sure?"

I nod, unable to open my mouth and make anything resembling words come out. If I was looking for a sign that I am way more affected by Cord than he is by me, I guess this is it. Every inch of my body feels like it's been licked by flames, but to look at him, you would think this was just any other rehearsal.

We run the number three more times.

By the time we hit the final pose on the last run-through, I'm exhausted, emotionally as well as physically. I guess Cord is a much better performer than I ever would have thought because when we're dancing together, he looks like he's seconds away from ripping my clothes off and bending me over the nearest couch. Then the music stops and he can't get away from me fast enough. When the music ends on our fourth run-through, my body goes limp in his arms. He doesn't let me fall.

When he sets me back on the ground, I head for my bag, chugging half a bottle of water in the hopes it will douse the fire burning through my veins.

"Are you heading out?" They're the first words he's said

to me since asking if I wanted to run through the number a few more times.

"Are we done?" I don't mean it in the final sense, but I watch Cord's shoulders tense up when I ask the question.

"I still had one more thing for you, but only if you feel up to it."

I tighten the lid on my water bottle. "My test. Right."

Cord's eyes rove over me, like he's trying to figure out what's going on in my head.

Good fucking luck, because I don't even know what's going on in my head.

"We can skip it, if you want. I think you're ready for your audition."

My audition. The real reason I'm here, putting myself through this back-and-forth and up-and-down cycle of torture that is being in Cord Donovan's presence. The reminder is a bucket of ice water dumped over my head.

"Let's do it." I toss my water bottle back in my bag and pull on the joggers I shucked when I got here. Even though I know whatever test Cord has cooked up will probably require the ability to see my body and how it moves, I also pull on an oversized sweatshirt, needing all the armor I can get.

Cord grabs a folding chair from the corner of the studio and places it in the center of the room.

My breath catches, because he can't be serious. "I don't think me sitting through another lap dance is going to prove anything at this point, and it's certainly not going to help me prepare for my audition."

Also, if I have to watch him dance for me again, watch him touch himself like he did that first night, I might spontaneously combust.

"You're not getting a lap dance." He sits down in the chair. "You're giving one."

My whole body tenses, my steps freezing me in motion. "You can't be serious."

He looks at me, looks *through* me. "I'm dead serious, Slippers. Think of it as the final boss. You nail this, and your audition tomorrow will be a walk in the park."

There are few things in this world I want less in this moment than to writhe my body all over his, but he doesn't drop his eyes from mine, like he knows I need the challenge.

"Fine." I stride purposefully to the center of the room, planting myself right in front of him. Reaching up, I pull the pins from my bun and let my hair fall down. Luckily, I was only in rehearsals today and not in a show so I used half as much hair product and my locks aren't stiff. I take a few seconds to rake my fingers through my long waves before tossing my hair over my shoulder. If Chloe taught me anything, it's the power of a good hair toss. "Give me your phone."

Cord slips it from his pocket and hands it to me and I don't miss the way his eyes linger on my hair. I find the song I want in his music app and hit play. The familiar opening beats of "Pony" echo through the room.

He smirks at me. "A little cliché, don't you think?"

I slide his phone across the room, spinning around so my back faces him, not bothering to respond. My hips begin to sway to the sensuous beats of the song. I hardly have to put effort into the motion anymore, it comes naturally to me, almost as if Cord's hands are resting on my waist, directing my body in the movement.

But I don't need Cord's hands to guide me anymore.

I spin back around, my hands fisting the bottom hem of my sweatshirt. Tugging it over my head, I make direct eye contact with him, and I don't miss the way his eyes trace down the bared expanse of my neck, and over the swells of my breasts, even though he's seen me in a leotard plenty of times by now.

I dance a little closer, giving him my back again, bending over as I slide my pants down my legs. I kick them off and come back to standing with another hair toss. Twirling around the chair, I place my hands on his shoulders, sliding them down his chest, pressing my breasts into the back of his neck as I do.

If I weren't so close to his mouth, I wouldn't have been able to hear the hitch in his breath when my fingers graze the waistband of his pants, but from this close, the sound is unmistakable. I drag my fingers back up over his stomach, letting them tangle in the fabric of his shirt as they do. He flinches when my skin brushes against his and I want to see his face, read the emotions I know can't stay hidden in his eyes.

I walk around him slowly, the intensity of his gaze burning through me as I turn my back to him once again. When Cord danced for me, he used this same motion, bending backward so his head landed in my lap. I reach for one of his hands, the same way he did with mine, tracing it over my collarbone and down the center of my chest. Of course, Cord's hands are much bigger than mine, and his thumb and pinkie end up brushing the sides of my breasts. I hold my breath so he can't see how much the slightest touch affects me.

I know the song is coming to an end, so I hair toss and spin one more time, straddling Cord's thighs and rolling my hips. Letting my eyes meet his, I take his hands and place them on the curve of my ass. He doesn't flinch this time, doesn't show any hint of being uncomfortable with the contact. He doesn't drop his gaze and I don't look away.

I roll my hips again and his fingers tighten, dragging me even closer. The room around us has disappeared, the only thing present in my senses is Cord. The clean laundry smell of him, the dark circles of his pupils, which seem to be expanding by the second. The strength of his grip as he urges my hips to roll and roll again.

I'm trying to focus on my breathing, but I can't seem to make my lungs function properly.

Instead of just rolling my hips this time, I swivel them, making a full circle. And that's when I feel it.

Cord is hard.

I repeat the motion, as if there was any way I could be wrong. But nope. I'm not wrong. I watch him watch me as I notice, but he doesn't say anything. Doesn't still my hips when I move again. If anything, he uses his grip on me to bring me even closer. My hands drift up over the cotton of his T-shirt, landing on his broad shoulders.

An inch separates our mouths now, our bodies so close I can smell the sweat on his skin and feel the flutter of his heart beating through my chest. When my hips continue to roll, Cord reaches down and adjusts himself, adjusts himself so that the aching center of my core brushes his hardness the next time my hips move over his.

I can't stop the gasp that escapes me. It's not that I didn't realize I was turned on by this whole thing, more that I didn't realize how much my body needed this contact until he gives it to me.

Somewhere in the foggy space of my mind, I hear the music end, but I don't stop my movement, don't stop grinding over Cord's lap like I'm a dog in heat. I don't think I can stop. I definitely don't want to.

I want to kiss him, but I'm scared if I do anything to pull us out of this trance, he'll realize what's happening and put a stop to the whole thing and I'm strung so tightly, my nerves so taut, that I think I might burst if I don't find some kind of relief soon.

I want more than this. I want his hands and his mouth to soothe this ache, but I don't know how to ask for it, don't expect him to reciprocate.

But wanting and needing more doesn't stop my body from dragging itself right to the brink. The tension builds inside me, low in my belly. My movements become more frantic and I lean into the grip of Cord's hands as he rocks my body against his.

My breath stutters audibly and Cord growls, his voice a rumble that hits me right where I'm aching. "Come for me, Allegra."

I don't know if it's his directive or that growl or the way my name sounds in his throat, but the orgasm rips through me, racking my whole body until I'm shaking in his arms. I cry out, too lost in the storm of sensations to be self-conscious about the noises coming from me.

Cord lets out a grunt of his own before burying his face in the crook of my neck, his hands moving from my ass up to my neck, holding me close.

Did he just . . . ?

I suck in a breath.

Of course, it doesn't really mean anything. He probably would have come if any half-naked woman had grinded herself to orgasm on his lap. It doesn't have anything to do with me personally.

The way his hands smooth soothing circles over my back feels a little bit personal though.

I wait for his hands to release me before I move again, not wanting to disrupt this fragile bubble we've created. Cord holds me for what feels like forever and not nearly long enough. The warmth of his embrace is steadying and safe and I would stay here all night if I could.

But as soon as he drops his hands from my back, I awkwardly push myself up and out of his lap.

I don't know what to say. I don't know what to feel.

That was one of the hottest things that has ever happened to me, and yet, I'm afraid to open my mouth and say the wrong thing and blow it all to hell.

"Are you okay?" Cord stays seated in the chair, giving me the freedom to move as far away from him as I need to.

But I don't want to move far away from him. I want to climb right back in his lap and let him kiss me senseless. Hell, I already am senseless. "I'm fine. Are you okay?"

Cord huffs out a hint of a laugh. "Yeah, I'm okay, Allegra."

I shuffle my feet for a second before I reach down to collect my discarded clothes. I tug the sweatshirt over my head and step into my joggers. I wait for him to say something else, but when he doesn't, I gather the rest of my things. "I should get home and get some rest before tomorrow."

He runs a hand through his hair, making the back stick up straight. "Right. You have an audition tomorrow."

"I have *the* audition tomorrow." It's as much a reminder for myself as it is for him.

He stands, adjusting his pants and folding up the chair. He takes it over to the other side of the room, leaning it against the wall. He doesn't cross back to the other side of the studio, where I'm still standing and fiddling with my bag even though everything is all packed up.

"Okay then. Thanks for the lessons. I guess just let me know when you want to do the performance." I shift my weight back and forth on my feet, waiting for him to say something, anything, about what just happened. Even if he thinks the whole thing was a huge mistake, I would rather hear that than this stilted silence.

"Will do."

I don't bother waiting any longer. I spin on my heel and race out of the studio. I refuse to let the tears that have been welling fall because I am not going to give Cord Donovan that satisfaction.

SEVENTEEN

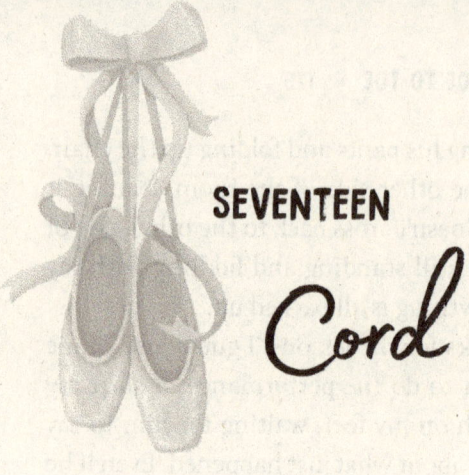
Cord

The moment the studio door thuds shut behind her, I start to follow her out. I don't know what to say about what just happened here, but I can't let her leave without saying anything. I force my feet into action, but by the time I get down to the ground floor, she's already gone.

"Shit."

I can't believe I let myself do that. I can't believe I let myself take advantage of her in that moment.

Dancing with her tonight, I've never experienced anything like it. The way we move together is seamless and sensual. Her body fits in my hands like it was sculpted just for me. I knew I was tempting fate with that fucking lap dance, knew there was no way I was going to be able to fully control myself with her dancing for me like that.

I didn't expect her to be just as turned on as I was.

My eyes fall shut, the memory of her writhing against my lap all too present.

I wipe the image from my brain before I get hard again. I need to think, to focus, and that's not going to help.

Back in the studio, I find my phone and pull up our text thread. I know there's nothing I can say to make it all go away, but I have to say something.

ME: God, Slippers, I'm so sorry.
ME: I shouldn't have let that happen.
ME: Not that I didn't want it to happen, because I did. Obviously.
ME: But I shouldn't have distracted you the night before your audition. I don't want to mess that up for you.
ME: I hope tomorrow goes well. And I hope you get the part you want. You've worked hard for it, and you've earned it.
ME: Anyway. I'm sorry again. And good luck tomorrow.

My fingers move without my permission, sending the string of unanswered texts like a complete fucking idiot. I stare at the screen for a solid ten minutes, waiting for a response. When one doesn't come, I lock up the studio and walk the two blocks to my apartment.

I guess this is it then. I won't ask her to perform the piece with me at Six Pact. It's probably better to just cut our losses now and move on. There was never a possibility of this being more than a business arrangement, and now, with her fully prepped for her audition, the arrangement has come to its end.

I step into a searing-hot shower the moment I get home. When I get out, my phone is lit up with new messages.

My heart lurches in my chest.

ALLEGRA: No apology necessary.
ALLEGRA: And thanks for the well wishes.
ME: Good night, Slippers.

She doesn't respond.

THE NEXT MORNING, I KNOW I NEED A DISTRACTION, OR I'LL spend the entire day worrying about what's happening at a ballet studio thirty blocks away from me. And one thing I promised myself a long time ago is that I would never again worry about what happens inside a ballet studio.

So I call the one person I know can talk me off any ledge.

Chloe is waiting for me at her favorite breakfast spot, a hole-in-the-wall diner with red pleather booths and grease stains on the chipped tables. She insisted if she was going to "drag herself out of bed," then I was going to treat her to her breakfast of choice. She's probably ordered one of everything on the menu since she knows I'm paying, but instead of being annoyed with her, I remember all the times when I would have given anything for her to indulge in a pancake breakfast.

I order my own coffee and an omelet, waiting until the first sip of caffeine has hit my system before I meet her eyes.

"You must have really fucked up if you are (a) awake this early and (b) offering to buy me breakfast." Chloe sips from her own mug, a knowing smirk on her lips. "Does this have anything to do with a certain ballerina who has made her preference for me as the favorite Donovan clear?"

It would probably be easier to just keep my mouth shut

and let Chloe deduce what's happening in my head without my input. "It might."

"Let me guess. I was right and you like her?"

I don't confirm or deny, my mouth twisting into a grimace.

"You like her and she likes you and something happened to let you know she likes you and now you're freaking out because you can't get over your shit and just be with her."

Sometimes having someone in your life who knows you so well is annoying, and this is one of those times. But at least I don't have to go through the trouble of putting my feelings into words.

Instead, I tip my head, giving her the acknowledgment she needs.

She sits back in her chair, crossing her arms over her chest. "It's been ten years, Cord."

"I know."

"When was the last time you checked in with your therapist?"

I rub at the tension lines on my forehead. "Too long ago, apparently."

"You should probably fix that."

"I will."

Our server delivers our order then, a stack of pancakes and a side of eggs and bacon for my sister that makes me regret my own breakfast selection.

Wordlessly, she cuts off a hunk of her pancakes and forks them onto my plate.

"Thanks."

She takes a bite, and for a minute there's just the silence

of our eating. She swigs from her coffee and levels me with a piercing stare. "Have you told her yet?"

I shake my head, burying my gaze in my omelet as if it's the most fascinating breakfast item I've ever seen.

"Why not?"

"It's not my story to tell, Coco."

She cocks her head to the side. "It is if you really care about her."

"I guess that's part of the problem. I don't know if I really care about her or not." The words taste sour in my mouth. A sip of coffee only makes the acidity burn worse.

"That's bullshit and we both know it." She stabs a bite of pancake. "You know I wouldn't care if you told her everything. I like Allegra, and I think she would understand. I don't think there's a professional ballerina out there who wouldn't understand. But if you're going to sit here and pretend like she doesn't mean anything to you, then you don't deserve her anyway."

"Ouch. Aren't you supposed to be on my side?" I reach over to steal another bite of her meal, but she pushes my hand away from her plate.

"Why do you have to always deflect, Cord? We went through something that was super fucked up. It sucked, for both of us. But you can't let it determine the rest of your life."

"I'm not." I sound like a petulant child. Something about debating with my sister brings it out in me.

"You're being ridiculous."

"You're being ridiculous," I mutter under my breath.

Chloe wipes her mouth with her napkin and throws it on top of her half-eaten meal. "Fine. Stew in your own misery. Maybe I'll swoop in and win Allegra for myself."

"Don't even think about it, Coco."

She glares at me. "Guess your feelings aren't as unclear as you want to pretend like they are." She pushes back her chair and stands, like she's about to storm out of the restaurant in a dramatic huff. Instead, she comes around to my side of the table and leans over to hug me. "Call your therapist. Like today. And tell Allegra the truth, Cord. If it's my permission you were waiting for, then you've got it."

With a final squeeze, she strides out of the restaurant, leaving me with the check.

EIGHTEEN

Allegra

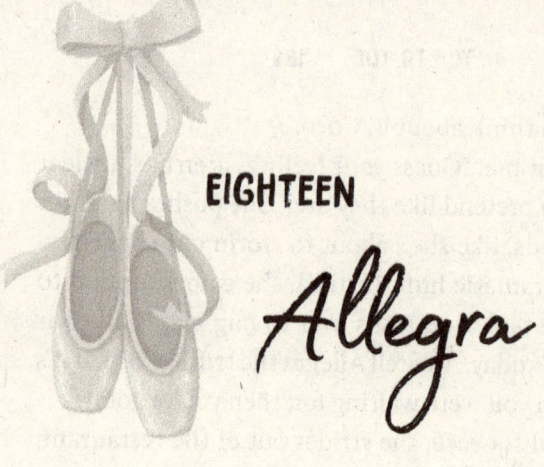

The morning of my audition, I dress in my sexiest leotard. It's one of the few I own that isn't pink. This one is black and low cut with tiny little straps that look like they could snap at any moment. I pair it with a fluttery black skirt and take a risk by leaving my legs bare, no tights.

Several other company members fill the audition room and as David teaches us the steps we'll audition with, I make sure I am in the front of the room. Close to his eyeline but also close to the mirror. As we practice the choreography, I watch myself, not looking for flaws like I would have done at any audition in the past. This time I'm looking for things I'm doing well, looking for things I like.

Cord's simple trick works. By the time it's my turn to perform, confidence is surging through my veins. I know I dance the steps well, but that isn't why I know I've nailed it the second I finished.

It's the look on David's face. Appraising, and appreciative, and if I let myself think on it too much, slightly leering.

I give him a smirk and a raised eyebrow, not backing

down, even when his eyes rake over my body from head to toe.

This part is mine.

And there's only one person I want to share the news with.

I don't have to initiate the conversation because by the time I push out of the studio doors, there's already a text from Cord waiting for me.

CORD: How did it go?
ME: Amazing. I don't think we'll know the results for a while, but I feel really good about it.

I feel more than good about it, but I don't want to jinx myself.

CORD: I knew you would nail it. I hope you're proud of yourself, Slippers.
ME: I am.
ME: Thank you.
CORD: My pleasure.

I still don't know if I can directly bring up what happened in the studio last night, but at the very least, I can see how he might be feeling about the future.

ME: Are you still planning on coming to Bethany's wedding on Saturday?
CORD: Only if it's okay with you.
ME: It is.
ME: I'd like for you to be there.
CORD: Of course you would, I look great in a suit.
ME: I've seen you in a suit in your opening act.
CORD: Should I also plan on taking this one off?

ME: Not at my sister's wedding, no.
CORD: Another time then 😉

My cheeks heat at the insinuation. I send him the pertinent info for the wedding and spend the rest of the day with a smile wide on my face.

WE DON'T TALK MUCH FOR THE REST OF THE WEEK, BUT NOT A day goes by where we don't exchange at least a couple of texts. There are no more lessons to schedule or plans to work out, but that doesn't stop us from finding a reason to reach out. I would be lying if I said a little thrill didn't race through me every time his name appeared on my screen.

I would be an even bigger liar if I claimed I didn't think about that lap dance most nights while lying in bed, sometimes with my vibrator in hand, usually imagining what it might feel like for Cord's fingers to be doing the work.

I let Bethany know Cord will be joining us for the wedding, and I finally break down and admit that things might not be totally platonic between us.

There's a lot of squealing (Bethany) and sighing (me) during our conversation and I'm ninety percent sure she's already planning our wedding, despite my insistence that I'm not looking for a relationship. Bethany has never been one to let a little thing like my thoughts and opinions get in the way of her plans for me.

The day of the wedding, I don't actually see Cord until the ceremony. I spend the morning doing my sister's bidding—willingly and happily—making sure she has everything she could possibly need at a moment's notice. Luckily, because of her intense planning and beyond competent wedding coordinator, everything so far has gone exactly to plan.

It isn't until I reach the altar and watch my baby sister walk down the flower-strewn aisle, sandwiched between our parents, that I fully let the meaning of the day sink in. Bethany is getting married. In just a few minutes, she's going to be someone's wife.

I watch Cassidy watch her walk down the aisle, and my heart fills to bursting. If ever there was a perfect match, it's these two. Cassidy calms my sister, while Bethany pushes Cassidy. They complement each other in every way, and as I listen to them exchange vows, I can't stop myself from thinking it might be nice to find my perfect complement one day. It's not a thought I allow myself to indulge in often, but if ever there were a time, I suppose this is it.

My eyes drift out over the crowd as the happy couple slide wedding bands on each other's fingers. And it shouldn't come as a surprise that my eyes go right to him.

Cord isn't looking at the brides like the rest of the crowd. Instead, he is watching me.

Our eyes meet and some foreign feeling grips my chest, a foreign feeling I'm not quite ready to acknowledge.

I'm really happy he's here, despite any lingering awkwardness.

I turn my attention back to the ladies of the hour just in time to see them share their first kiss as a married couple. The guests burst into applause, cheers ringing around the garden of the local wine bar where Bethany and Cassidy shared their first date.

Bethany reaches to grab her bouquet from me and we share a smile. I want to tell her how proud I am of her, how happy I am for her and Cassidy, but there isn't time, and I don't really need to voice the sentiment. I can tell by her grin that she already knows.

I watch my sister and her new wife be showered with bubbles as they exit their ceremony, before I link arms with Cassidy's brother and follow in their wake.

Cord is sitting in an aisle seat, and as I walk past him, I instinctively reach out my hand. He meets my palm with his. It's the quickest brush, the slightest hint of contact, and considering the last time we touched, it should feel like nothing.

Instead, it feels like everything.

Once the hoopla of the ceremony dies down, I head right for him, ignoring my mother's directive to not go far because we still have family photos to take.

"Hi," I say when I finally spot him on the crowded patio where cocktail hour is being held. The sun is setting and the twinkle lights strung in the trees wink on, making the whole area look like a fairy tale.

"Hi." He hands me a glass of champagne. "You look beautiful."

"Oh, this old thing?" I swish the skirt of the long chiffon dress my mother picked out for me. It's too formal for the venue, and it's, of course, ballet pink.

For a second, neither of us says anything, we just stand and stare at each other, awkward smiles plastered on our faces.

Then a wedding guest bumps into me, pushing me into Cord's space.

His hand darts out to catch my elbow, keeping us from a collision. The guest moves away, but Cord keeps a hold on my arm, keeps me pressed close to his side.

"Thank you for coming. I'm sorry we haven't had much

chance to talk." I swig half of my champagne, nearly choking on the bubbles.

"You had official duties. I didn't mind." His fingers loosen their grip on my elbow, trailing down my forearm and leaving an explosion of goose bumps in their wake.

"I think my official duties are almost coming to an end, and then hopefully we might get the chance to talk?" My voice rises on the not-total question. But we do need to talk, I think. Our conversations since the night of the lap dance have all been casual. Not forced or stiff, but certainly not addressing the orgasm in the room.

"I think that might be a good idea."

I try not to read too much into his words, his expression, the tone of his voice, but it would be impossible not to. He doesn't exactly sound enthused by the prospect, not that many would be by the whole *we need to talk* line.

"Allegra!" My mother's voice echoes around the patio.

I swig the last of my champagne, handing the empty glass to Cord. "I'll be back as soon as I can. You okay here?"

"There's an open bar and a charcuterie table, I'm just fine." He nudges me with his elbow. "We'll talk later."

I rush back inside the wine bar where the reception will take place, the industrial metal vibes a complementary opposite of the outdoor area, before my mother has the chance to completely lose her shit, or worse, discover me standing with Cord. Family photos take forever, and by the time I make it back to Cord, guests are being shuffled off to their dinner tables. Luckily, Bethany has seated me on the opposite side of the room from my parents.

As Cord and I settle into our seats, I introduce him to the other guests at our table. Everyone makes casual conversation as dinner is served and it warms me to hear the love and laughter surrounding Bethany and Cassidy on their big day.

After dinner, the couple shares their first dance, followed by a dance with their dads. Despite the plethora of emotions I've felt throughout the day, watching my sister and my father dance is the first moment that brings a tear to my eye. Applause rings around the room as the song comes to an end. The DJ then invites everyone out to the dance floor, the slow and steady beat of an old love song spilling through the speakers.

Cord's hand finds a spot on the small of my back. "Shall we?"

I nod, wiping under my eyes to hopefully clear any remaining trace of tears.

He leads me to the dance floor and I let myself be swept up in his arms. This is the kind of dancing I'm not usually comfortable with, but I know Cord well enough at this point to let him lead.

His grip on my hand tightens before he spins me twice, pulling me even closer in his embrace when I land back in his arms. "I've been wanting to talk to you about the other night, but it felt like a conversation we should have in person."

I'm tempted to close the distance between us even more, if it means being able to avoid looking directly at him. "I don't know that it needs to be a conversation. Unless you were upset about it, or I made you uncomfortable."

He leans closer, his lips brushing the shell of my ear. "Did it seem like I was uncomfortable, Allegra?"

I force my lungs to expand. "Maybe not in the moment, but I would understand if you felt weird about it looking back on it."

"Do you feel weird about it looking back on it?"

I hesitate before answering. "No."

"I don't either." Cord spins me out, pulling me back in and shifting our position so my back is pressed to his chest. "It was one of the hottest things that ever happened to me."

I really hope he doesn't feel the shiver racing up my spine at his declaration, but given our position, it's unlikely. "Me too," I admit in a whisper.

He spins me out again, returning us to our original position, his hand low on my back, our other hands joined. "I like you, Allegra."

I swallow, because surely he can't mean that, not in the way I want him to mean it.

"But I understand how important your career is to you," he continues. "I know the time commitment it's going to require when you get this part." There's an understanding there, in the depths of his eyes, and I know he really means it.

Other people I've dated in the past have said they understood that I have a demanding job that always comes first. But they inevitably would grow frustrated with me when I couldn't put them first, when I had to miss dates or go on tour, and they weren't my priority.

Cord's hand slides down my jaw, gently gripping my chin and lifting my gaze to his. "I don't think we can let anything like that happen again, Slippers."

It isn't what I'm expecting him to say, and it stops the breath in my chest. "Oh."

"Not because I don't like you, but because I think I could like you too much." His voice softens as the song fades out. He looks like he wants to say more, but those perfect lips of his don't open again.

The DJ gets back on the mic, letting the wedding guests know it's time to party before shifting the music to a popular dance tune. Someone flips the switch on a disco ball and the twinkling lights illuminate the dance floor. The crowd around us immediately transforms from couples swaying peacefully to groups jumping up and down to the beat.

"Let's just have fun tonight, okay?" Cord has to yell the words in my ear to be heard over the combination of the music and the crowd singing along to it.

I nod, not sure I have the power to make my voice loud enough to answer back.

I know I will be thinking about Cord's words for maybe the rest of my life, but for right now, I turn my attention to celebrating my sister. When she grabs my hands, pulling me into the center of the circle, I lose sight of Cord.

I miss him the second he's gone.

NINETEEN

Cord

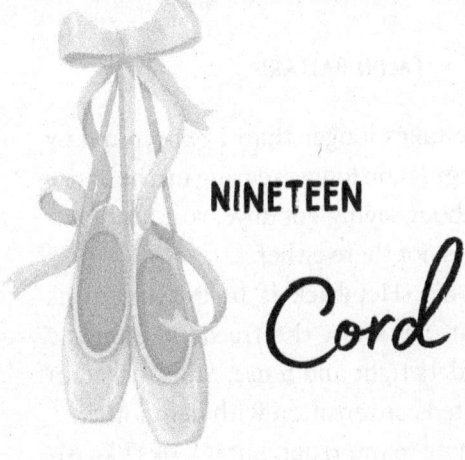

I watch Allegra from the outer edge of the dance party. Her hands are in the air, hips swaying as she bounces to the beat of the catchy pop tune. I've never seen her look so free. I've never seen her look more beautiful.

I chug the remainder of my beer, handing off the empty glass to a circling server. I wish I were out on that dance floor with her, our bodies pressed together, sticky with sweat, drunk on adrenaline and good vibes.

But I've come to an upsetting conclusion: Chloe is right.

If I have any real thoughts about wanting to take things further with Allegra—and I think it's time I stop denying that I do—then I need to tell her everything.

But tonight is not the night to lay all of that at her feet. Tonight is the night for her to celebrate with her sister, and from the look of it, she doesn't need me here to do that. I head for the bathroom, tucked in the corner of the venue with a long line of guests waiting at the door. After this, I'll tell Allegra I need to head out and make plans to see her soon, at a time and place when we can talk and actually hear each other speak.

The bathroom line takes longer than I expect and by the time I emerge, Allegra is no longer tearing up the dance floor. I can't leave without saying goodbye, so I head outside to the bar, but she's not there either.

Eventually, I spot her. Her back is to me, her arms crossed over her chest. She's lost the freedom from the dance floor, her shoulders tight and tense. She's locked in what looks to be a heated conversation with her mother.

Normally I would hate to interrupt, but it looks like Allegra might be in need of a save.

Crossing the patio, I try to catch Allegra's eye, give her a heads-up that I'm approaching, but her back is firmly to me and her mother isn't paying me a lick of attention.

Which is unfortunate, because if she were, maybe she would have tempered her next words.

"You don't know anything about him, Allegra. The man makes a living taking off his clothes, for god's sake."

Scratch that. I don't see a woman like Mrs. Hart tempering anything, no matter who is there to overhear.

"The man makes a very good living running a successful business. The taking off of his clothes is just a bonus."

I can't fight the smile at her defense of me. She's got a little spark, this woman.

"Really, Allegra. Listen to yourself. We are so close to getting what we want, what we've been working your whole life for. Are you really going to throw it all away for a man?"

Her shoulders stiffen even more, her back going ramrod straight. "I'm not throwing it away for anyone, Mom."

I hate that she doesn't point out that *she* is the one who has worked so hard, not her mother. She isn't the first ballerina with the weight of her mother's former life choices resting on her shoulders, but I hate that when Allegra gets this part—as I know she will—anyone else might try to share in the credit.

"He's a good person, and if I get this role, it will be because of the help he has given me. I wish you would just give him a chance."

"He's going to ruin your career if you are seen with him."

"That's a little dramatic."

Her mother moves a step closer to Allegra, though she doesn't bother to lower her voice. "Did you even bother to google this man? Do you know anything about his history?"

My hackles start to rise. I move from my mostly hidden position, walking as fast as I can toward her, but I know I'm going to be too late.

"Cord Donovan used to dance with the Pacific Ballet. But he was fired. Do you know why?" She doesn't pause, doesn't give either of us a chance to stop her. "Because he punched his director, Allegra. He beat up his director because of jealousy about a girl."

"Cord would never do something like that. I'm not going to listen to this anymore." Allegra spins on her heel, turning around to find me waiting. Her eyes widen and shame paints her cheeks a pink the same color as her dress. "Oh. You're here."

"I'm here." I don't bother to acknowledge her mother, keeping my attention solely focused on Allegra. "I was coming to say goodbye."

She glances over her shoulder, where her mother stands with a triumphant smile. "How much of that did you hear?"

"Enough." I shove my hands in my pockets so I don't reach for her. "Your mother isn't wrong, Allegra." She isn't completely right either, but there's no point in denying that what she claims is the truth.

Her mother's smile grows. "I'll leave you two to say goodbye. Allegra, don't take too long. You don't want to miss your sister's whole wedding."

Allegra doesn't respond to her mother, her eyes glued on me.

I jump in before she can question me. "I was going to talk to you about all of this, but I didn't want to ruin your night."

"You've had plenty of chances to talk to me before tonight, Cord."

"I know." I gesture to a nearby bench. "Can we sit?"

For a minute it looks like she might refuse, but she finally folds herself onto the wooden bench, arms and legs both crossed tight. "You danced with Pacific Ballet?"

I nod. This is the easy part. "For five years. I started dancing because of Chloe—she always loved ballet more than me. We trained together our whole lives so when we got hired together, it felt like a dream."

"But you hate ballet."

I shrug, studying the pattern of the brick because it's easier than looking at her. "I didn't always. I never loved it like you do, but I didn't always hate it. I love to dance. And I loved performing—that much hasn't changed. And I liked the physical challenge of it."

"So what did change?" Her voice softens, some of the tension draining away.

I chance a look at her. Her hazel eyes are on me, open and listening. I know once I tell her this, it will change everything, just as I know there's no chance for us if I can't be completely honest. "Chloe had an encounter with one of the choreographers. Nothing physical, at first anyway . . ." I trust that Allegra will pick up on what I'm saying without me having to spell out the details. "When she told me about it, I convinced her to go to the director of the company and report it. I went with her. We did all the right things, followed all the steps they told us to take."

"And they didn't believe you." She says it with a certainty only another dancer could deliver.

"I think they believed her."

"They just didn't care."

"The choreographer was a big name and they wanted to keep him happy."

"Jesus, Cord. I'm so sorry that happened to her."

"That's not the end of the story, unfortunately." I lean my elbows on my knees, clasping my hands together.

Allegra places a hand on my thigh, a solid comfort.

"He did it again. Probably because she had the audacity to report him. Something Chloe probably wouldn't have done without my encouragement."

She scoots closer to me, her thigh pressing against mine. "That wasn't your fault, Cord."

I shrug again. I know it wasn't my fault—years of therapy helped me finally accept that. "I know that, deep down. But when she told me it happened again . . . well . . . I didn't exactly have the calm and measured response I did the first time."

Allegra slips her hand in between mine. "No one could blame you for that."

I thread our fingers together. "Everyone else in the company did. They fired both of us. Blacklisted us, too. I had no desire to be a part of ballet anymore, but Chloe would have gone somewhere else if she'd been able to. Dancing was her whole life, and she lost her career because of me."

"I don't think she believes that, just as I know it isn't true."

Chloe doesn't blame me, of course she doesn't. But that's only because she's a better person than I am.

I sit back, keeping our hands clasped together. "So yeah. That's why I hate ballet."

She angles her body toward mine. "Your feelings are pretty well justified, Cord."

I turn toward her, tucking a stray strand of hair behind her ear, knowing I haven't finished being completely honest. "When I called you on opening night..."

Her eyes widen as she thinks back on the conversation. "Shit. I'm so sorry, Cord. I had no idea."

"Why are you apologizing?"

"Because you had to hear that. It must have been extremely triggering for you and I had no idea."

I squeeze her hand. "You aren't the one who should be apologizing."

She bites her lip. "I know. But if it weren't for me begging you for those lessons, none of this would be happening."

"If you hadn't begged me for those lessons, I wouldn't be sitting here right now, about to say fuck my boundaries because I think I'm falling for you, Slippers." My heart pauses in my chest. I can't believe I just said that out loud.

"Oh, Cord." Her entire face softens, a small tugging on her lips. "I feel the same, you know I do."

"But?"

She goes back to worrying her lip. "But ballet is my life. Being in a relationship with anyone right now would be close to impossible."

"And being with a disgraced former dancer would be

even worse?" I try to keep the hurt from turning to venom, but I don't do a very good job.

"That's not what I meant." Hurt lines her eyes and I mentally kick myself for being the one to cause it.

"I know you didn't."

"I don't know if the strength of our feelings matters here, Cord," she whispers.

I untangle my fingers from hers. "We don't need to make any decisions right now."

She nods. "Yeah. I think a couple of days to think things through would help."

It's not a rejection, but it sure as hell feels like one.

I stand, straightening my suit pants and buttoning my jacket. "Well, you know where to find me."

She rises next to me, slipping her hand into mine and tugging me to face her. She opens her mouth to speak, but no words come.

So instead, I lean down, brushing my lips against hers. It's the softest kiss, not enough to satiate my desire for her, but not enough to stoke it either. "Talk to you soon, Slippers."

If she responds, I don't hear it. I'm already on my way out the door.

TWENTY

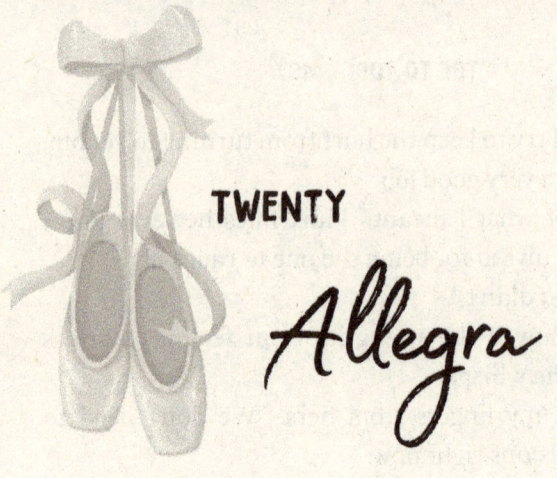
Allegra

I skip class the day after the wedding. I haven't done that in I can't remember how long. I've danced sick and hurt, the morning after a late night out and the day after getting dumped.

Somehow my conversation with Cord last night feels so much worse than any of that.

I'm glad he felt safe enough to open up to me and tell me about his past, though I think I will always wonder if he would have been so honest if my mother hadn't found out what she did. I think there's a small part of him that thought I might think less of him, but really, the opposite is true.

I like him more than I thought I did. But I still don't care about him more than I care about my career. I still can't see a day when I care about any partner more than my career. And so, despite the deep ache in my chest when I replay our conversation in my mind over and over, I know walking away now, before I'm in too deep, is the right thing to do.

Monday my phone rings minutes before my alarm is set to go off. I reach over to my nightstand, blindly grabbing for it, my brain barely able to distinguish between my ringtone and my alarm.

"Hello?" I don't bother to check who's calling before answering, assuming anyone who's calling this early has a good reason.

"Allegra? Did I wake you?"

I sit up straight in bed the second David's voice comes through the speaker. "Nope, I'm awake. Just doing some stretching and getting ready to go work out." It's only a partial lie, as that's what I would be doing in a few minutes.

"Glad to hear it." He clears his throat.

I hold my breath in anticipation, waiting for him to tell me why he's calling.

He takes his time and I'm sure there's a part of him that's enjoying dragging this out. "I'm sure you're wondering why I'm calling so early."

Obviously.

"I wanted to be the first to congratulate you."

I suck in a breath, not willing to celebrate before he's said the exact words I've been longing to hear for most of my life.

"I'd like to offer you the role of Dominique. Assuming you're still interested."

Internally, I squeal, jumping up and down on my bed. Externally, I let myself grin, but I keep my tone cool. "I'm absolutely still interested. I would be honored to work with you on this piece and create this role."

"I'm not going to lie, Allegra, I had my doubts. But you

really sold it during your audition. I watched your body move in ways I didn't think you were capable of."

I know his words shouldn't give me the ick, it's his job to evaluate my body and the way it moves. Luckily, he can't see my face and the way I blanch. "Thank you." Not sure it was a compliment, really, but I go with it.

"Rehearsals will start next week and we should have a contract in your inbox by Friday." He pauses. "I'm taking a chance on you, Allegra. And I don't think I need to mention that earning this part is the first big step toward a permanent position as principal. Don't let me down."

"I won't."

David doesn't say goodbye, the line just goes dead.

I check the screen, making sure he's really off the line before I let myself freak out. That internal celebration becomes external. I leap on top of my bed, jumping around like a little kid, pumping my arms and squealing with excitement. I flop back onto my bed and dig my phone out of the crumple of sheets, pulling up Cord's contact info before I remember I can't really call him.

We said we were going to take a couple days to figure things out, but if anything, getting this part maybe does the work for us. How can I call him to celebrate the thing that is sure to keep us apart?

I call my mom instead, still tucked under the sheets of my bed, and let her tears of joy bolster me further. I want to call Bethany, but she left on her honeymoon this morning and I don't want to interrupt her. I text her instead, knowing she'll be happy for me, but letting her respond on her own timeline. I text Lucy too, and she responds with all the appropriate emojis. The love from my circle feels good, but I can't help but feel like the only person who would really understand what this means to me is the one person I can't share the news with.

ON TUESDAY NIGHT, WHEN I PUSH THROUGH THE DOOR OF Chloe's studio, her eyes immediately widen.

She hesitates for only a moment before coming over and wrapping me in a hug. "Hi. I wasn't sure I would see you again."

"You can't get rid of me that easily. You did help change my life and all."

Chloe pulls away, still holding me by the elbows. A slow smile spreads across her face, making her blue eyes—Cord's blue eyes—sparkle. "Does that mean you got the part?"

I nod, still unable to fully believe it myself. "I got the part."

She squeals so loud, the other dancers stretching turn to us in alarm. "I'm so proud of you, Allegra!"

Given everything I know now, her genuine excitement means even more.

She lowers her voice. "Does Cord know?"

I shake my head. "I'm assuming he told you about the wedding?" I wait for her to nod yes, though I know Cord would have told her everything by now. "I wasn't sure if he would want to hear from me."

"Oh, sweetie." She gives my arm a squeeze. "Let's talk after class, yeah?"

I spend the next forty-five minutes focusing on the freedom I feel when I'm spinning around the pole, the laughter and the comradery with the other people in the class. It's another good reminder that dancing is supposed to be fun.

When the final member of class has said goodnight and the door has clicked shut, Chloe turns to me. "How are you feeling?"

"Right in this moment? Like my vagina is going to be sore tomorrow."

She laughs at my deflection, but rolls her eyes, tugging on my arm so I'm forced to sit next to her on the floor, our backs pressed up against the mirror, legs splayed in front of us. We both instinctively point our toes.

I let the silence linger for a minute. "I'm so sorry about what happened to you, Chloe."

She gives me a soft smile. "It's not your fault."

"I know, but that doesn't mean I'm not sorry."

"It can be really hard to realize that this thing we love so much also has the potential to do a lot of damage, not just to our bodies, but to our hearts and souls."

I nod. It's a realization every dancer comes to at some point in time. The quiet lingers between us for a moment. "I don't want to hurt him," I say softly.

She threads her arm through mine. "I know. And I'm not going to sit here and lie and say that that won't happen."

"So you think we should just call it now before the hurt gets worse?" I hold my breath, not sure what I want her answer to be.

"I didn't say that. I can see how a relationship between the two of you would have its challenges."

"But?"

"But I've never seen my brother happier than he has been over the past few weeks, the past couple days notwithstanding." She nudges me with her shoulder. "I think that's mostly because of you."

My heart clenches with how badly I want that to be

true. "Is there anything I can do, you think, to reassure him?"

"Just be there. Show up and don't let him walk away because he's scared of getting hurt." She leans her head on my shoulder. "And know that he's a bit of a stubborn bastard a lot of the time."

I laugh. "How did you get to be so wise?"

"Years and years of therapy, my friend."

CHLOE'S WORDS LINGER, BUT DESPITE HER CLAIM THAT CORD and I could make it work, I don't reach out to him. Too scared of what might happen if I do, just as scared of what might happen if I don't. Instead of allowing myself to linger in the doubt, I turn all my focus and attention where it really needs to be: on this new ballet.

DAVID'S HANDS CIRCLE MY WAIST, DRAWING ME CLOSER TO HIS body. He presses close against me, his chest to my back, so close his breath warms the nape of my already sweaty neck. He holds me for longer than he should need to before he demonstrates the next step and lets Sam, the dancer playing my lover in the new ballet, step into his place.

We've been in rehearsals for about a week, and it's been nothing like I expected and also exactly what I expected. Gone is the express request to put hands on my body; David uses me like a doll, posing me, moving my limbs however he sees fit. He takes his time with me, showing Sam exactly what he wants. Sam is nice, and a good partner, but he dances with me the same way David choreographs me—like he owns me.

I don't miss the way David's hands often linger, often drift.

I miss dancing with Cord.

It's not a thought I ever expected to have weeks ago, and yet it crosses my mind at least once during every rehearsal.

I haven't spoken to him since the night of the wedding. Haven't spoken to Chloe since that night at the studio. Bethany is still on her honeymoon, and since we aren't rehearsing with the corps yet, my ballet days are often spent with just David and Sam, sometimes joined by the other soloists.

It's not the first time I've felt lonely in my adult life, but the isolation is almost overwhelming, suffocating, to the point where I come home from the studio and just sit and stare into space. Not even the Real Housewives can drag me out of this funk.

Lucy watches me with concern as I change out of my company class shoes and switch to my rehearsal shoes two weeks after landing the part of my dreams. Company class is the one time of day I can count on being surrounded by other people, but it doesn't do much to assuage the loneliness that engulfs me the rest of the day.

"How is everything going with the new ballet? I'm looking forward to working on the new choreo," she says, her eyes scrutinizing me in a way that would make me uncomfortable if my brain was working correctly these days.

"It's good. I think it's going to be really interesting."

"Is it everything you thought it would be?"

I open my mouth to tell her it's everything I wanted it to be and more, but I can't form the words, can't let myself lie to her.

She reaches out a hand, squeezing my forearm. "Can we go get some dinner when you're done with rehearsal?"

My first instinct is to deny her request, because it would be much easier to go home and sit on my bed and stare at the wall. But I know I should accept, know that I can't exist like this for much longer. "Sure. That might be nice."

"I'm not going to let you cancel, Allegra. I'll be waiting for you out front when you're done, okay?"

I nod, blinking away tears that have no business forming. "Thank you."

I can't say rehearsal is easier knowing that I have something to look forward to afterward, but it does at least pass by faster than it has been recently.

True to her word, Lucy waits for me outside the front doors of the studio when I finish with rehearsal. She doesn't ask me where I want to go, as if she knows making even the simplest decision might be enough to push me over the edge.

She leads us to a small café and we sit outside in the warm evening air. It's almost summer, in those blissful few short weeks when the weather is warm without being overly humid. I order a sparkling water and Lucy gets a glass of wine. Before our server can leave the table, I change my order and ask for a glass of wine, too.

Lucy makes small talk until our drinks are delivered, waits for me to take a large swig of wine before she folds her arms on the table and levels me with her insightful stare. "All right, Allegra. Time to fess up. What the hell is going on with you?"

I don't bother trying to deny her; I let everything spill from me in one convoluted chunk of a story. Lucy doesn't interrupt, and when I finally finish telling her everything, she doesn't offer me meaningless platitudes.

She leans back in her chair, arms still folded across her chest. "Shit, Allegra. I don't know what I was expecting, but I never would have guessed you'd gone and fallen in love with a stripper."

"He's not a stripper," I murmur. My throat is parched after so much talking and I quench my thirst by downing half of my wine. "I'm not in love with him," I say, the lie obvious even to me.

"So what are you going to do?"

I shrug, stabbing my straw into the ice in my glass of water. "I don't think there's anything for me to do. I got the part, that's the most important thing. Now I need to focus on not fucking up this chance to show David I'm worthy of a full-time promotion."

Lucy swirls the wine in her glass. "I'm going to say this in the nicest way I know how."

"That doesn't bode well."

She flicks my elbow. "You look fucking miserable, Allegra. And you have ever since you got this part. It might take everyone else a while longer to notice than it's taken me, but they will notice."

"I'm sure it's just a phase. Once I get more comfortable with the new demands, everything will feel a lot better."

She raises her eyebrows. "We both know it's not the new ballet making you feel this way."

I know the new ballet is definitely responsible for a huge chunk of what's making me feel this way, even if inadvertently, but I don't bother to correct her. "I'm not going to let a man, a man I wasn't ever even in a real relationship with, derail my entire career, Luce."

"I would never suggest you do. But clearly, this isn't working for you."

"What isn't working for me?" Maybe if I play dumb, she'll get tired of this line of questioning and leave me alone.

Instead, she shoots me down with a single glare. "You and Cord. You not being with Cord. It's making you miserable, and if you don't do something about it, it's going to start affecting your performance, so if nothing else, you need to handle the situation for the sake of your career."

"He hasn't even tried to contact me since the wedding."

"You mean the wedding where he opened his heart and told you his most painful secret?"

"Only because he got caught and called out."

"I can't believe I'm saying this, but maybe he's scared." She leans her elbows on the table. "Normally I'd be the first to call that line a crock of shit when it's coming from a man, but I think in this case, it might actually apply."

"Why would he be scared?" I ask, hoping she can convince me. Hoping there's some way to fix all of this, some way for me to keep Cord and the ballet.

"Think about it, Allegra. He went through this terrible situation with his sister, the person closest to him in the world. Now think about the things you've told him about David, the things he had to have inferred. You think he wants to let himself get close to someone who already has a relationship with her director that mirrors the one his sister had with her abuser?"

My breath catches in my chest as Lucy lays it all out there for me. The comparison between David and the choreographer who assaulted Chloe makes my skin crawl, but she's not wrong. Even though things with David have never fully crossed the line, he's definitely prodded that line to its full extent.

Of course Cord would be wary of putting himself in another situation where someone he cares about could get hurt.

"You're right," I admit, finishing off my glass of wine. "But I think all you've proven is that the two of us have no business being together."

She shrugs. "I don't know, Allegra. I find it hard to believe you guys can't find some kind of middle ground. Maybe he just needs to know that you want him to be there for you."

"Or maybe he was right to walk away. Maybe if I care for him, I should respect his decision and give him his space." It would be easier that way. Even if not seeing him right now is making me miserable, I know it will get better with time. I know I'll feel his absence in my life a little less each day.

"Did he ask for space?"

"He said we should take a couple of days to think about things, but then I never heard from him."

She levels me with a look. "And how many times have you tried calling him?"

I ignore that pointed not-question. "What do you think I should do?"

Lucy gives me a knowing smile. "You know what to do." She signals for the check and pays for the whole thing before I even have a chance to get my card out of my wallet. "Look, there's a small chance that I'm reading this situation all wrong. Maybe Cord really does need this space from you, even if I'm sure it's hurting both of you in the moment." She signs the receipt and turns her full attention on me. "But don't you think you owe it to yourself to try?"

I don't answer her rhetorical question because I know she expects a resounding yes and I can't give it to her. I don't know if I owe it to myself to try. I don't know if I can handle it if Cord rejects me, if he doesn't want me the same way I want him.

And I don't know what I would say to him if he asked me to choose between him and this ballet.

No. That's a lie. I know what I would choose.

I don't want Cord to get hurt and that feels like an almost inevitable conclusion. But maybe Lucy is right. Maybe Chloe is right. Maybe I owe it to the both of us to at least try.

TWENTY-ONE
Cord

"No. That's not it. That was all wrong."

Noah sets down the pretty dancer he had lifted over his head. His shoulders are tense and he levels me with a glare. "I think maybe it's time to call it a night."

I run a hand through my hair, tugging on the ends in frustration. "I want to get this right."

"Clearly something isn't working here. Let's let Ivy go, it's getting late. We can start fresh next rehearsal." Noah nods to Ivy, the dancer we hired to perform the piece I originally choreographed on Allegra. Choreographed *with* Allegra.

Which may or may not have something to do with the reason why none of this feels right.

It's been three weeks since the wedding and I haven't heard from her. Thanks to Chloe, I know she got the part. When my sister told me the news, I was so elated it felt as if the good news were my own. Then the realization quickly set in. Even after all we went through to get there, Allegra didn't call me when she found out she got the part.

That ripped out what was left of my heart.

I don't know what I expected when I left Bethany's wedding, but in my mind, it didn't have to be goodbye forever. Just goodbye while we both think about this and figure out what we want to do.

Allegra has made it pretty clear what she wants to do. And so, even though I was willing to put everything from my past aside and give it a shot, I don't think I have any other choice but to respect her wishes.

Ivy scampers out of the studio the moment Noah gives her the go-ahead and I mentally curse myself. I never wanted to be one of those directors, and here I am, taking out my own issues on an innocent dancer.

When the door closes behind her, I sink into one of the armchairs in the sitting area, my head falling into my hands.

Noah sits down next to me but doesn't say anything. His silence is a gift, but I know it won't last for long.

"I'll apologize to Ivy."

"Good."

We sit there and I know he's waiting for me to say something, to open up and tell him what's going on, but if I voice it all out loud, that will make it real and then I might have to actually address my feelings.

"You know I will sit here all night if that's what it takes."

I sigh, sitting up and leaning back in the chair. "I know. There's no point in trying to out-stubborn you."

He grins. "Glad my reputation is well established. So . . . what the fuck was that all about?"

"I think that was mostly about one Allegra Hart."

"Yeah, I figured that much out on my own. How about you tell me what actually happened?"

A quick glance at Noah shows he's leaned forward in his seat, ready to listen, and if history is any indication, probably offer me some damn good advice. So I spill. I tell him everything, putting my feelings for Allegra into words that I haven't even been able to express to Chloe.

Noah doesn't say a word, though he does reach out to grasp my shoulder at one point and it's a point of solidarity I desperately need.

When I finally finish, Noah leans back in his seat and whistles low under his breath. "Shit man. Your life these days is looking a lot like the telenovelas my abuela used to make me watch after school."

I wish he were wrong. "Yeah. I know. There's a lot of things about ballet I don't miss, and the constant company gossip is one of them. And yet, here I am again, wrapped up in ballet drama."

"What are you going to do?"

I glare at him. "I thought the point of telling you all my problems was so that you could solve them for me."

He shrugs. "I'm not a miracle worker."

I search for something to throw at him, but nothing is within easy reach. "All right then. If you were in my shoes, what would you do?"

"Technically I would never be in your shoes because I wouldn't have let Allegra's career keep me from being with her." He smirks but then tempers his attitude. "I also didn't have the experience with ballet that you and Chloe did."

"So helpful, thank you."

Noah leans forward, resting his elbows on his knees. "Look, man, I don't think anyone aside from you and Allegra can figure this out. Maybe she's taken some space and realized she doesn't have time for a relationship while she's working on this new ballet. That blows, but it doesn't mean the two of you have no shot in the future." He reaches over and pats my knee, harder than he needs to. "So maybe in the meantime, you need to focus on figuring out if you want to be with her, and if you do, how you can manage it without it damaging your mental health."

I sit with that for a second. "Fuck, man, that was actually good advice."

He grins, his bright white teeth sparkling. "I know." He stands and gathers his things, giving me a half-hearted noogie on his way out the door. "Let me know if you need the name of a good therapist!"

I DON'T ACTUALLY NEED THE NAME OF A GOOD THERAPIST BEcause I already have one of my own. Granted, I haven't seen her in a while. Once Chloe and I got settled in our new careers in New York, with all of our problems in the past and on the other side of the country, I didn't really need the weekly check-ins.

Now, I am in desperate need of one.

I schedule an in-office meeting, taking the first available appointment, which means I'm up early a few days after my conversation with Noah.

The waiting room hasn't changed much in the years since I've been here, still done up in neutrals with bland art hanging on the walls and fake plants situated in the corners. Because I'm the first appointment of the day, I don't have to wait long before Dr. Leeds shows me into her office.

The interior is more of the same, the boring tones of the lobby repeated.

I settle myself on a beige armchair and Dr. Leeds takes the one across from me. There's also a small sofa, but sitting there always made me feel like I was in therapy in a movie, not in real life.

Dr. Leeds, a middle-aged white woman who reminds me of my mother—in a good way—smiles warmly as we both settle into our seats. "It's good to see you again, Cord."

I return the smile. "Thanks. You too. Though I guess I wouldn't be seeing you if everything were going well."

"Therapy doesn't always have to be for when things are wrong. Maintenance is important, too."

"Right." I stretch out my legs, running my hands over my thighs to adjust my pants. "Unfortunately, I'm not here for maintenance."

She nods, opening her notebook and reaching for a pen. "Why don't you tell me why you're here then?"

"I met a girl. A woman, I mean. I met a woman and I really like her."

Dr. Leeds keeps nodding, her eyes studying me so intently that I focus on the painting behind her.

"And she's great, it all could be great. Except she's a ballerina."

"Ah." It's a simple sound of acknowledgment, but it holds weight.

"Yeah. And not only that, from what I can gather of her current director, she is dealing with some harassment issues."

Dr. Leeds raises one eyebrow. "What kind of harassment are we talking about?"

"She insists he's never crossed the line, but I called her one night when she was leaving the theater and it sounded like she was escaping a situation that might not have ended well."

"And how did that make you feel?"

I huff out a mirthless laugh. "Triggered. Really fucking triggered. If I could, I would have gone down to the theater and given that asshole a piece of my mind."

"But you didn't."

I look at her, her calm expression helping to soothe my racing heartbeat. "No. I didn't."

"Why not? You know who this guy is and where he works, why didn't you go give him a piece of your mind?"

"Because she wouldn't want me to do that. And it's not my place."

Dr. Leeds nods and jots something down on her notepad. "All right then. Where do things stand with the two of you now?"

I run a hand through my hair. "Nowhere, I guess. I ended up telling her everything about my past, she ended up getting this lead role, and we haven't spoken in almost three weeks."

She keeps nodding. "Now, let me ask you this. Are you here today because you want me to give you permission to have a relationship with this woman?"

I open my mouth to answer, but nothing comes out. "I don't think I need permission necessarily."

"You don't need it, but is it something you are looking for?"

I let out a long breath. "I think what I'm looking for is some indication of whether or not it would be unhealthy for me to be with her."

"I can't answer that for you, Cord."

"Come on, doc, for the amount of money I'm paying you," I say with a smile.

She ignores that. "What I can tell you is this. In order for you to have a healthy relationship, with anyone, you must communicate. It sounds like you have taken the first steps as far as that is concerned, by telling her about your past."

I nod, failing to mention I really only told Allegra because her mother forced my hand.

"But I think you also need to realize that communication might not be enough. The truth of the matter is sometimes people's lives are simply incompatible."

It's the exact opposite of what I want to hear. "But isn't love supposed to conquer all?"

She shrugs. "Perhaps it can, but I don't think it's helpful to sugarcoat the situation. She has a job that holds a lot of trauma for you. It doesn't sound like she is going to be giving that up anytime soon."

"I wouldn't want her to." I know how hard she has worked, know how much this opportunity means to her.

"So you have to figure out if you are willing to give her the space to be in a career that is going to upset you sometimes."

"And if I'm not?" I realize as I sit here that I want to be. I want the chance to try this with Allegra, if she is willing to have me. But wanting it doesn't necessarily mean I'm ready for it.

"Then maybe now isn't the right time." Dr. Leeds sets aside her notebook. "Or maybe she's not the right person."

Something deep in my gut recoils at those words. Maybe now isn't the right time. Maybe I need to focus on doing some more work internally before we give this another go. The last thing I want is to be the reason Allegra begins to resent something she loves with her whole heart, and I don't know if I'm capable of not letting my past with ballet color how I feel about it in the present.

But there's something lodged right in my chest, letting me know she is definitely the right person. It hurts too much to think otherwise.

TWENTY-TWO

It takes another two weeks after my conversation with Lucy before I make up my mind. It's two more weeks of rehearsals where I feel more like Ballerina Barbie than I do like an accomplished and trained dancer. Two more weeks of missing the way Cord asked for my thoughts and opinions, the way he always made sure I was comfortable. Two more weeks of just plain missing him, really. The loneliness may have abated somewhat, but I fear that, without Cord in my life, it might not ever fully dissipate.

I borrow a short-sleeved black wrap dress from Lucy and wear some of the lingerie from my photo shoot underneath. Not because I'm planning for things to go like that, but because part of the dance Cord and I choreographed requires me to strip down to my undies and no one needs to see my faded cotton granny panties.

When I get to Six Pact, there's about an hour before the next show starts. I greet Warren with a timid smile.

"Haven't seen you around in a while." He smiles but crosses his arms over his chest in case I had any notion of getting past him and backstage without his permission.

"I've had a lot going on." It's on the tip of my tongue to ask how Cord is doing, but I don't want to put Warren in that spot. Instead, I hand him a folded piece of paper. "Could you give this to Noah?"

"Noah?"

I nod, biting my tongue so I don't spill the whole plan. The fewer people who know, the better.

Warren takes the paper from me. I thank him and head down the block to a nearby coffee shop. Fifteen minutes later, my phone vibrates.

NOAH: Are you sure about this?
ME: I am.
ME: Unless you think I'm making a huge mistake?
NOAH: Look, I have no idea how Cord is going to react, but I do know he's been a miserable little shit lately so it can't hurt.
ME: I appreciate your help.
NOAH: See you soon.
NOAH: And good luck.

I blow out a breath and check the time. I don't want to get to the theater any earlier than absolutely necessary, don't want there to be any chance he sees me before I'm ready.

I wait until I know the show has started, then give it a few extra minutes so I miss Cord's opening act. The woman working at the front of the club marks off the fake name I used to make a reservation and shows me to the last open table in the theater, all the way in the back corner. Perfectly out of sight.

I'm tempted to order a drink because, god knows, I need it, but I also don't want there to be anything sloshing around in my stomach when the time comes. So I ask for a water, flashing the server an apologetic look and vowing to leave as generous a tip as I can afford.

It's impossible to focus on the show, the screams and the abs all a blur around me. I'm sure I look completely out of place, sitting here by myself and not participating, but no one seems to pay me much attention, which is what I need.

When the firefighter act comes out onstage, I take a deep breath. Noah is the lead in this one, and when it's over, he's going to give me the cue. The music fades out and Noah helps his audience participant down the stairs of the stage. He gestures to the DJ, who hands him a microphone.

Noah's voice booms through the speakers, deeper and slower than his normal conversational tone. "How's everybody doing tonight?"

The room erupts in a deafening roar.

"Well, your night is about to get even better. Because we have something special in store for you tonight. I'm going to need my main man Cord Donovan out here on the stage, please."

The shrieks increase at the sound of Cord's name, and they don't die down in the sixty seconds it takes for him to be shoved out onto the stage. He's wearing a black button-down shirt and black pants and he's never looked more beautiful.

He also looks confused—and more than a little annoyed.

Noah claps him on the back and I stand, making my way slowly through the crowd to the front of the stage. When Noah sees me, he hands the mic back to the DJ and whispers something to him. A second later, the opening notes of our song chime through the sound system.

Cord's face falls as he recognizes the song, and the closer I get to the stage, the clearer I can see the dark circles under his eyes. It's impossible for him to look terrible, but he certainly doesn't look happy.

He crosses to the DJ booth, giving the universal sign for "Cut the music," but the DJ lets the song keep playing.

I reach the stairs and fight back the urge to puke. I've never once had stage fright before, not even when I was a kid. I was raised on the stage, but it takes a mini pep talk to convince my feet to move.

Cord turns to exit the stage, clearly frustrated and upset, which is of course when he spots me.

I freeze when his eyes meet mine. I'm pretty sure the audience is completely losing their minds, but at that moment, all I can see is him. All I can hear is Alicia singing about how sad life is without you.

Cord looks at me, then looks at the audience. I've put him in a terrible position, made it impossible for him to ignore me. He gives me a nod and I finish climbing the stairs.

I look down at my feet, realizing I still have my plain black heels on. I toe them off, leaving them at the edge of the stage.

Cord stalks toward me and I meet him in the middle. His hand finds its place on my neck. "What are you doing here, Slippers?" The words are low, inaudible to anyone but me.

"I missed dancing with you," I breathe.

His grip on me tightens, but he doesn't respond. We fall effortlessly into the choreography, even though we haven't practiced these steps in weeks. Everything from my time with Cord is permanently engraved on my brain. Every sense of him is engraved on my body. And when he wraps me in his embrace, I know that no matter what happens next, I was meant to come here. We were meant to dance this dance, at least one more time.

We reach a point in the steps we never actually practiced, when our "characters" undress each other. Cord easily finds the tie of my dress, tugging it loose. I let the fabric slip from my shoulders, tossing the dress offstage. My hands move to the buttons of his shirt and while my fingers work, his fingers unfasten his pants, unzipping so that when I've pushed his shirt to the floor, all he has to do is drop his pants.

We're both stripped down to our undergarments, but I don't even have time to appreciate the carved lines of him before I'm swept back in his arms.

It shouldn't come as a surprise, but the feel of his bare skin against mine is potent, heady. My fingers brush his stomach and his stroke my lower back, like we need the reassurance that we're here and this is happening.

I don't ever want this to end. I want this dance with Cord to last forever. I need this excuse to keep touching him, to keep his hands on my body.

But as with all good things, it must come to an end.

I leap and he catches me. My legs wrap around his waist, his hands support me, latched onto my upper thighs. His fingers brush the edge of my panties and my arms wind around his neck.

The music fades and we're face-to-face, locked in our intimate embrace.

There is still so much to say and discuss, but the power of his gaze takes my breath away, leaving me speechless.

The room explodes once again, this time in applause like nothing I've heard before. But none of that matters, I can barely bring myself to acknowledge it.

I wait for Cord to set me down, but instead he keeps me wrapped in his arms and carries me offstage, never breaking my gaze. There's so much hidden in the depths of those blue eyes, but I can't make any sense of it. Can't make any sense of anything other than the feeling of being in his arms. The feeling of being safe, and cherished.

We reach the wings, out of view of the audience. I vaguely hear the sound of the next act starting, and the accompanying shrieks.

Cord still doesn't let me go. "Come home with me?"

I nod, still unable to form silly things like words.

Only once I've agreed does he set me on my feet. A stagehand who must have been lurking nearby hands him our clothes, including my shoes. He helps me slip into my dress. I tie it and step into my heels while he quickly dresses. Then he takes my hand in his and tugs me toward the exit.

"Don't you need to wait for the end of the show?" I whisper.

"Fuck the show."

We walk down a long hallway of dressing rooms and when I catch Noah's eye, he flashes me a wink and a smile. It helps calm some of the nerves, because Cord hasn't looked back at me once since pulling me away from the wings.

The walk to Cord's apartment is only two blocks from the theater, and they're silent. It would freak me out beyond the usual, except he keeps a tight hold on my hand, our fingers laced together. Every few seconds, he squeezes, like he's worried I might disappear while he isn't looking. And he doesn't look at me, not once the entire walk.

Not until we enter his apartment building and travel up to the top floor. I'm not sure what I'm expecting his place to look like, but somehow it fits the exact vision I have for him. It's bigger than my studio, of course, but still a modest size, two bedrooms if the doors down the hallway are any indication. The walls in the living room are painted a deep navy blue, but the city lights through the huge windows brighten up the space, as does the large cream-colored sofa that looks cushy enough to sink into. Beautiful photographs hang on the walls, most of them city landscapes, not just from New York, but from all over the world.

It's gorgeous.

Cord slips out of his shoes the second he crosses the threshold and immediately drops my hand and darts to the opposite side of the room, striding toward the huge windows framing the nighttime lights of Hell's Kitchen.

Well. That's enough to make my stomach completely churn with anxiety.

I toe off my heels, following his example. And then I follow in his steps, slowly, in case he wants me to stay hovering by the door despite dragging me all the way here.

"I like your place," I say tentatively when I've made it about halfway to him, several feet still separating us.

"Thanks." He turns toward me and nothing in his eyes says stop, so I keep walking.

"Did you change your mind? About inviting me here? I can go if you want."

He shakes his head. "I don't want that. I want you to stay."

"I'm sorry for just showing up at the theater. I probably should have texted you first, but I was too afraid you would tell me you didn't want to see me ever again."

He runs a hand through his hair. It's still slightly damp with sweat and the motion makes the back stick up. "Honestly, that's probably what I would have said."

My heart drops into my butt. "Oh."

He reaches for one of my hands, pulling me closer. "But I'm glad you just showed up. I don't think I realized until I saw you standing there just how much I've missed you, Slippers."

I lace our fingers together. "I missed you too, Cord. A lot."

Blowing out a breath, he keeps our hands joined but takes a step away from me. "But even though I'm happy to see you, I don't know that it changes much of anything."

"I'm still a ballet dancer."

"And I'm still a rigid motherfucker too wrapped up in the past."

"Hey." This time I tug, though I wouldn't ever be able to move him if he didn't want to come willingly. "That's not fair."

"Now that you know everything, you understand why it's been so hard for me? Why I don't think I could ever let this get serious between us." Even as he says the words, his eyes dim, the blue seemingly fading right in front of my eyes.

"I understand." I reach for his other hand and he gives it. "But I wouldn't be here if I could just accept that, Cord."

"Slippers . . ."

"Look, I'm not going to lie to you and say ballet isn't my priority. It is. I worked my ass off to get this part—you understand that better than anyone—and I'm not giving up right when I'm on the cusp of being made a principal." I take a deep breath. "And I'm also not going to pretend like my director isn't problematic. He has said and done things that are one hundred percent inappropriate. I've never reported him, and as long as he doesn't take things any further, I don't think I ever will."

Cord's jaw tenses. "That night when I called you, when he cornered you in the hallway, don't you think he would have taken things further if he hadn't been interrupted?"

"Maybe. I don't know that for sure, and neither do you. But even still, this is my career, my body, and my boundaries. I will stay true to them." I know what would happen if I reported David for the "minor" infractions he's committed so far, and any favorable result wouldn't be worth what I would have to go through on my end. I understand that that line doesn't work for everyone, but it does work for me, and that's what matters.

Cord considers my words for a long minute. "I respect that."

I reward him with a small smile. "Thank you."

"But I don't know where that leaves us."

"That's up to you, Cord. I respect your boundaries, too, and if this is too much for you, then I will walk out that door and never look back." Just saying the words is a knife in the gut and my fingers instinctively tighten around his, but I try to put on a brave face. "But I don't want that. I want us to try. I want us to compromise and meet in the middle and find a way to make this work."

"I want that too," he says quietly.

My heart lightens . . . until I hear his next word.

"But . . ." This time it's his grip that tightens. "I'm not

going to lie to you, Allegra. I'm scared that I can't do it. I'm scared that I don't have it in me to accept your world in the way you deserve."

I nod, untangling our fingers. "I understand." I know when it fully hits me, the loss of him, for real this time, it's going to run me over like a stampeding bull, and so I move toward the front door, wanting and needing to escape as fast as possible.

"But I want to try, Allegra."

I halt in my tracks, spinning slowly to face him once again. "You want to try?"

He nods, a slow grin spreading across his full lips. "I want to try. If you think you can be patient with me."

"Patience is my middle name." It's definitely not, but for a chance with Cord Donovan, I'll file the paperwork and change it.

This time he moves toward me, cupping my cheeks in his hand. "I wouldn't do this if I didn't think this was something real, Allegra. Promise me you think this is something real, too?"

"It's something real, Cord. Very real."

For a minute he doesn't move and I lose myself in the depths of his crystal-clear gaze. He's so beautiful, he takes my breath away.

And then his mouth presses gently to mine and new life is breathed into me. His lips are soft and slow, they move against mine with the lightest of touches. I let him command it, his hands tilting my head to deepen the kiss. I sink into him, leaning into his weight to support me as my brain goes fuzzy.

My hands find their home at his waist and when I tug on his hips, he lets me move him closer. Our bodies press together and the heat of him warms me. His lips continue their exploration and I think I could kiss him forever.

He grazes his teeth over my bottom lip and I gasp, my hips moving of their own accord. Cord grunts at the contact. My lips part and he teases me with just the tip of his tongue.

We've barely kissed and somehow this is the most erotic thing that has ever happened to me. Every single nerve in my body is on high alert, but it's my heart that melts when he pulls away from me, his eyes roving over my face like he can't believe I'm standing here.

"I've been thinking about doing that since the moment I first saw you outside of the theater."

I roll my eyes. "You have not. You couldn't stand me when we first met."

He shakes his head, moving his hands from their position cradling my face, trailing them down my arms and around my waist. "It was never you I couldn't stand, Slippers."

I don't let him expound on that thought, not wanting to derail the moment. I rise on my toes and bring my lips to his, my arms tightening around his neck. Taking control of the kiss, I open myself to him, exploring him with my tongue. He lets me take the lead, and the control is heady.

I feel the moment his resolve snaps, when something in him demands to take over. His tongue sweeps into my mouth as his hand finds its way to my hair. This kiss is devouring and hot and kind of messy. His other hand palms my ass, and the hard length of him presses against my belly.

"I want you, Cord," I mutter against his mouth when we part the slightest bit so we can breathe. I trail my hands down his chest, over his stomach, cupping him over the fabric of his pants.

"I want you, too, Allegra. So fucking much. But we don't have to do anything tonight. We can take this slow if you want." His mouth moves down the curve of my neck as if to persuade me otherwise.

But he doesn't need to persuade me. I feel like I've been yearning for his touch for months. And I don't want to wait any longer.

I pull away from him, ever so slightly, just enough so I can see his eyes. "Where's the bedroom?"

His pupils widen. "You sure?"

"One hundred percent." I kiss him quickly. "And I still remember my word." I know I won't need to use it.

"In that case." He hoists me up once again, just like at the end of our routine. Somehow he manages to resume kissing me, even as he walks us down the hallway to the last door.

I wish I had time to fully take in the space, absorb all the details of Cord's most personal and intimate room, but that would require me to part from him, and that's not happening anytime soon.

He sits carefully on the edge of the bed, settling me on his lap, my thighs tucked around his hips. It's reminiscent of the night of the lap dance, and I can't help but groan when the image floats into my head.

"Are you thinking about the last time we sat like this?" He shifts the neckline of my dress so his mouth can trail along my collarbone.

"Yes." I roll my hips, delighting in the grunt he releases. "I wanted to kiss you so badly."

"I would have let you."

I tug a little on the long hair that falls over the back of his neck, forcing him to bring his eyes to mine. "I'm kind of glad we didn't. I like that we waited until we could be fully honest with each other."

He places a soft kiss on my lips. "Me too." His hands trace over the muscles of my calves, up to my thighs, slipping under the skirt of my dress. "Though I really hope I don't come in my pants tonight."

"Not going to lie, I hope you don't either."

Cord's fingers toy with the lace tie of my dress. "Is it okay if I take this off?"

I do it for him, practically ripping the damn thing off.

His eyes linger, tracing me from the swells of my breasts down to the barely there lace covering my butt. "You wore this in one of the pictures you sent me."

"Be honest, how often have you looked at them?"

His gaze meets mine and the blue of his eyes is blazing. "Every fucking day. Sometimes twice a day."

It's the hottest thing anyone has ever said to me, and my mouth lands on his as my fingers work the buttons of his shirt. Once he's bared to me, I let my hands roam everywhere. It's not the first time I've touched the ridges of his abs or the defined lines of his pecs, but I explore them with a new freedom. I tug on the waistband of his pants and he somehow manages to keep me wrapped around him while standing to kick them off his legs.

Stripping *is* part of his job.

Nothing stands between us now except for some cotton and lace and it's too much. I unhook my bra, tossing it into the corner of the room.

Cord cups my breasts in his hands, and his gaze is reverent, like the man has never seen a pair of tits before. He swallows thickly. "You're so fucking beautiful, Slippers."

"I always hated them," I say, even as my head falls back as his fingers stroke my sensitive skin with his gentle touch.

"Seriously? Why?"

"They're too big for ballet." I may be trim and toned, but my boobs sprouted when I was thirteen, and they've been a problem ever since. Ballet is all about clean lines, not breasts that practically spill out of my leotard.

"They're fucking perfect. You're fucking perfect."

He doesn't let me argue, his tongue flicking over my nipple before he sucks the peaked bud into his mouth.

No partner has ever paid attention to my breasts the way that Cord does, and before I know what's happening, I'm rocking over the hard length of him, the orgasm building slowly, deep in my belly.

"Cord," I moan, too close to the edge to be embarrassed by the way I'm shamelessly humping him while his mouth works over my skin. I dig my fingers into his hair, silently demanding more.

His teeth graze over me and his first bite is gentle. I cry out, tightening my grip on his hair, and his second bite is a little less so.

The orgasm doesn't rip through me, it's a slow and steady build that lasts for longer than I thought possible. Cord works me through it, his mouth never faltering, delivering me the kind of delicious torture I've never experienced before.

When I finally come down, I collapse in his arms.

He chuckles, rubbing soothing circles over my bare back. "That was the sexiest thing I've ever seen."

"Holy shit. I've never . . . that's never . . . I didn't even know that was possible."

He chuckles again, and I feel the vibration of it on my cheek that's pressed to his chest. He scoots back on the bed, bringing me with him. Tucking me into the crook of his shoulder, he settles us both, his hand moving to my hair, combing through the long strands.

"If you keep doing that, you're going to put me to sleep." I murmur the words into his chest, brushing a line of kisses over his pec.

"It's okay if you do."

I prop myself up on my elbow so I can see him. "Do you not want this to go any further tonight?"

"I want this to go as far as you want it to, Allegra."

I trail my fingers down his chest, over his stomach, along the waistband of his underwear. "I already told you that I want you." I slip a single finger underneath the elastic, following the line of hair leading to his straining erection.

He sucks in a breath and opens his mouth to speak.

"Do not ask me if I'm sure again. I told you I am, and I know exactly what to say if I change my mind." I slide my hand into his underwear, wrapping my fingers around the thick length of him. "But I'm not going to."

Cord's mouth crashes into mine and he flips us over, the movement dislodging my hand from his boxer briefs. He kisses me desperately, our tongues mingling, teeth clashing. Gripping both of my wrists in one of his hands, he raises them over my head.

"Keep your hands up there. If you keep touching me, we're going to have a repeat lap dance experience."

I grin against his lips. "When you say it like that, it sounds like a challenge."

"You are trouble, Slippers." His mouth begins its descent, trailing lightly over my still sensitive nipples, spending more time exploring the dips and curves of my belly.

"Are you just now realizing that?" I gasp when he licks the crease of my hips, and they buck underneath him.

Cord's mouth licks along the edge of my panties and he settles himself between my thighs before looking up at me. "Can I taste you, Allegra?"

I squirm a little under his weight and his question. "I already came once, you don't need to."

"I know I don't need to. I want to." He trails a single finger down my center, causing my hips to buck once again. "I've been dreaming about the taste of you since you sent me those pictures, thinking about it constantly since you came on my lap."

My breath stutters in my chest. No one has ever spoken to me like that before, with such hunger and wanting, with such bare desire. It's enough to make my skin tingle, for a wave of goose bumps to explode over my flesh. "I . . . I . . . I can't normally come that way."

He keeps his eyes on me, even as his fingers run light trails over the swirls of the lace still covering me. "Do you not like it?"

"It's not that." It's just that every man I've been with has put in a perfunctory sixty seconds of lapping at me with no finesse, making it very clear he would rather be doing anything else. I've only really been with one woman and we never got past making out and some light fingering before she got tired of my schedule and dumped me.

But I can't tell him any of that. I pull my eyes to the ceiling so I don't have to look at him.

"Allegra." He waits for me to meet his stare. "I want to taste you. I want to devour you. I want to explore you with my tongue and find all the magical places that make you scream. If I spend twenty minutes between your thighs and you don't come, it will have been time well spent because I am going to enjoy every single second of having my mouth on you."

"Jesus, Cord."

He grins, and his thumbs hook into the waistband of my underwear, dragging them slowly down my thighs. "If you don't like what I'm doing, you can tell me, but don't you dare stop me because you think some sort of self-imposed time limit has elapsed. Got it?"

All I can do is nod, too transfixed on the hungry look in his eyes as he flings my panties across the room and settles back in between my legs.

"Use your word, if you need it."

Somehow I know I won't.

Even still, I can't bear to watch him, so I let my eyes close and lose myself in the sensations.

Cord starts slow, light kisses pressed over my inner thighs. He moves closer and closer to my center, and by the time I can feel his breath on my aching core, I am burning up inside. His fingers part me and the very tip of his tongue dances over me, tracing me open.

He groans and the sound shoots right through me. "You taste so good, Allegra. So fucking good." He murmurs the words against me and I can't stop myself from bucking against his face.

He continues to deliver slow and exquisite torture, his tongue gliding over my clit in teasing strokes. I've never experienced anything like it, but I force myself to focus on the pleasure, not concerns about whether or not Cord is enjoying himself. His moans and grunts let me know that he is.

His tongue flicks my clit with a soft back-and-forth motion, and I can't hold back the cry. My eyes pop open, unable to be screwed shut any longer. When I look down at him, he's looking back at me. His mouth never stops working, but I watch his hand as he grips himself, stroking his thick cock while his tongue drives me over the edge.

I come even harder the second time, my vision going cloudy as the orgasm rips through me.

He strokes me through it before moving up my body, leaving a trail of wet kisses over my skin. When he kisses me, I taste myself on his tongue and groan.

"Just when I think you can't get any sexier, Slippers." He locks his forearms, looking down at me as I lie beneath him. "Watching you come is the hottest thing I've ever seen."

I'm still catching my breath and can't seem to form any words, but I can feel a flush spreading over my cheeks and down my chest. "That was incredible," I finally manage.

He lowers himself over me and kisses me softly. "Good."

I slip my hand in between our bodies, finding him so hard and ready. "Will you tell me what you want? How can I make you feel as good as you've made me feel?"

He hesitates for a mere second. "Will you ride me, Slippers?"

TWENTY-THREE

Cord

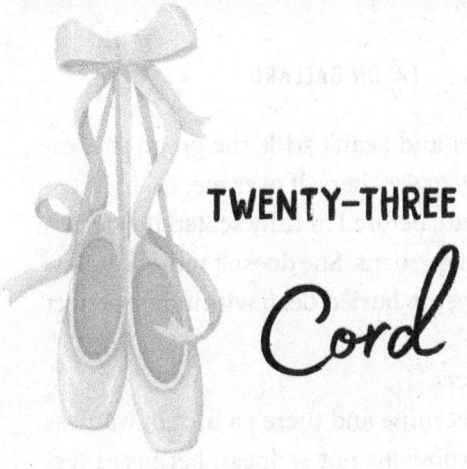

Allegra doesn't answer. Instead, she pushes me so I'm lying flat on my back. It's an unexpectedly sexy move. "Condoms?"

I reach into the nightstand drawer and pull out a shiny foil packet.

She takes it from me, opening it and covering my cock. My eyes flutter at her touch and I force myself to not buck in her grip, to not spill all over her hand.

Allegra straddles my hips and I don't think I've ever seen a more beautiful sight. I don't think I've ever been this hard, this ready before. But there's something uncertain in the small smile she gives me.

I reach up, cupping her cheek, stroking along the length of her jaw. "Giving you pleasure brings me pleasure, Allegra. I want to watch you take that pleasure for yourself. However it feels good for you is going to feel incredible for me."

She nods, a little more confidence in her next smile.

I take my dick in my hand, notching it at her entrance.

She's so warm and wet and I can't stifle the groan that escapes me as she slowly lowers herself over me.

It takes a full minute before I'm fully seated inside her, and we let out matching groans. She doesn't move for a few seconds, and I relish being buried deep within her perfect body.

"Look at me, Slippers."

Her hazel eyes meet mine and there's a hint of wetness shining there. But I know it's not sadness, because I feel it too. This overwhelming sensation of this being right where I am meant to be.

She plants her hands on my chest and swivels her hips. I suck in a sharp breath as she repeats the motion. Our eyes stay locked, and our pleasure stays synced.

I slide my hands over her thighs, gripping her hips. My thumb grazes over her clit and she gasps. I want to hear that sound every day for the rest of my life. "This okay?"

She nods, her hips continuing to roll over me while I continue to stroke her clit. I can tell when her orgasm starts to build and thank fucking god because I don't know how much longer I can hold out. She starts to tighten around me and I know she's close. I cup her breast with my free hand. Her nipples are pink and slightly swollen and it doesn't take more than a few soft pinches before she throws her head back, her breaths coming in short pants, her pussy squeezing my cock and driving me to the edge.

"Do you think you can come with me?" she chokes out.

"If I feel you coming on my cock, I won't be able to hold back." I'm fighting for my life, waiting for that final release to take her before I let go.

"Good."

She increases her pace, moving over me faster. My hips begin to buck underneath her, thrusting deeper until she cries out my name, letting the orgasm pull her under.

"Allegra, fuck fuck fuck." I grasp her hips, my fingers digging into her skin. I explode inside her, coming harder and longer than I thought possible.

Her hips continue their swivel, slow and easy as we both come down.

I sit up, wrapping my arms around her. She buries her face in my neck, breathing in deeply.

"Did you just lick me?" I keep her pressed close to me, even as the sensation of her tongue dancing over my skin makes me shiver.

"Yup. You taste as good as you look."

I laugh, one hand stroking her back while the other moves to tangle itself in her hair. "That was incredible."

"That was beyond incredible." She twines her arms around my neck, and I hope she stays here in my lap, in my arms, forever.

"Will you stay tonight?"

I wait for her to tell me that she can't. That she has to wake up early for rehearsal or class and she needs to go home and sleep so she can be at her best for ballet. But instead, she surprises me.

"Of course."

We take a minute to clean up. I'm back in bed before she is and when she exits the bathroom and slides under the comforter, snuggling into my side, I let out a breath I didn't know I was holding. I kiss the top of her head. She kisses the spot on my chest right where my heart beats. And we fall asleep in each other's arms.

HER ALARM GOES OFF AT SIX A.M., A RATHER RUDE AWAKEN-ing to a pleasant night's sleep.

My arm is wrapped around her waist and I pull her into me after she hits snooze. "It is way too early for that shit."

She groans, nestling into my embrace. "I know, but I need to go back to my apartment and change. Then I need to get a workout in before class at nine."

"There's a gym here, you know." My grip on her tightens and my hips press into the round curve of her butt, letting her feel how hard I already am for her.

"Please do not tell me you know a much more fun way to burn some calories."

I laugh. "I meant there's an actual gym here in the building, but I'm also down for a more creative workout if you're up for it." I trail my mouth along her neck, my teeth nibbling her sensitive skin.

She fights it for a second, but it doesn't take long for her to press back against me, for her hand to snake around and bury itself in my hair.

But when the snooze goes off, she slides out of my embrace and climbs out of bed.

Posed in the bed like the hero on the cover of a romance novel, the sheet draped over my hips, tenting my arousal, I watch her hunt around the room for her clothes. She does everything she can not to look at me, escaping into the en suite bathroom to change as I concede defeat.

While she's changing, I force myself out of bed and slip

into a pair of gray sweatpants. Heading into the kitchen, I start the coffee and try to keep myself from grinning like the absolute besotted fool I am.

Allegra emerges from the bathroom, her hair pulled back, her eyes bright.

"Coffee?" I hold up the freshly brewed pot.

She nods and I hand her the travel mug I've poured for her, assuming she needs to make a quick exit to keep her schedule on track. I don't want to let her go; I want to throw her over my shoulder and carry her straight back to bed, but I promised I would respect her schedule and I can't very well break that promise our first morning together.

"Do you have a show tonight?" she asks, sipping carefully from the steaming mug.

"Not on Sundays. What's your schedule like for the day?"

"I'm going to go home and change, get a quick workout in, then go to class."

I know from experience that there aren't official classes or rehearsals on Sundays, just as I know how directors keep a watchful eye on who shows up for non-mandatory meetings. It doesn't surprise me that Allegra shows up even when she doesn't have to.

Still, I hope that doesn't mean she can't find time for me today. "Can we meet up when you're done?"

She hesitates, and I see those arguments bouncing around inside her head. I want to show her that we can do this, that I am supportive of her needs.

I set my mug on the counter, my hands landing on her waist and pulling her to me. "How about I take you out for dinner? I'll come to your neighborhood and I promise I won't try to score an invite back to your place after."

She smiles. "What if I want to invite you back to my place after?"

I nuzzle her neck, my mouth finding the sensitive spot at her pulse point. "Then I will come over and deliver as many orgasms as you'd like and then leave you to sleep in peace." Somehow, I think we both know that's not how it would go down, pun intended, but we can pretend.

"Okay fine. But I'm only agreeing to dinner. No orgasms."

I trace my tongue over the exposed edge of her collarbone. "What if I can't keep my hands off of you at dinner? I might have to slip my fingers under your skirt, tease the edge of your panties. Will you wear lace ones again?"

Her breath hitches in her chest. "I'm gonna wear pants."

I dot a line of kisses up her neck and along her jaw. "But if you do that, I can't take you into the restaurant bathroom, bend you over the counter, and fuck you while you watch in the mirror."

She fumbles setting her mug down on the counter, her hands cupping my jaw and bringing our mouths together. "You're terrible," she mutters into my lips before tugging me against her, our tongues sliding over each other.

I sense when she's on the verge of capitulating and dragging me back to the bedroom. I choose that moment to pull away. Her eyes are bright and her lips, swollen. I give her a wicked smile. "I'll see you tonight, Slippers."

It takes a minute for her to focus, and then her cry is indignant. "You did that on purpose!"

I shrug. "I don't know what you're talking about." I pick up my mug and take a calm sip, like I wasn't just about to take her on the kitchen counter. "You should get going. I don't want you to be late to class."

She turns on her heel, ready to huff out of the kitchen, but she pauses to press a single soft kiss to my lips. "I hate you."

"No you don't." I flash her a wink. "I'll pick you up at seven."

"Our date is canceled." She grabs her purse and heads for the door.

"Sure thing," I say with a laugh.

I SPEND MY DAY THINKING ABOUT HER, FIGHTING THE URGE TO slip into the bathroom and bring up those photos on my phone, get myself off to the memory of the way she rode me, of her taste on my tongue. I manage to restrain myself, but just barely.

I'm waiting outside her front door at seven and even though I buzz at the door to come up to her apartment, she bounds down the stairs and out to the sidewalk a few seconds later, like she was standing by the door waiting for me.

She's dressed in a floral print sundress, a jean jacket slung over her arm in case it gets cold. Her hair is down and slightly wavy, her face bright with a wide smile.

I greet her with a chaste kiss, the two of us grinning like utter fools when we part. Slipping her hand into mine, I tug her down the sidewalk. "Come on, I found a cute spot for us to try."

"A cute spot, huh?"

I bump her hip with mine. "You heard me. How was class?"

"It was good. Sundays are usually pretty casual since they're not mandatory."

I lead us to a hole-in-the-wall Italian place, tensing slightly when I see the hesitation on her face. I know dining out can be tricky sometimes, but I did my research, and there are some good options on the menu if she wants to eat something leaner than the lasagna I plan to get.

I order us a bottle of wine and offer some suggestions for an appetizer, wanting her to make the choice.

She bites her lip, and I try not to think about how sexy the move is.

I reach across the table, giving her hand a quick squeeze. "Athletes watch what they eat, Allegra. You don't have to eat anything you aren't comfortable with."

Her relief is immediately apparent and I wonder if her dates in the past have made her feel guilty or self-conscious about her food restrictions. I know there are real issues when it comes to ballet and body-shaming and unhealthy habits, but I meant what I said. Show me a professional athlete out there who doesn't pay close attention to what they're eating. No one would fault a football player watching his food intake, why don't we offer dancers the same courtesy?

When the server comes back around, Allegra orders the caprese salad to start and the grilled salmon entrée.

"That actually sounds good. I think I'll take that too," I tell our server, handing him both of our menus.

She smiles and I feel like I could conquer the world.

"So what did you get up to today?" She swirls the wine in her glass and takes a tiny sip.

"Got in a good workout, spent some time at the theater, worked on a couple of new routine ideas." I shrug, taking a much larger sip from my own glass.

"Do you normally work on Sundays?"

"It depends on what I've got going on, honestly. But I discovered pretty early on that owning my own business means I don't work a normal schedule, and days completely off are few and far between."

The server delivers our appetizer and Allegra cuts off a piece of tomato, swiping it through the thick balsamic vinegar.

"That's something I can certainly relate to."

"How are you feeling about the new ballet so far?" I spear a tomato and scoop up the extra mozzarella Allegra discarded.

She hesitates before answering.

I pull my eyes from the salad and look at her. "It's okay to talk about it, Slippers. We don't have much of a chance as a couple if you can't talk to me about the most important thing in your life."

Her cheeks flush and she buries her gaze in her glass of wine. "Are we a couple now?"

"Well, we're here on a date and I did give you multiple orgasms last night, so . . ."

She shoots me a warning glare as the flush travels down her cheeks to her neck. "Say that a little louder, why don't you."

I open my mouth as if to comply. She rips off a chunk of bread and throws it at me. I drag it through the remaining balsamic on the salad plate and pop it into my mouth.

"Okay, but seriously," she starts when I've finished chewing. "Are we a couple now? Is this a real thing?"

I reach across the table for her hand. "I thought we established last night that this is a real thing, Allegra."

"I know, but maybe that was just the heat of the moment talking."

"It wasn't for me."

Her fingers tighten around mine. "For me either."

I grin. "Good."

Our server delivers our main dishes at that moment, and we spend the rest of the meal chatting about everything and nothing. She fills me in on the new ballet and I tell her about the new numbers I'm thinking of adding to the show. She gives me great feedback and I try to focus on the passion in her voice when she talks about dancing.

When the server asks us if we want to see the dessert menu, I ask for the check. There is only one thing I'm interested in for dessert, if you know what I mean, though I plan to hold to my promise to deliver her to her door and allow her to get to bed early. If that's what she wants.

The walk back to her building goes by too fast, even though we walk at a glacial pace, earning several dirty looks from people trying to pass us on the crowded sidewalks.

When we get to the front door of her building, I pull her to a stop. I want nothing more than to join her upstairs, but I will stick to my word. I cup her cheeks in my hands and kiss her softly. "Thanks for making time to see me tonight."

She smiles, the disappointment visible in her eyes. "Thank you for dinner."

I brush back a strand of her hair, tucking it behind her ear. "I know you have to get up early tomorrow and I know that you're in the midst of very important rehearsals, so even though I want nothing more than to take you upstairs and ravish you, I'm going to say goodnight."

She groans and pulls me in for another kiss. "What if I want you to come upstairs and ravish me?"

I laugh, keeping our lips pressed together. "I'm glad you do, but I'm not changing my mind. I kind of like that you're going to go to bed tonight wishing you were in my arms."

She pouts, and I want to suck that bottom lip between my teeth. Instead, I force myself to take a step away from her.

"You're being very mature and responsible, and I don't think I like it."

"You'll thank me in the morning." I lean in, placing a single kiss on her neck. "If I got ahold of you again tonight, I don't know if you'd be able to walk in the morning. Let alone dance."

Her breath catches, and something sparks in her eyes. She sighs dramatically and rises on her toes to kiss my cheek. "Fine. Guess I'll just have to go upstairs and take care of myself then. I'll think about you as I stroke myself, picture all the things I want to do to you next time."

I swallow thickly, the cheeky minx. She knows exactly what she's doing, leaving me with that image in my head.

She turns away from me, unlocking the door to her building and blowing me a kiss, before she lets the door thud shut behind her.

I want to be good. Really I do, but the thought of Allegra touching herself is enough to make me leave all good intentions behind.

ME: Let me In.
ALLEGRA: I changed my mind. You were right. I should just get some sleep tonight.

Well, shit.

ME: Okay. Have a good night then, Slippers.

She's laughing when she pushes open the door to her building. "I'm just messing with you. Get your ass in here."

I grin, lifting her off the ground and carrying her over to the elevator. The moment the door of her apartment closes behind us, clothes are flying in every direction.

I make her come four times that night, and twice more the next morning.

The next day she texts me to tell me her director said she danced better at the rehearsal than she ever has before.

It's going to be hard to keep my ego in check after that.

TWENTY-FOUR

Allegra

The next week is the blissful montage. You know the scene in every rom-com where the couple is gallivanting around, holding hands and kissing and staring at each other like they are the only two people in the world. I've never felt rom-com montage feelings before, but along with a continuous stream of orgasms, Cord gives me those feelings.

I'd been so worried that being with him would affect my performance in the new ballet, but if anything, the wild amounts of sex the two of us are having, coupled with that honeymoon-stage euphoria mean I am the perfect embodiment of my character. David lavishes me with praise and drops more than one hint about a promotion on the horizon.

Everything is perfect, and I've never been this happy in my life.

So when Cord texts me on a Saturday afternoon as I'm packing up my stuff after class, two weeks after we slept together for the first time, a grin splits my face the second his name pops up on my screen.

CORD: What do you say you come to the theater tonight and we do our dance again?
ME: You mean the great Cord Donovan wants to dance with little old me?
CORD: Only if the esteemed Allegra Hart will lower herself to being seen onstage with me.
ME: Sounds good.
ME: I'm leaving class now, gonna swing by my place and shower and then I'll head over.
CORD: Cool. I'll send a car for you.
ME: 😒 I'm perfectly fine taking the subway.
CORD: But if I send a car for you, you'll get here sooner and we can make out in my dressing room until it's time for us to go on.
ME: . . .
ME: Fine. I'll be ready in 20 minutes.
CORD: See you soon 😊

"Good lord, woman, if you don't stop making eyes at your phone screen, everybody's going to think you're watching porn." Lucy nudges me with her foot.

I'm still sitting on the floor of the studio, and it isn't until I finally look up from my phone that I realize everyone else has already left. I hop to my feet, tucking my phone in the pocket of my joggers. "Haha. I guess I could just say I'm preparing for my role."

Lucy raises an eyebrow. "If I had insinuated you were sneak watching porn in the sacred studio a month ago, you would have (a) turned a shade of red brighter than the sun and (b) been mad at me for a week."

I shrug, turning toward the door, walking quickly because I only have twenty minutes to get to my place, shower, and make myself look presentable. I wonder which set of lingerie I should wear under my dress this time.

"Okay, seriously, Allegra," Lucy pants as she rushes to keep up with me. "I know you and the stripper guy are hooking up, but this seems like it might be something more."

I bite my lip, but it doesn't stop the grin from spreading across my face. "And what if it is?"

"I think that would be amazing. You deserve someone who makes you happy, and you seem happier than I've ever seen you."

A niggle of worry lodges itself in my belly. "Do you think David noticed?" There's no explicit policy about company members having partners, obviously, but David has never made it a secret that he looks down on those in serious relationships. How can one be entirely devoted to ballet if there's a significant other involved?

"I think everyone has noticed, sweetie. But who cares?"

I shoot her a look. "You know he does."

"Fuck that, Allegra. David is your boss, he has no right to dictate what happens in your personal life. Morally or legally."

I come to a halt as we reach the front of my building. "I know, but legal or not, David always seems to get his way."

Lucy hoists her bag farther up on her shoulder. "Again, fuck that. You're dancing beautifully, you've got the lead role in a new ballet, and your skin is fucking glowing. Lean into it, babe." She checks her phone for the time. "What have you got planned tonight?"

"I'm heading over to Cord's theater, actually. We're going to do our number tonight."

Her eyes widen. "Fun!"

"You should come! The show is amazing and I can introduce you to everyone after." Even though Cord and I haven't performed together since that first night, I've been to the theater several times over the past couple of weeks and have had the chance to hang out with most of the guys.

"Yes! I'm in!"

I unlock the front door of my building. "I'll text you the info, I've got to go get ready!"

"See you tonight!" she calls over her shoulder, already turned and heading toward her place.

I take the quickest shower of my life, dress in one of my fancy lingerie sets and the black wrap dress, and grab my ballet bag so I can do my makeup in the car.

Cord greets me at the front entrance when I arrive and I ask him to put Lucy's name on the list for the evening. He seems excited about the prospect of meeting one of my friends and I love that he isn't shying away from meeting my ballet people. Despite my trepidations, and his, so far he hasn't had any issues with hearing about my daily routine or the happenings at the studio. It makes me hopeful, which is a little scary, but there's not a lot of room for fear when Cord looks at me like he can't believe his luck.

Our routine is even better the second time, there's no hesitation or awkwardness, it's just us, acting out a scenario that's pretty damn close to how our real relationship has played out. Tonight, when the music fades out, Cord kisses me, and the already deafening cheers grow even louder.

Cord carries me offstage, our mouths still joined together. We break the kiss, but he doesn't put me down until we're back in his dressing room.

"Any chance you want to hop up on that desk and let me have my way with you?" We're still pressed together, Cord's mouth finding its way to my neck the second the door closed behind us.

"Maybe next time," I say, even as I capture his mouth in another kiss. "I want to go watch the rest of the show with Lucy."

Cord sighs and it's very dramatic. "All right. I suppose I'll just have to feast on you later."

I groan, because the offer is tempting. But Lucy has already been on her own for the first part of the show and I really do want to watch with her. So I push Cord to the opposite side of the room and grab my dress from the pile that one of the stagehands dropped off for us. I tie the dress and slip into my shoes, kissing him once before heading out.

Lucy, of course, has managed to make friends with the people around her. She tries to introduce me to everyone, but it's too loud to hear anything. I ask our server for a sparkling water and enjoy watching the rest of the show.

Cord doesn't come back onstage until the final number, when all of the guys come out for one last hurrah. After the number ends, the lights dim onstage and rise in the house and it takes my eyes and ears a minute to adjust to the bright silence after the screams die down.

More than one person stops to compliment me on the routine, even more than that tell me how lucky I am to have been able to kiss Cord. I don't bother bragging, telling them I can kiss him whenever I want because sometimes I forget to believe it myself.

The rest of the crowd clears out and Noah is the first one of the performers to find me and Lucy at one of the tables in the back of the theater. I introduce them and definitely notice how his eyes linger on hers, and how her eyes drink him in from head to toe.

Hmmm. I make a mental note of that possible connection and vow to explore it further. Lucy is a firecracker and Noah is a sweetheart, the two might be the perfect pair. Cord and a few of the other guys join us and we decide to head next door to the nearest bar. It's a little divey, but the music is good and kept at a normal volume so we can all actually hear one another.

Cord, Noah, Lucy, and I find a four top while the rest of the crew claims the pool table in the back.

"So that was an experience," Lucy starts us off, raising her glass to the center of the table.

The rest of us clink our glasses against hers and drink. I'm having another sparkling water, with a slice of lime so it feels fancy. Tomorrow is Sunday—no rehearsals—but I plan to do my normal Sunday routine of working out and going to company class, so even as we're chatting, I'm keeping an eye on the time.

"What did you think of the show, Lucy?" Noah leans back in his chair, crossing his arms over his chest, not because he's defensive but because it makes his biceps bulge.

"Honestly?" Lucy stabs the ice in her old fashioned with her straw. "I was surprisingly impressed."

Noah scoffs and Cord shoots me a knowing smile, his hand finding a place on my knee and squeezing gently.

I come to Lucy's rescue, not that she really needs it. "Not going to lie, I felt the same way the first time I saw it."

"Yeah, you were so impressed, you coerced this guy into working for you." Noah shoves Cord's shoulder, knocking him closer to me.

"Excuse me, I was not working for her. I was blessing her with my vast amount of knowledge."

"And it paid off." Lucy raises her glass again. "To Allegra and her lead role!"

We clink glasses again, and even though I'm not drinking alcohol, a warmth fills my belly and spreads through me.

"Cord, are you dying to see Allegra perform the new ballet? I've only seen hints of her solos during rehearsals, but so far everything looks like it's going to be incredible." Lucy gives me a mock salute.

I smile and squeeze her arm.

But Cord doesn't say anything in response. His hand drops from my knee and he becomes seriously interested in the shape of the ice cubes in his drink.

Lucy and I exchange a look.

"I, for one, am really looking forward to watching Allegra dance this part. God knows she's earned this opportunity. I'm sure you can't wait to see her, too." She keeps going, digging in further when all I want is for her to back off.

This question should have a very simple answer. An answer Cord isn't giving.

His jaw tenses and he still refuses to look up from his drink. "I don't go to the ballet. So while I'm sure Allegra is going to be amazing, I won't be there to see it."

An immediate cloud of fury overtakes Lucy's face, but I shoot her a pleading look. She purses her lips and her eyes tighten, but she doesn't say anything.

"What do you mean you won't be there to see it?" I ask quietly.

Noah pushes his stool back from the table. "I need another drink. Lucy, care to join me at the bar?"

Lucy waits for me to give her a nod, a signal that I'm okay, before she joins Noah. Of course, the look she shoots Cord as she walks away from the table would make a lesser man tremble in his boots.

Once they're gone, Cord sits back in his seat and sighs. I wait for him to answer my question because I don't know that I have the strength to ask it again.

"I was planning on having this talk a little closer to opening."

"About how you don't plan to be there for the most important opening night of my career?" I try to keep my voice neutral, but his response is so unexpected, such an out-of-the-blue dart to the chest, that I don't think I do a good job moderating my tone.

Cord reaches for my hand, and I let him take it. "There's still a lot we haven't talked about when it comes to my past with ballet, Slippers."

I raise my eyebrows. "Is it worse than what happened with Chloe?"

He shakes his head. "No. That was the breaking point. The moment when we could no longer ignore all the ways ballet was hurting us. But that one single moment in time was the culmination of a lifetime of small abuses." His fingers tighten around mine. "I know you know exactly what I'm talking about, Allegra, because I know you've witnessed them and experienced them yourself."

He's right, of course. The world of ballet has a lot of problems, and though the community at large is working to correct many of them, they still exist. Everything from teachers fat-shaming young girls to the pervasive need for perfection at any cost. Ballet dancers put our health and safety at risk pretty much every day, just by dancing the way we do. As a kid, I was always told those who raised a fuss were too weak to hack it. I know better now, but that doesn't mean I don't tolerate a lot for love of the art.

"What I choose to tolerate is my own business, Cord."

"I know, and I would never try to tell you otherwise. I respect your boundaries, Allegra. And I need you to do the same for me."

I let out a long breath. "And one of your boundaries is never seeing another ballet, ever again?"

"I have a problem supporting an institution I know to be abusive." He finally meets my gaze and his eyes are defeated.

It's the sadness that does me in. I know it's going to take me some time to process this latest revelation, but I know, more than anything else, that I want Cord to be happy.

"Okay."

"Okay?" There's a tinge of hope in his repetition.

"Okay. If that is a boundary you don't want to cross, then I respect that. I don't like it, of course. I wish you could be there to see the payoff of all your hard work with me, but I respect your decision."

He leans in and presses a soft kiss to my lips. "Thank you, Allegra."

"I'm in this for the long haul, Cord, and I realize that's going to come with some compromises." I know in my heart it's the right thing to say, just like I know deep down that I really mean it. But it feels a little bit like I'm lying to him, and I hate that. I pull out my phone, making a show of checking the time. "I should probably head out."

Lucy appears at my side at the exact right moment. "Should we share a cab?"

I nod, grateful.

"Are you sure you don't want me to call a car for you?" Cord stands when I do, his hands shoved in his pockets.

"We're fine, I'm sure we won't have an issue getting a cab." I flash Lucy a look.

"I'll meet you out front," she tells me. I watch her whisper something to Noah as she passes by him at the bar on her way.

"Will you let me know when you get home?" Cord looks like he's fighting to not reach for me.

I put him out of his misery, tucking myself into his embrace. "I will."

He takes my cheeks in his hands when I pull away. "Allegra, I . . ."

I wait for him to fill in the blank, but he doesn't. So I kiss him softly, say my goodbyes to the rest of the guys, and push through the door of the bar.

TWENTY-FIVE

Cord

It's never good when the chime of my phone registering a new text message is what drags me from sleep. It either means I slept too late or something is going massively wrong with the show.

Of course this morning there's an added layer of dread as I reach for my phone, groping blindly through eyes that aren't quite fully open yet. I know Allegra said she was fine with my boundaries and me not going to see her perform, but there was such sadness in her voice when she said goodbye. I hate myself for being the cause of it. If she hasn't already texted to end things, I should probably be the one to do it for her. All I'm going to bring into her life is more pain.

But the text isn't from Allegra, it's from my sister.

CHLOE: Ummmmm, have you seen this?

She's included a link to a TikTok, which I can't open because I refuse to download TikTok, which she well knows.

ME: You know I can't see that but it better be important for you to text me this early.
CHLOE: It's 9:00.
CHLOE: Here's a different version.

This one is a link to Instagram, and I click on it warily.

My blood runs ice-cold the moment I realize what I'm watching.

I hit call. Texts aren't going to cut it. "Fuck, fuck, fuck."

Chloe lets out a long sigh. "So this wasn't intentional."

"No, it wasn't intentional. Fucking hell, why would I want this out on the fucking internet?" I push out of bed, running a hand through my hair and tugging at the roots, hoping a jolt of pain might help me think more clearly.

"Well, if you read the comments, you would know that everyone is drooling over the two of you. I wouldn't be surprised if this sells out your shows for the rest of the year."

"I don't need a viral video to sell out shows, Coco. And you know this isn't about me." Striding down the hallway, I find my laptop and open it up, needing to see how bad this has gotten, how widespread. I google Allegra's name and nothing related to the video comes up. Thank god.

I find the video—it's posted on just about every social media platform—muting the sound so I can continue my conversation with my sister uninterrupted. "This is bad, Coco."

"It's one viral video. You know how these things go, it will blow over in a week when the next big thing comes along."

I scrub a hand over my face. "It might blow over for me, but what about her? Can you imagine how the company would have reacted if something like this would've happened when we were still dancing?"

She sucks in an audible breath. We don't talk about our old company, ever.

"I'm sorry. I shouldn't have said that." The last thing I need this morning is to piss off my sister.

"You don't have to apologize, Cord. It's been a long time. I don't mind talking about it." She pauses for a second. "And I can imagine how it would have gone over with the company. Maybe you should call Allegra and see if you can get ahead of this?"

I nod even though she can't see me. "Yeah. I probably should."

"This isn't your fault, Cord."

I snort. "She never would have been onstage with me if I hadn't asked her to."

"Allegra is a grown woman who is perfectly capable of making her own decisions. Don't infantilize her because of your own need to take the blame for everything."

"Shit, Coco. It's too early for that."

"Not sorry. Call me later." She hangs up without saying goodbye.

I know I should call Allegra right away, hopefully catch her before anyone else does. But first, I turn up the volume on the video and scroll back to the beginning. I watch the whole routine, finding myself swept away in what's captured the attention of strangers on the internet. God, she's gorgeous. And this dance. It's sexy and powerful, *she* is sexy and powerful. My heart clenches at the thought of this thing we created together possibly being the cause of something that brings her pain.

I want to think that this is no big deal, that I'm catastrophizing unnecessarily. But I know ballet better than that.

I open my phone, focusing on steadying breaths as the FaceTime connects. I know it's bad form to FaceTime without warning, but I need to see her, make sure she's really okay. And I need her to see me, too.

"Allegra."

"Cord, what the hell is going on? Why is everyone acting like someone died? Did someone die?" Her eyes are wide, sleep still crusting in the corners. She sits among a pile of blankets, still in her bed. She never lets herself sleep in, and I hate that this is how she has to wake up.

I pinch the bridge of my nose, half relieved she doesn't know yet and mostly dreading I now have to be the one to tell her. "No one died. Everyone is fine, physically speaking."

She lets out a long breath, dragging her fingers through her tangled hair. "Okay. Then why is everyone freaking out?"

I hesitate for a long second.

"Just tell me. Please."

"Someone posted a video of our routine after the show last night and it's going viral." I blurt out the truth in one quick breath.

Relief washes over her and I can't help but feel like she doesn't truly understand what the repercussions might be. "How viral?" she finally asks.

I purse my lips. "Last I saw the original video on TikTok had over a million views. But that doesn't include all the duets and shares. I don't actually have TikTok so I can't check on the real numbers."

She sighs, pairing it with a soft smile. "Well, if it's only on TikTok, then we should be fine."

I shake my head. My laptop is still open next to me and each time I refresh the search page, more and more results pop up. "The video that blew up is from last night, but since that one, people are discovering videos from our first performance, too. And those are everywhere, Slippers."

"What do you mean everywhere?"

"Facebook, Instagram, Twitter . . ." My email chimes and I navigate to my inbox, the tab open on my computer. "Shit. I just got an email from a local news network." Fuck the internet.

"Jesus." She rubs a hand over her forehead. It looks like the reality might be setting in.

"I won't say yes to anything until you've decided how you want to handle this." I can already tell this is going to be good for me, business-wise at least. We weren't exactly hurting for ticket sales, but this is the kind of exposure you can't buy, and I know it's going to give Six Pact an all-around boost. And while the New York flagship might be doing just fine, this could really help some of our newer locations, like the one in Texas.

"I have no idea how to handle this." The realizations begin to sink in and I watch them play out over her face. "Shit." Her skin goes ashen, her hazel eyes lined with worry.

"I know. I'm sorry, Slippers." I want to reach through the screen and hug her.

"It's not your fault."

"It happened at my club, and I'm the one who pressured you into performing with me. And I'm the one who will reap the benefits of this." I close my eyes, unable to bear looking at her for a moment longer. "It seems like I'm doing nothing but letting you down lately."

"Hey."

I open my eyes.

She meets my gaze. "You are not disappointing me. And you didn't pressure me into anything. I love dancing with you." Her phone beeps with another incoming call and the lines around her eyes tighten. "I should go. My mom is calling and she's probably having a heart attack about seeing my butt."

"To be fair, it is a pretty spectacular butt."

She smiles and it seems genuine, which makes me feel slightly better. "I'll call you later, okay?"

"Of course. Let me know if there's anything I can do to help."

She waves and the call ends, leaving me staring at a blank screen. My inbox dings again, and again a minute later. My phone rings a few seconds after that.

I shut my laptop and switch my phone to Do Not Disturb, adding Allegra's name to the allowed contacts. I know I'm going to have to deal with all of this at some point, but first, I need about a gallon of coffee. Something tells me even that won't be enough.

TWENTY-SIX

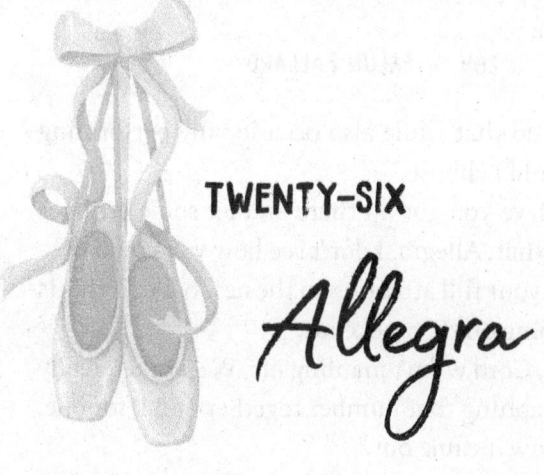

"Hi, Mom." I mentally prepare myself for the ire I know is coming. Before talking to Cord, all I knew was that my phone was blowing up, messages from Lucy and my sister, and many, many from my mother. Now that I know why, I know nothing good is coming my way today.

"Hi Mom? That's all you have to say to me right now?"

"It is the traditional greeting one bestows upon someone when answering a phone call."

"Now is not the time to get smart with me, young lady. Do you know how many people have sent me texts and emails asking what my daughter is doing dancing onstage at a strip club?"

I sigh, making it nice and loud so she can hear it. "It's not a strip club, Mom. I was dancing, performing a routine, the thing that is my actual job."

"Your job is to be an upstanding and hardworking member of one of the most prestigious ballet companies in the world. That is the career I have pledged my time and money to for your entire life."

As if she needs to remind me.

"And I can do that while also occasionally performing elsewhere should I choose."

"I can't believe you got up there and let some stripper maul you like that, Allegra. I don't see how you could possibly be giving your full attention to the new ballet if this is what you're doing on the weekends."

"First of all, Cord wasn't mauling me. We worked really hard choreographing that number together and I, for one, am proud of how it came out."

There's a long moment of silence while she readies her next argument. When she speaks again, her voice is layered in fake sadness meant to guilt me into doing exactly what she wants. "I don't think you understand just how much I sacrificed for you, Allegra. I don't think you've ever truly known how much I gave up to be your mother, and how much I gave up for you to be able to have the success you do now."

Tears fill my eyes, because even though I spent most of my life trying to be the perfect daughter and the perfect dancer, the perfect everything, this isn't the first time she's said something like this to me. On the rare occasion I asked for a day off. When I told her I didn't want to leave school to focus on dance. When an injury was taking longer to heal than expected and I was hesitant to get back to class.

I wasn't planning on having this moment of reckoning today, but this video seems to have forced my hand. "You made a choice to do that, Mom. You made a choice to give up ballet when you got pregnant. You made a choice to have me. You made a choice to try to relive your own youth by dictating mine."

"Dictating? Really, Allegra."

"I love ballet and I love my job and I love my life, but I am not going to sit here and be chastised for doing something that makes me happy. And dancing with Cord makes me happy."

"Of course. This is about that boy."

"He's a thirty-three-year-old successful entrepreneur actually."

"He's a thirty-three-year-old disgrace to the ballet community, is what he is."

I suck in a breath. "That's not fair."

"I know exactly who Cord Donovan is. He physically attacked his director and was fired from his company."

"That's not the whole story, Mom." I don't know why I'm bothering because it's easy to see she has had her mind made up since long before this video became an issue.

She scoffs. "So this is the kind of man you want to align yourself with?"

"Yes. He's exactly the kind of man I want to be with. And I will be with him. I will keep dancing with him. If you decide you can no longer emotionally and financially support me because of it, then I understand." Nausea roils through me at the thought of losing my safety net, but it feels good to finally stand up to her.

"This conversation isn't over, Allegra."

"Goodbye, Mom." And then I do something I haven't done since I was a teenager. I hang up before she does.

I DRESS QUICKLY, BEHIND SCHEDULE BEFORE THE DAY'S EVEN really begun. I skip my morning workout, needing to get to the studio and get focused before class begins.

The second I walk into the studio, it's clear every single

person in the room has seen the video. I make a beeline right for Lucy, who's here on a Sunday for once, probably for this very reason.

I sink down next to her on the floor, pulling my shoes out of my bag so I have somewhere to direct my attention.

"How are you doing?"

I shoot her a look. "How do you think I'm doing?"

"Have you talked to Cord?"

I nod. "Yeah. He was the one who told me. There's not much he can do about it at this point. I guess the two of us will need to figure out what we do from here, if anything."

"It's good publicity for the club, at least."

I tug on my pointe shoes, securing the ribbon tighter than I need to. "If only the same could be said for the ballet."

Lucy shrugs, sticking her legs out in front of her and bending over to stretch. "I don't know. I think the whole thing could be used as a sort of preview for the new ballet, if you put the right spin on it."

"Somehow I don't think David will see it that way." I've barely had time to think about how he's going to react, and I don't really want to.

"Have you heard from him yet?"

I shake my head. "After the lecture I had to endure from my mom, I turned off my phone."

"Probably a wise move."

Brianna, David's assistant, comes in then and motions for us all to take our positions for company class. And, unsurprisingly, class is a bit of a disaster. I can't get out of my head, can't stop thinking about how David is going to react. I mess up even the most basic of steps, and though she doesn't call me out, I know Brianna notices every mistake

I make, just as I know those errors will get reported to David when class is done.

Brianna dismisses us and immediately glides over to me, her graceful movement out of sync with the severe look on her face. "David wants to see you in his office."

I swallow thickly, nodding and following her out of the studio because what other choice do I have? Lucy shoots me a tight smile as I walk by. Everyone else turns away from me like I'm branded with a scarlet letter.

"Would you like me to stay?" Brianna asks when we arrive at the door to David's office.

I nod, unsure my voice is actually working at the moment.

She reaches over and gives my shoulder a quick squeeze before knocking on the door and pushing it open.

The two of us slip into the chairs in front of David's desk. I give myself a second to breathe before I raise my eyes and look at him.

If I could hear my mother's anger through the phone lines, I can feel David's wrath just by looking at him. I guess we're not taking this whole thing as a publicity opportunity then.

I know better than to speak first, but he lets the silence drag on so long I almost open my mouth to offer my defense. Right when I'm on the verge of cracking, his tirade begins.

"Do you have any idea what you have done, Allegra?"

I resist the urge to tell him that I danced with my boyfriend and everyone should probably stop acting like I killed someone.

"I have been fielding calls from board members, trustees, donors, the press. I have spent my entire day trying to answer for your impetuous, immature, selfish decisions, and I'm wondering why I'm bothering to defend you. Why I'm explaining away the unexplainable. So perhaps to start, you should tell me what the hell you were thinking getting up onstage at a strip club and dancing around in your underwear?"

I take a deep breath. Responding out of anger isn't going to get me anywhere. I need to be measured and matter-of-fact if I'm going to get him over to my side. "I started working with Cord Donovan when I was preparing for my audition for *La Courtesan*. I knew that I had the skills to dance the part, but I also knew that I was lacking in the performance aspect of the character." I raise my eyebrow ever so slightly, hoping it's a reminder of the words he said to me. Words that I could have reported, but did not.

"Taking outside classes is highly discouraged, Allegra, and you know that." He glares at me.

"Discouraged but not forbidden. And no one can deny the results." I pull my shoulders back. "Dancing with Cord helped me find this character and embrace my sexuality onstage. The routine we performed this weekend was one that we worked on during our lessons together."

"That does not explain to me why you thought it was okay to perform the piece in front of an audience." David's stare is penetrating and I can't help but feel like nothing I say is going to make any bit of difference.

"Cord asked me to perform the piece to test it in front of an audience, and I did. If you think about it, the piece going viral and being connected to the company could be used as a publicity tool when it comes time to promote the new ballet." It's the exact wrong thing to say and I realize it the moment the words are out of my mouth.

"You think I am going to promote my ballet being tied

to a group of shirtless idiots who prance around while women throw money at them?"

My cheeks flush with rage. "That is not what the show is, and it's not who the dancers are either. But even if that were the case, there wouldn't be anything wrong with that."

"You're right. I don't really give a shit what a bunch of nobodies who couldn't hack it in ballet choose to do with their time." His fists clench. "But I do care when one of my dancers and therefore my company get dragged into the debauchery."

I fight not to roll my eyes. "If it's this big of an issue, then I won't dance the piece with Cord again until after the new ballet opens."

He huffs the kind of laugh that lets me know he finds none of this amusing. "You won't dance up on that stage ever again, Allegra. Not while you're a member of this company." He pulls a piece of paper from his desk. "Let me remind you that you are under contract here. You are legally not allowed to dance for anyone other than BNY without express written permission. I could fire you right now for breach of contract."

My heart stops in my chest. Of course I was aware of this clause in our contracts, but it's mostly seen as perfunctory. Dancers perform with other companies all the time, and as long as it doesn't interfere with their company schedule, it's never a problem. I certainly have never had to seek written permission before.

David smirks when a minute passes and I don't say anything. "Lucky for you, we're too far into rehearsals and your understudy isn't up to the task, so you won't be getting fired. Not today anyway."

It doesn't bring me much relief.

David leans forward, his arms crossed on his desk. "Here's what's going to happen. You are obviously not to go anywhere near that theater, let alone step foot on its stage."

I nod, keeping my head down so I don't have to look him in the eye. It sucks that I won't get to visit the guys at rehearsal, or watch the performances, but if this is what it takes to keep my job, then it's what I'll do.

"And you will not be seen with Cord Donovan, at his theater, at this theater, anywhere in the entire fucking city."

My head snaps up. "What? I can't see him at all? You can't tell me to do that."

"Of course I can. Your contract also has a morality clause and since you are a subject of high public interest right now, all eyes will be on you. If you are seen in public with a man who is damaging to BNY's reputation, the morality clause can be invoked."

I wrestle down the tears because I will not let this man see me cry. "That isn't fair, and you know it. You don't have a right to dictate my private life."

"Your private life isn't private right now, Allegra, and that has nothing to do with me. These are the consequences of your own actions."

"So my options are break up with my boyfriend or be fired?" Even just saying it out loud is ludicrous.

David shrugs, and I know he's smart enough not to give me a direct ultimatum, especially not with a witness sitting in the room. "I'm not telling you what to do, I'm just advising you of the extremely difficult position you have put me in."

"You *are* telling me what to do." I fight not to sound like a petulant teenager, but I don't think I succeed.

"I'm simply reminding you of the specific clauses of the legally binding contract you signed." He sits back in his chair, hands laced together and resting on his stomach. "Now if you don't have further questions, I have work to do."

I practically jump from my chair, needing to get out of this room before I completely lose it. Brianna calls my name as I run down the hall toward the dressing room, but I ignore her. I don't know how I'm supposed to focus on a rehearsal right now, but I do know I need a minute by myself before I can even think about dancing.

Closing myself in a bathroom stall, I let my back fall against the tiled wall, one hand covering my mouth to tamp down on the sobs pouring from me. I don't have my phone with me, but I don't even know who I would call in the moment. Certainly not Cord.

Cord.

How the hell am I going to tell him about this? We just decided to give this a chance and now I have to tell him we can't be seen in public together. I have to believe it won't be forever. Eventually the online hype will die down and at that point I can get away with doing whatever I want outside of the ballet studio. But until then, our relationship just got a lot more complicated.

But I can't think about that right now. Cord, and our relationship, will have to wait a few more hours.

I unlock the stall door, splash some water on my face, and blow my nose. My eyes are still red and puffy and everyone in the room is going to know something major just happened.

But I pull my shoulders back as I enter the studio. It's just me and Sam and our understudies today and Sam flashes me a sympathetic smile as we take our first positions. I know I can't let on that anything is wrong, not to Sam, not to the assistants, and most definitely not to David.

And so I drop the mask in place. I've been wearing it my whole life. When I was tired and sick and injured and burned-out, but couldn't allow myself to take a single day off from ballet, I shut down my brain and let my muscle memory take over. It's like I'm floating, hovering over the rehearsal room while some puppet who looks just like me completes the steps down below. I let my body move to the music, and I forget about everything else.

TWENTY-SEVEN

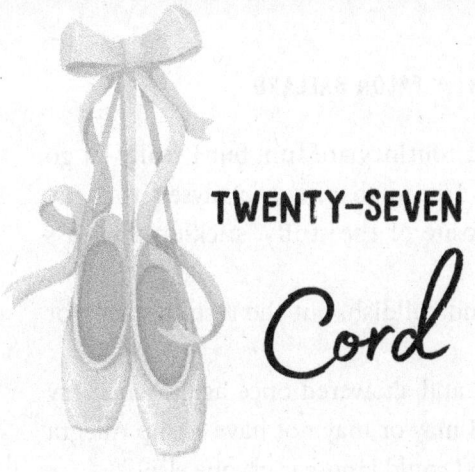

Cord

I head to the gym pretty much the moment I hang up the phone with Allegra. I know she has a busy day ahead of her and I don't want to spend the entire thing waiting for her to text when I know she won't have time to. I expel my frustration on the weight machine, then shower and head to the Six Pact studio. We don't have rehearsal or anything scheduled, but I would rather be here than in the office.

Chloe checks in throughout the day, Noah sends me an "oh fuck" text, followed by an offer to talk if I need to. I appreciate their support, but there's only one person I need to talk to right now and she's too busy dealing with the ramifications of my stupidity.

I hate myself for putting her in this position, but I hate ballet more. Who the fuck cares if she goes out and dances for fun? If anything, her asshole director should be grateful for the free publicity. Something tells me he won't see it that way.

My frustration continues to build, so I harness that energy and put it into the one thing I know will bring relief. I choreograph a new number, and I let myself have fun with it. All of the Six Pact routines are fun, but I really let go with this one, as if I need to prove to myself that my company is the opposite of the stuffy, stick-up-their-ass BNY.

It may be petty and childish, but the results speak for themselves.

I'm back at home and showered once again when my phone finally dings. I may or may not have set up Allegra with her own alert so I could ignore everyone else.

ALLEGRA: Are you home?
ME: Sure am. You coming over?
ALLEGRA: Is that okay?
ME: Of course. I've been counting down the minutes until I get to see you.
ME: Want me to send a car?
ALLEGRA: I'm already at the subway. See you soon.

My finger hovers over the keyboard. I send her a heart emoji, but I don't get any response. She's probably already lost service. At least, that's what I tell myself.

I buzz her up when she arrives, but it takes way longer than it should before I hear her knock at the door. I'm about to go out and look for her when she raps tentatively. I know it's only a door knock, but it doesn't sound good. My stomach sinks, but I shore up my nerves. Today was hard for me, but it was inevitably much more difficult for her. My only job right now is to make sure she is okay.

I take one look at her and immediately know she is not okay. Pushing the door open wide, I usher her in, wrapping an arm around her shoulders. "What happened? What's wrong?"

She snuggles into my side and I feel a flash of relief. It

doesn't last long as she covers her face with her hands to try to hide her tears. I lead her to the couch and help her sit.

I sit across from her, pulling her hands from her face and keeping them clasped in mine. "Allegra, you're freaking me out. What happened?"

She takes a moment to sniffle and wipe her eyes before she starts talking. "David saw the video, obviously, and he called me into his office and told me I was violating my contract by performing at the club without permission."

I suck in a sharp breath. "Did he fire you? If he did, we can fight it, Allegra."

She shakes her head, her eyes locked on our grasped hands and avoiding mine. "He didn't fire me. At least not yet." She takes a shuddering breath. "He told me I'm not allowed to perform at the club anymore."

I tighten my fingers around hers, trying to control the anger threatening to overtake me. "Okay. I mean, that's a dick move, but to be expected, I suppose."

"There's more," she says quietly. Her eyes move from our hands down to the rug. "He told me I'm not allowed to see you in public anymore."

There's a minute of deadly silence.

"He's trying to dictate what you do in your personal life now, too?" It takes everything in me, every ounce of self-control, to keep my voice level and calm. On the inside, I'm a roiling mass of fury, but if I'm being truly honest with myself, the fury is just a mask for the underlying hurt. Because some part of me, a big part of me, already knows where this conversation is going.

"He told me since my contract includes a morality clause, and since we're the subject of high public interest right now, that I can't be seen with you." She finally raises her eyes to mine; they're still filled with tears and I want to stalk my way over to the BNY building and beat the shit out of the man who put them there. "But that doesn't mean we can't be together. We just have to stay out of the public eye until things die down."

My jaw clenches. "What does that even mean, we have to stay out of the public eye?"

She swallows thickly, and I see the hope there, the hope that we can find a way to make this work. Too bad it's the hope that kills you. "It just means we can't be seen together for a little bit."

"How long? How long does David want us to confine our relationship to our apartments?" My tone shifts and I know she notices.

She pulls her eyes from mine once again and I know she isn't telling me everything. "I don't know, Cord. I think that depends on how long it takes for the hype of the video to die down."

"That could be months, Allegra." I pull my hands from hers and shift my position on the couch so I'm facing away from her.

"I know, but we're so busy anyway, it won't be that hard. Those couple months will go by in a flash." She's pleading with me, and a big part of me wants to give her what she wants.

She wants me to say it will all be okay, that we can hide our relationship and not go out in public together for however long her damn director decrees it so. But I quit living my life to appease ballet directors a long time ago. I gave up the one thing I worked my whole life for so that ballet didn't get to dictate who I am and what I do.

"Are you really asking me this? We've only been together for a couple of weeks, Allegra."

Tears spill over her cheeks and the sight of them makes my stomach clench. "This isn't my fault, Cord. I didn't ask to be in that video. I didn't ask for it to go viral and invite the scrutiny of everyone at BNY. I don't want this, but it's the only way."

I scoff. Even though a part of me knew this is where we were headed, I'm still in disbelief that she would actually go along with this. "So if I'm not willing to hide out because of the whims of one asshole ballet director, you're going to break up with me?"

Her mouth drops open in shock. At least the tears stop flowing, so I no longer have to fight the urge to wipe them all away. "Are you serious? You would rather break up than give this whole thing a little while to calm down?"

I turn back to her, her eyes full of pain and dismay. I want to be willing to do whatever it takes to take away that pain, but I know I can't. "This isn't just about the video and not being out in public, Allegra. It's about you choosing ballet over me."

She purses her lips and shakes her head. "I'm not choosing ballet over you."

"Oh yeah? Did you tell David to go fuck himself with his bullshit demands? Did you tell him to take his morality clause and shove it up his ass?"

"No, I didn't, because that's not how I choose to talk to my boss. You might be okay with that, but I am not."

I run a hand through my hair. "I knew this was going to happen. I honestly just didn't expect it to happen so soon."

"What is that supposed to mean?" Her words are cutting,

and I'm almost relieved she is letting anger replace the hurt.

"I knew you would choose ballet if it ever came down to it."

"I told you ballet is my priority from the beginning, Cord. I have always been honest with you about that. It doesn't mean I care for you any less."

"It sure as hell means you don't care for me more." I stand, gesturing for her to rise with me. "I think you should go."

Her eyes widen, cheeks flushed. "This conversation isn't finished."

"Then let's finish it. Your director won't allow you to see me. I'm not going to hide my relationship." I shrug, as if this all means nothing to me. Maybe if I pretend hard enough, it will be true. "So you choose, Allegra."

She stands, moving closer to me, resting her hands on my chest. She smells like rosin and it's such a powerful sensory memory I almost recoil at her touch, but the warmth of her palm over my heart feels too good. "Don't do this, Cord. It doesn't need to be an either-or. I know it isn't ideal, but we can make this work. I don't want to lose you." Her tears flow again, and this time, I do reach out to gently wipe them with my thumb.

I sigh, giving in to the overwhelming need to comfort her. I pull her into my arms, letting my chin rest on the top of her head. "Don't cry, Slippers. I don't want to lose you either."

My gut clenches at the thought, as it starts to hit me what is really happening here. She's going to pick ballet. I always knew she would, and yet, being here and faced with the reality of it is more painful than I could have even imagined. She's going to walk out that door, leave me, and I'm going to be left with the remains of my heart, ballet once again holding the hammer that shattered it.

"Let's figure this out, okay? I know we can." She rises up on her toes, reaching to press her lips to mine.

But I take a step back, breaking contact between us. If I let her kiss me now, it might erase the truth of what I know needs to happen here. "I don't see how we can figure this out. I wanted this to work, more than you could possibly know, but I should've trusted my instincts. Ballet is toxic, and I don't think I can be with anyone still in it."

For a minute, all she does is blink, eyelashes wet. "Are you breaking up with me?" she whispers.

I shake my head. I'm not the one who wants this. "This is the choice you're making, Allegra. I don't want it to be this way, but if you're going to choose ballet, going to choose him, then I don't see any other way."

She nods and I watch her face change. She thinks I'm being unreasonable, and maybe I am. But the fact that she doesn't see what this is doing to me, putting me in the same traumatizing situation as before, shows me that this was never going to work in the first place.

She wipes under her eyes and takes another step away from me. "If that's how you feel."

She hovers there for a second, like she's waiting for me to change my mind. And if she stands there for much longer, I just might. There's a part of me—not a small part—that thinks I might have loved her. But even if I did, or if I do, this isn't going to work. It's better to cut our losses now before we get in too deep.

Heading toward the front door, she grabs her purse and lingers. I keep my eyes glued to her, wanting to drink in every single second of her presence. But I don't stop her.

In a way, I'm doing this for her. It would be easy to give in, tell her we can figure this out. But it would only lead to more heartache in the end.

When it becomes clear I'm not going to change my mind, she opens the door. And walks away.

TWENTY-EIGHT

Allegra

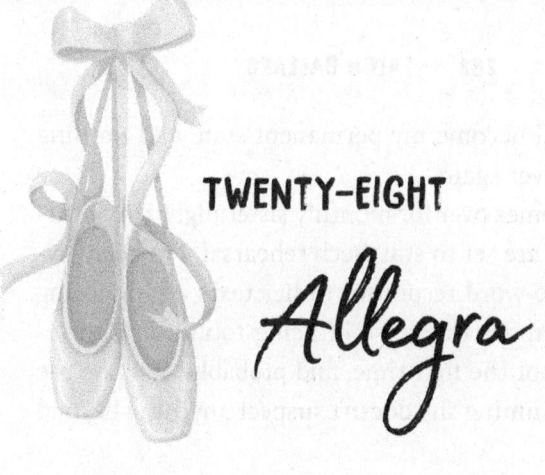

I don't let myself fall apart on the walk to the subway or on the train or during the trek up the stairs to my apartment. I don't cry as I unlock the door and kick off my shoes and make myself a reheated leftovers dinner. I don't pick up the phone and call my sister to complain about Cord and the terrible position he put me in.

Maybe ballet has taught me to mask my feelings a little too well, because I don't cry at all.

I move through the next few days in a haze of indifference, a state of numbness unlike anything I've ever felt before. There's three weeks until tech rehearsal, a month until the premiere of *La Courtesan*, and the excitement should be building. I should be looking forward to my first starring role, the promotion that might follow.

But I feel nothing.

And maybe it's better that way. Maybe it's better to lock up all the emotions and shove them to the back of my mind, where they can stay forever as far as I'm concerned. Maybe if I pretend hard enough, for long enough, this numbness will become my permanent state and nothing will hurt me ever again.

Bethany comes over for monthly sister night the Saturday before we are set to start tech rehearsal. I've been giving vague, one-word responses to her texts and ignoring her calls, all under the guise of being too busy with rehearsals. It's not the first time, and probably won't be the last, so I'm assuming she doesn't suspect anything beyond the ordinary.

But I can't hide from her forever, not when she lets herself into my apartment and takes one single look at me, standing in my tiny kitchen pouring two glasses of wine.

"Oh, honey."

Apparently, all it takes is those two words and I dissolve into the puddle of tears I've been holding back for two weeks. I drown in them, choke on them, let them consume me. I sink to the floor and let Bethany cradle me like I used to do to her when we were little and she got hurt.

She strokes my hair and whispers calming platitudes that mean nothing. But most importantly, she lets me cry.

When the tears finally subside, she leads me into the bathroom, taking a makeup wipe to my skin, clearing me of snot and tears and mascara remnants. She holds a tissue to my face like I'm a little kid, forcing me to blow my nose.

Then she guides me back into the main room, depositing me on the bed before grabbing the two glasses of wine from the kitchen counter. She hands me one and sits facing me on the bed, both of us with our legs folded up like pretzels.

"Is this about the ballet or the boy?" she finally asks.

Fresh tears replace the ones I just wiped away. "Both I guess. But mainly the boy."

She nods, sipping her wine. "Want to fill me in or is it what I think?"

"He asked me to choose." I take a tiny sip from my own glass of wine. It burns a little on the way down, my throat raw from all the crying, but it warms my belly and so I take another drink.

She keeps nodding. "Right. So as I expected."

I pull the sleeves of my sweatshirt over my hand, using it to dab at the tears that seem to keep on coming. "You really thought he would do something like this?"

Bethany sighs, leaning back on the pillows. "Look, I don't know the whole story and I don't know everything about Cord's past, but Mom sent me that article about him getting fired, and clearly there's some underlying explanation, but also clearly the guy has some deep-seated resentment about ballet."

"And you think he's right. About ballet I mean." I stare into the depths of my wine as if it can solve this problem for me. It can't, but it can bring back my numbness, so I keep drinking.

"I've never hidden my feelings about ballet. It has a lot of problems, despite also making a lot of progress. But it doesn't really matter how I feel about it, or even how Cord feels about it." She pats my knee. "You are the one who has devoted your life to this, and you are many things, Allegra Hart, but you are not stupid. And if this is what you want to do with your life, then you know I support you."

I wait for her to finish.

She only hesitates a second before tacking on, "And he should've supported you, too."

"I get it, though. I told him we couldn't be seen in public together or David would fire me."

Her eyebrows shoot up to the top of her forehead. "Fuck, I hate that guy."

"I get that I was asking a lot of Cord."

"But you expected him to go with it?"

"I expected him to put our relationship first."

She purses her lips, and I know exactly what she's thinking.

"I know I didn't put him first, but you can't sit here and tell me you think I should give up my job, my entire life's greatest passion, for a man I've known a couple of months."

"Well, when you put it like that," she grumbles.

I finish the rest of my wine and cross the three steps to the kitchen to refill my glass. "There is no way for me to win here, B. Either I give up Cord and keep dancing or I keep Cord and quit ballet."

"Neither of them should have forced you to make that choice."

"But they did. And I did." I plop back down on the bed. "And here we are."

"Want to drink so much wine you forget about all your problems?"

"Yes. Obviously."

I am, as we have established, not a drinker, so it doesn't take much. Three glasses of wine and two episodes of *Summer House* later, I crash into blissful oblivion, the dulcet tones of a Paige DeSorbo takedown echoing in the background.

TWENTY-NINE

Cord

I sit at one of the tables in the middle of the audience at the Six Pact theater. It's a seat I've occupied hundreds of times, in a building I practically lived in in the early days of the show, before I made enough money to buy the space for myself. And yet everything about it just feels wrong.

I rub a hand over my face, forcing my eyes back to the stage. Noah and Ivy are rehearsing their number. Our number. Noah and Ivy are good, better than good really, but something about their performance is still off.

I've watched the viral videos of us a million times by now. I told myself it was for practical purposes—I needed to be able to teach the choreography. I would have erased the whole damn dance from my mind if I could, but my marketing team expressly forbid me from ignoring this opportunity. Millions of people have watched the video, are clamoring to see the dance in person, and I would be foolish not to capitalize on that kind of popularity and demand. Tickets for the show are sold out for months. And I need to give the people what they want.

Of course, what they want is me and Allegra. And I can't give them that.

My stomach clenches. As soon as I think of her, my body rebels against me. It's hard to breathe, hard to keep food down, impossible to think straight. Impossible to keep myself from aching for her, from wanting her with such a need I almost forget why I let her leave.

That's what's missing, I realize, from Noah and Ivy's performance. The want, and the need. Sure, they're both attractive people, but they don't want each other. Not the way Allegra and I wanted each other. There's no way to fake that.

Unfortunately, no amount of tortured rehearsal is going to give them that spark.

I wait for them to finish their run-through before I stand. "I think that's enough for today. That was great. You guys are ready." I don't believe it, not truly, but I also know there's nothing I can do to give them the extra edge. Maybe they just need to find it when it comes time to perform for an audience.

Noah's hands rest on his hips, his chest heaving as he regains his breath. "You sure?"

I nod. "You know I wouldn't put you out there if I didn't think you could handle it."

Ivy crosses the stage and grabs her water bottle and her bag. "Cool. I'll see you guys tomorrow night then. I've gotta run and teach a class." She waves over her shoulder as she exits the theater.

I start for my office, but before I can get far, my steps are cut off by a block of muscle. "Did you need something, Noah?"

"Yeah. I need you to cut the shit and tell me why you're

making us do this dance." He crosses his arms over his chest in a move that would probably intimidate someone who didn't know he's a teddy bear on the inside.

"The dance has gone viral, Noah. You know this. People want to see it."

"People want to see you, Cord. You and Allegra."

"Yeah, well. That's not happening."

"You could wait until her run of *La Courtesan* is up if she's too busy right now, you know. People will wait for the performance if it's going to be the one they want." He raises an eyebrow. "Don't you think she's worth the wait?"

"Of course she's worth the wait," I say softly. "But this isn't about a conflict of dates, Noah. She doesn't want me." It's the first time I've voiced the sentiment out loud. Despite Chloe badgering me for details, I haven't been ready to talk about it, and so I've just been stewing, making myself fucking miserable.

Noah pushes me into a chair, taking the one opposite for himself. "Tell me what happened, Cord."

I shut my eyes for a second, as if that will help keep the walls in place. But it's a fruitless attempt. I know Noah will sit and wait for me to be ready, so I don't keep him waiting, relaying everything that happened after the video went viral, everything she said to me, and everything I said to her. Reliving that night sends my body into meltdown mode again. I think if I had to do it a hundred more times, it would hurt the same each and every time.

I don't think losing her is ever going to not hurt.

Noah lets out a low whistle when I finally finish. "Jesus, Cord."

"I know. I knew it was going to happen, and yet I'm somehow still surprised that the moment she had a choice, she chose ballet." I'd been a fool to let myself hope that what we had was something real.

Noah looks at me as though I'm an idiot. "She only chose ballet because you made her choose."

"I didn't make her choose, her fucking asshole director made her choose."

Noah shrugs. "I mean, the guy does sound like a dick, but he's not the one dating her. He's her boss. You are the one who was supposed to stand by her and support her."

My mouth drops open, incredulous. "Are you trying to say this is my fault?"

"Of course it's your fucking fault, you complete moron. She told you from the beginning that ballet is her life, that she's worked too hard for this opportunity to give it up, and at your first chance to stand by her and lift her up, you gave her an ultimatum. You know how much this part meant to her and you expected her to what? Quit the show?" Noah's voice rises and I've never heard him sound so angry before. It's only the shock of it that keeps me from yelling right back.

"So what, I was supposed to just hide our relationship? Never be seen in public with my own girlfriend?" My hackles raise, my shoulders along with them, tight with tension.

"Yeah, Cord, you could have hid your relationship for a few weeks. I wouldn't think it would be too hard to be confined to your apartment with your megahot girlfriend. I would have relished the opportunity myself." He grins, winking.

I punch him in the shoulder. "Take it easy over there."

"Just saying. There are worse things." He leans back in his chair. "You seemed to really care about her."

"I do. I did." I cross my arms over my chest, heart aching.

"Then why would you ask her to do that?"

"You seem to be suggesting that I'm the one who fucked up here."

Noah laughs. "I'm not suggesting it, Cord. I'm flat-out telling you, you fucked up."

"Maybe I did, but I don't think it changes anything. Clearly ballet was always going to come between us. It was inevitable."

He shakes his head slowly, like a parent who could not be more disappointed. "Whatever, man." Pushing back his chair, he heads for the dressing rooms in the back of the theater. "Fix your shit."

I flip him off, but he doesn't see because he doesn't turn around. I trust Noah, and he knows me better than almost anyone. If he thinks this was all my fault, he's probably right.

The thought knocks me back into my seat.

I rise from the table in a daze, heading for the front exit so I don't have to cross paths with anyone on my way out.

This isn't my fault. I told Allegra what I needed from her, and she couldn't do it. Sure, maybe what I was asking was too much, but she knew that from the beginning.

Just as you knew the choice she would make from the beginning, a voice in my head whispers. It sounds, unfortunately, a lot like my sister.

I walk the two blocks back to my apartment, even though I've come to think of it as the scene of the crime. I've been spending as little time here as possible. But maybe it's time to face reality. Allegra and I were never meant to be. There are some issues that just can't be solved by a compromise or a conversation or some choreography. Love doesn't actually conquer all. I've always known that, now it's time to accept it.

THIRTY

Allegra

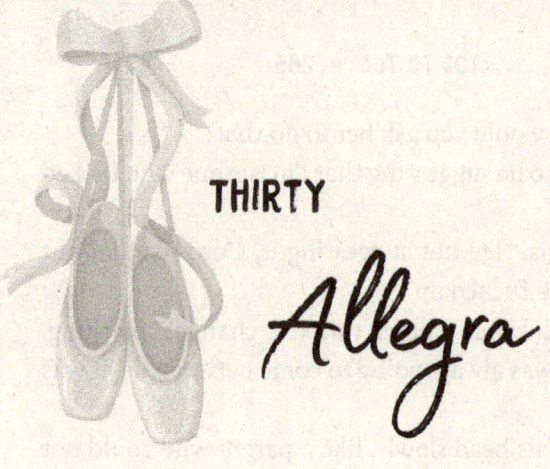

Tech week is always a blur, but this one even more so. Thank god for Lucy, who, after pestering me for three days straight, finally got the whole story out of me. She cursed Cord's name to high heavens, claiming she never liked him anyway and promising to block Noah if he tried to text her again. I told her that was highly unnecessary and fought the urge to ask her to ask Noah how Cord is doing.

Truthfully, I'm grateful for her vitriolic response to the situation because I don't have the energy for it myself. It's time to really focus on this part and on making sure my first leading role isn't my last.

Lucy keeps me rested and fed, admonishing me for coming to class when I don't need to, piling my plate high during lunch and dinner breaks.

I'm fitted for my costumes and lighting is designed to best highlight my movements. We rehearse the entire ballet from start to finish without stopping and I survive. David even offers me praise every once in a while, in between all the shouting and demands.

Sam is a good partner and we work well together, and it's only once a run-through or so that I imagine what it would feel like if Cord were dancing with me instead. Only in our characters' most romantic moments do I let myself picture Cord's blue eyes and all the feelings, the words I never got to say, the emotions I never got to express. Purely to benefit my performance, of course.

When opening night finally rolls around, I try to treat it like any other day. I wake up, work out, go to the studio. I stretch and run through my barre exercises. I practice one part of the ballet that has been giving me trouble and I nail it. I eat a healthy lunch and find my spot in the dressing room. I do my makeup and slick back my hair.

When flowers arrive for me, I don't hope they could be from him. I read the card from my parents and relish the words written in my mom's flowy script: *I'm so proud of you*. It's not the first time she's said them, but it does feel like the most important. We haven't talked much since the explosive phone call the morning of the video. Things have mostly just gone back to normal, both of us happy to sweep the whole thing under the rug.

When it's time to go out to the stage, I don't try to peek through the curtain to catch a glimpse of the audience. I know my parents are out there, and Bethany and Cassidy. I know Lucy will be beside me onstage. That's all I allow myself to care about.

I know Cord won't be there, sitting in the audience, and I don't bother checking, because I can feel it deep in my bones, this absence of him.

A more romantic person might have imagined Cord rushing onstage with a bouquet of red roses, sweeping me up in his arms and telling me it's all going to be okay. That he was a fool, that he made a mistake, that of course we can make it work.

I'm not a more romantic person.

Sometimes things just aren't meant to be.

What *is* meant to be is this night.

I step out onstage with the lights still dim, the curtain still closed. I take a deep breath and hit my opening pose. And when the curtain rises and the lights find me, I dance better than I ever have in my entire life. I let myself feel every beat of the music, every breath of the steps.

And I don't need anything else in this moment. I worked for years for this, sacrificed so much of my life for this. And I absorb every single second, imprinting it all on my brain to examine later, because in the moment, all that remains is me and the music.

I leave everything that's left of me out on that stage.

The curtain comes down after the final beat of the music and the roar of the applause fills the theater, ringing in my ears. Sam sweeps me up in his arms, and, gasping for air, I let myself smile and laugh because holy shit, I did it.

My limbs tingle with excitement and exhaustion as we take our bows and the standing ovation lasts for a lifetime. I find my family in the audience, my mom wiping her tears while Bethany hoots and hollers like she's at a hockey game and not one of the most prestigious theaters in the world.

I don't look for Cord because I won't allow his absence to taint this moment.

David strides onto the stage, looking dapper in his perfectly fitted tuxedo, absorbing his own round of applause with a smarmy smile. He has a microphone in one hand and a bouquet of roses in the other. He hands me the flowers and kisses my cheek before shaking Sam's hand and taking center stage.

David raises his hand and the applause dies down. "Thank you so much for being here tonight to celebrate the premiere of my new ballet, *La Courtesan*." He pretends to shake off the cheers that follow, but we all know how much he enjoys this part of his job. "I could not have dreamed of a better leading lady than our very own Allegra Hart." David gestures for me to join him as the applause rings out once again. "And I couldn't think of a better moment to announce her promotion to principal dancer at Ballet New York."

I hear the words, I hear the screams, I feel the arms of my company members circling me and hugging me. I know a smile is wide on my face. I know I make eye contact with David and say thank you, though I don't know if he can hear me.

And still, none of it seems real.

The numbness I've blanketed myself in in order to survive the past few weeks isn't so easy to shake off, and its protection has begun to hinder even my positive emotions. Until I greet my family in the lobby after changing out of my costume and Bethany screams—a literal scream—before throwing herself into my arms.

"You did it! I'm so fucking proud of you and you fucking did it!" Her grip on my neck is too tight, but I don't even care.

I let myself sink into her embrace. Once again, it's the presence of my sister that makes it all real and stirs a flood of emotions. I don't hold back the tears, even though I know they're making a huge mess of my makeup. They keep flowing as I hug my dad and then my mom, who holds on tight, but doesn't say anything. When she finally lets me go, I see her own tears trailing down her cheeks, and I don't need her words.

We go out to celebrate and I stay out later than I should, but it doesn't matter because I'm floating on a cloud and I sleep like the dead and wake up the next morning as a principal dancer for Ballet New York.

All my dreams have finally come true.

~~~

I WAIT FOR DANCING THE LEAD ROLE IN A NEW BALLET TO FILL the hole in my heart. But while the Cord-shaped wound scabs over and hardens, it doesn't close up.

We start rehearsals for our next production, even as *La Courtesan* continues its run. I have a solo role in this one, smaller than a principal, but still important. David tells me to learn the principal role as an understudy, and I take it as a sign of his confidence in me. He continues to give me instructions and corrections, but he seems about as happy with me as he ever is with anyone.

And I don't know exactly what it is I'm waiting for. It's been six weeks since Cord and I had our breakup conversation. I haven't let myself cry about him, not since that night with Bethany. I try not to let myself think of him, and I mostly succeed.

It isn't until I climb into bed each night, exhausted from hours of rehearsals and classes and performances, that his face occupies my mind. I dream about him often.

Only once do I pick up the phone, think about reaching out. But he made his wishes clear and I refuse to leave my happiness in someone else's hands again.

THIRTY-ONE

Cord

It takes me a couple of days, but I finally make that therapy appointment. And then I make another one, and another. It's been six weeks since Allegra walked out of my apartment, and I've seen my therapist more than I've seen my dancers. There's no such thing as an overnight success, not in dance or in therapy, but it does seem to be helping, at least a little.

On the opening night of her ballet, I spend the day at the theater, needing to keep myself occupied. Noah and Ivy premiered their routine the week before, and while there was still something missing, the crowd ate it up and our publicity team seems to be at least temporarily satisfied, so I take it as a win.

For a second, at the end of the night when I'm leaving, I think about jumping in a cab and making my way uptown. I think about showing up outside the stage door and begging for a second chance. But I dismiss the idea almost as soon as it comes. I made our whole relationship, including its demise, about me. I don't need to make her opening night about me, too.

When I wake up the next morning, I immediately head over to the *Times*' website, searching for her name. Pride washes over me as I read the review of *La Courtesan*, but it's not pride I feel when I look at the accompanying photos: one of her leaping across the stage, and one of her tucked under David's arm at the end of the show when he announced her promotion to principal. There isn't a word to describe that feeling.

I'm on my third read-through when my phone chimes with a text.

CHLOE: Did you see the article in the Times?
ME: No.
CHLOE: Liar.
CHLOE: But here's the link on the off chance you're telling the truth.
CHLOE: Looks like the new ballet is a hit.
CHLOE: And Allegra Hart "is sure to dazzle audiences with her brilliant debut as principal."
CHLOE: Her performance is "electrifying" and her dancing is "hypnotic."
ME: Whatever point you're trying to make, I think you've proved it.
CHLOE: You should go see her.
ME: No.
CHLOE: I know how much you miss her.
ME: Then you know how painful it would be for me to see her up on that stage, living out the dream she's worked for her whole life, and know that I asked her to give it all up.
ME: You know how much it would hurt to see her again and know that I completely fucked it all up.

I stab at my phone screen, angry at my sister, angry at ballet, but most of all, angry at myself. Really, there's no one to blame but myself.

CHLOE: If that's how you really feel, then why do you insist on continuing to be such a stubborn ass?
CHLOE: If she means this much to you, then is it really worth holding some stupid arbitrary line?
ME: She deserves better than me.
CHLOE: Well, at least we agree on that much.

My phone stays blissfully silent for a moment, but it doesn't last, as I knew it wouldn't.

CHLOE: You deserve to be happy, Cord. And Allegra could do a hell of a lot worse than you. You know you're my favorite brother.
ME: I'm your only brother.
CHLOE: Point still stands.
CHLOE: Promise me you'll think about it?

I don't like lying to my sister, so I take my time before I respond.

ME: I'll think about it.
CHLOE: I love you.
ME: Love you too.

I spend the rest of the day puttering around my apartment, considering Chloe's words. When the sky darkens outside my windows and I'm still in my pajamas and haven't left the apartment all day, I collapse on my sofa, reaching for my laptop.

I have to scroll back deep in the cloud, but I find what I'm looking for eventually.

Pressing play on the video, I lean back against the couch cushions and steel myself.

On the screen of my computer, I watch a heavy red curtain rise, already knowing what waits on the other side, but seeing the whole picture with fresh eyes. I'm holding my pose, waiting for the music to strike and swell before I begin. Dressed in blue tights and a velvet jacket, ten years younger, I almost don't recognize myself. But then I begin to dance and finally recognize the boy on the stage.

Aside from the viral video of my dance with Allegra, I haven't seen myself perform in years. The director of our ballet company used to make us watch our recorded performances so he could dissect them, pointing out even the slightest of missteps. It's a practice I never adopted—and certainly haven't carried on for myself.

I wait for the old instincts to kick in, for the critiques to form in my mind. I wait to see the misery hidden in my eyes, unclear to the audience, but obvious to anyone who knows me.

But none of that comes. I don't find a myriad of issues with the height of my jumps or the strength of my lifts. I don't care about the slight wobble at the end of my turns.

And it isn't misery I see in my eyes. It's joy.

So much of ballet has been tainted, but this, here onstage, is what I always loved the most. Being onstage made me feel alive and powerful and creative and fulfilled.

I let everything else that happened around it wipe the love of the dance from my mind . . . and from my heart.

When the video ends, I click on another. And another. I watch Chloe and me dance together. I watch myself fly across the stage with a wide smile on my face. I watch myself launch my partners into the air, always there to catch them. I see my strength and the length of my lines and the balance in my turns.

I don't realize I'm crying until drops land on the keyboard of my laptop, sparkling against the silver keys. I dig the heel of my palms into my eyes, as a half laugh, half sob escapes me.

I pick my favorite video of Chloe and me dancing together and send it to her. My phone rings five minutes later.

"Hey," I say, glad I cleared the tears from my voice, even though I know she will still hear them.

"Hi." She clears her own emotion from her throat. "I haven't seen that in a long time."

"Me either. I almost forgot how much fun we used to have up there."

"The most fun. I always loved dancing with you."

"Even when I threatened to drop you on your head?"

She laughs. "Even then."

"It wasn't all bad, was it?"

"No, it wasn't all bad." She takes in a deep breath. "I'm sorry, Cord. I'm sorry if my experiences colored the way you feel about your own."

"Don't apologize, Coco."

"I know it wasn't my fault. But I hate that what happened to me ruined ballet for you."

"It didn't. Or at least, it doesn't have to," I amend. "No matter what happened, it made us who we are today, and that's something to be proud of."

"Yeah. God knows you wouldn't have that fancy-ass apartment on a ballet dancer's salary."

I choke out a laugh. "Very true."

A comfortable quiet falls between us.

"Does this mean you're going to go get your girl?"

I smile, for the first time in weeks, the thought of Allegra striking something other than despair in me. "Yeah, I think that's what it means."

THIRTY-TWO

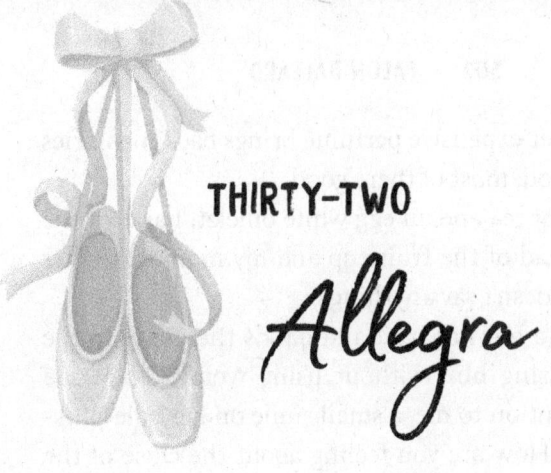
Allegra

Only one weekend remains of *La Courtesan* and it's hard to believe after all the work we put in, the whole thing is almost over. I'll be sad to say goodbye to the show, the role that changed my whole life. But I'm looking forward to what comes next. Maybe there's a small part of me that thinks that leaving behind this role, this last remaining connection to Cord, will help me fully move on.

My mom insists on meeting me for breakfast on Friday morning, with our final show scheduled for the following night.

I don't want to go, but I've been successfully avoiding her for a while—and at least I know she won't badger me too much with a show to prepare for or offer me guilt-ridden money now that I've earned a raise along with my promotion.

So I meet her at a café near my apartment. She's there when I arrive, a mug of black coffee already sitting on the table. She stands to hug me and I let myself lean into it. My mother isn't exactly known for being comforting, but still, the smell of her expensive perfume brings back memories of my childhood, most of them good.

I order a hot tea and an egg white omelet. I ask for the potatoes instead of the fruit cup and my mom raises her eyebrow but doesn't say anything.

She orders a bowl of fruit and hands the menu to the server, dismissing him without using words. Then she turns her attention to me, a small smile on her pale-pink-painted lips. "How are you feeling about the close of the show?"

I fiddle with the string of my tea bag. "Sad, of course. It's always a little sad when a show closes. But I'm excited to see what comes next."

"Has David mentioned when you'll get your next principal role?"

I shake my head. "He hasn't announced anything for the rest of the season yet, but I'm sure I'll get some good parts."

Her head tilts to the side as she studies me. "And yet, you don't seem very happy, Allegra. You've finally achieved everything we've ever wanted, and yet, you don't seem happy."

"I am happy," I insist, and it's not a total lie. I'm not unhappy, at least.

She sips from her mug. "Bethany told me a little bit more about what happened with that boy."

I make a mental note to kill my sister, but for now I focus my ire on my mother. "His name is Cord."

"Right. Cord." She folds the corner of her linen napkin, then unfolds it, then folds it again. "I really am sorry that things didn't work out between you."

I snort. "No, you're not."

She sighs. "All right, maybe I'm not sorry, exactly. I do think that now more than ever is the time to put all your focus where it belongs—on ballet." As if I could ever misconstrue her words.

"I am focused on ballet, Mom."

"But you miss him."

I shrug, letting my eyes roam around the café so they don't have to meet hers. "I mean, sure, I do. But that doesn't change anything. I'm not giving up ballet for a man." I don't mean the words to pack a punch, but from the look on her face, they hit her right in the gut.

My mom takes a deep breath. "I know you probably think that I pushed you so hard in ballet because I regretted my own choices, the ones that led me to give up dance when I met your father."

I don't think, I know. But I don't voice the thought, instead staying silent and letting her continue.

"But that's not the whole story, Allegra. The truth is that I stopped dancing because I wasn't good enough."

I study her face as she tells me something she's never told me before. The lines around her eyes are slight, even less prominent on her forehead thanks to her regularly scheduled Botox appointments. But the tension is visible, even with her surgical perfection.

"I danced for so many years, and I worked so hard. But I didn't have the natural talent that you do. It didn't matter how hard I worked, it couldn't change the fact that I didn't have the innate ability needed in order to move out of the corps. And I wanted it, desperately. I was so jealous of the girls in my company who made it look so easy."

"It's not easy for anyone." Even the most naturally gifted dancers still have to work their asses off.

"I know that now, and I knew it then too. But still, when I met your father, it felt like an out. It felt like an opportunity to quit with some amount of grace, and an excuse no one could really blame me for. Who wouldn't give up their job for a chance at true love?"

I suck in a breath. I don't think she meant that to be a pointed hit, but it sure feels like one. "Why are you telling me this now?"

She reaches across the table and pats my hand. "I want you to have everything you ever wanted, Allegra. Not just in ballet, but in life."

"So now you want me to get back together with him?"

"Would that make you happy?"

I swallow the last of my tea; it's turned lukewarm and bitter. "I don't know if a reconciliation is even possible, Mom."

She shrugs her shoulder and leans back in her seat so the server can deliver our breakfasts. "You've accomplished everything in life you've set your mind to, Allegra. If you want it, want him, you'll find a way to make it happen."

I SPEND THE HOURS BEFORE OUR FRIDAY-NIGHT PERFORMANCE like I always do: stretching, applying my makeup, fixing my hair, readying my shoes. But I can't get my conversation with my mother out of my head the entire time.

The notion of "we just want you to be happy" has always felt like a foreign one. Because what does that even mean? How do you know when you're really truly happy?

And isn't that something that I should be able to identify?

There's no question in my mind that being onstage

makes me happy. Yes, it comes at a cost, but the way my heart soars when I'm leaping through the air... that has to be true happiness.

But what about those moments with Cord? The soft kisses and the way his hand spanned my back when we danced together? Being with Cord made me feel just as weightless as being onstage.

Do I need both to achieve this much-sought-after true happiness? And what does it mean for me that I can't? Am I doomed to this half life forever?

There's a knock on my dressing room door as I'm doing my final makeup touch-ups and for a second, I let myself think that it might be him. Maybe I can have both love and ballet.

But it isn't Cord who sticks his head through the door. It's David. He grins when he sees me sitting in front of the mirror, stepping into the small space and closing the door before I have a chance to respond. His hands land on my upper back and he squeezes gently. "You look marvelous, Allegra."

"Thank you." I smile at him in the reflection, but my mouth is tight.

"I just wanted to stop by tonight because I know tomorrow night will be chaotic with all of the show-closing hullaballoo." He doesn't remove his hands, moving them so they cup my shoulders. "You've exceeded my expectations, Allegra. Truly, when I envisioned this part, I didn't know that anyone would be able to dance it the way I wanted, but you have made this role and this performance your own."

My smile softens, turning genuine at his praise. "Thank you, David. That means a lot. I really appreciate you giving me this opportunity."

"You earned it." He leans down a little, his breath searing my neck. "And I must say, I admire your dedication to the show, and to the company. I hope you see now that I was right to tell you to stay away from that stripper. It allowed you to dance to your full potential."

My stomach turns. Of course he would chalk up my performance to something he did.

I pull my shoulders back, shrugging away his grip. "That had nothing to do with my performance. I'm dancing well because I worked hard, not because of any inappropriate demands you made."

Shock crosses his face for a fleeting second before he hardens his gaze. "It is not inappropriate for me to ensure my dancers follow the rules set out in their contracts."

"Yeah, well, it's a bullshit rule if you ask me." I pick up my scarlet lipstick, swiping it slowly and carefully over my bottom lip, taking deep breaths to still my trembling hands. I can't believe I just said that to my director, the man who holds my entire career in his grip.

I wait for the explosion of anger from him, but it doesn't come.

Instead, David studies me with his head tilted to the side. "I like seeing this fire in you. Nothing is more important in ballet than passion."

My mouth drops open, but I cover the shock by blotting my lipstick with a tissue. "I agree." I should take this opportunity to tell him that if I want to date Cord, I will. But it's a moot point when I remember that Cord no longer wants to date me.

"I'll see you out there." David offers me a final smirk before letting himself out the door and closing it behind him.

I slick on another coat of red lipstick before heading out to the stage.

THE CLOSING PERFORMANCE OF *LA COURTESAN* IS BITTER-sweet. On the surface, it's a night just like hundreds of others I've had before it. I prepare for this show the same way I have for every ballet I've danced with BNY over the course of my career.

But there's a different charge of electricity in the air when the curtain rises and the lights brighten. This is likely the last time I'll ever dance this part, this part that will forever be linked to my name. And so I make a point to enjoy every second of it. To flash Sam plenty of coy smiles and inject a little more swivel into each twirl of my hips.

It's the most fun I've ever had onstage. And when the lights dim after not one but two standing ovations, the mood backstage is nothing but celebratory.

Tomorrow, we will all take the morning off and let ourselves sleep in. I'm looking forward to the much-needed rest, but tonight I'm looking forward to sharing the bliss with my company members.

Lucy finds me in my dressing room, offering me a congratulatory hug before darting off to the bar to save tables. I'm one of the last to leave the theater, the rest of the company already headed over to the bar across the street. I wanted to take my time, changing out of my costume and unpinning my headpiece, leaving the final physical remnants of my character behind. Now that I've had a quiet moment to say goodbye to Dominique, I'm ready to celebrate my accomplishments, really let myself savor the experience. I might even let myself have more than one drink, since I don't have to wake up early the next morning.

A figure steps from the shadows as I push through the doors of the theater, and I freeze, about to turn and run back to the safety of the dressing room.

It only takes a second, but I recognize the figure.

"What are you doing here?" My fingers tighten around the strap of my bag, like I'm waiting for him to try to steal it.

Cord steps farther into the light, pulling a bouquet of coral sunset-colored roses from behind his back. He lets out a long breath before he speaks. "I couldn't pass up my last chance to see you dance your first leading role, Slippers." He holds out the flowers.

I take them, cautiously, the paper crinkling in my tight grip. "You watched the show?"

He nods. "I did. You were beautiful. Perfect. I couldn't take my eyes off you, Allegra."

"You watched the show?" I repeat like the idiot I am. But I remember how adamant he was, how resolute about not supporting ballet, and that was when we were still a couple.

"I did." He moves a single step closer. "I hadn't realized, until recently..."

"Hadn't realized what?" I push when he doesn't finish his thought.

"How much I miss ballet." He runs a hand through his hair. "I focused for so many years on all the problems, I forgot how beautiful it can be. How beautiful it is."

I tuck the flowers into my arms, like I've been given silent permission to accept them. "I'm happy you came."

"And have you been happy otherwise? I heard about your promotion, you must be thrilled."

"Everything here has been going really well."

He nods, like it was the exact answer he expected. "Good. I'm happy for you, truly." He falls back a step. "I'll let you get to wherever you're going. You have a lot to celebrate tonight and I don't want to take up too much of your time. I just . . ." He doesn't finish this thought either, just takes another step away from me.

"Cord."

He freezes and his face is so shielded, I can't read a single one of his emotions.

"Why did you really come here tonight?" Something suspiciously hope-like is prying at the edges of my heart, but I need more from him before I can let it in fully.

He sighs. "I needed to see you. Needed to see that you were all right, and that you made the right choice. And I think you did. Watching you up there tonight, it was clear that you were made for ballet. You were made for the stage and that role. You were made to be a ballerina."

"I didn't want to have to make a choice at all, Cord."

"I know. And trust me, I regret putting you in that position. I have ever since the moment you walked out of my apartment."

My head cocks to the side. "Then why didn't you reach out?"

"I didn't know what to say. And I think a big part of me wanted you to realize you made a mistake, that you should have picked me." He chuckles, but there's no humor in it. "But you didn't make a mistake. Not going to lie, that stings a little, but I meant it when I said I was happy for you. I am." He sounds like he's trying to convince himself along with me, but there's something genuine in his eyes, some hint of emotion that lets me know he does really mean it.

I clear my throat, shuffling closer to him. "Did you make a mistake? When you asked me to choose."

His eyes meet mine and that first breath of contact knocks the air out of my lungs. "I did. I made a huge mistake. The biggest mistake of my life."

This time I take a full step, making it clear I'm purposefully crossing closer to him. "Are you going to do anything about it?"

His eyes widen slightly. "Is there anything I can do?"

I shrug. "You're here. That's a good start."

"What about what David said? I don't want you to put your job at risk." He runs a hand through his hair. "Looking back on it, I can't believe I ever even suggested you should walk away from ballet. It was incredibly selfish of me, and I could never forgive myself if I somehow caused you to lose out on your dream."

"Let me worry about David." I nudge his elbow with mine. "I'm giving you your shot here. Make your argument. And make it good."

He laughs a little, and this one feels genuine. Then he takes a deep breath to steady himself. "Allegra, I did a really shitty job of showing it, but I think you should know that I'm in love with you."

My mouth drops open. Going in hard from the get.

"The past several weeks have been some of the worst of my life. One, because I'm selfish and I absolutely hated not having you in my life. But mostly because I hate the position I put you in. I hate that at the first chance you gave me to support you and love you, I failed. I fucked up, and I have spent the past few weeks hating myself for it. For letting you down."

"Cord." I take his hand in mine, lacing our fingers together.

"There's more." He clears his throat and pulls me in so our hips are flush. "I realized I still have some unresolved anger about things that happened in the past. So I went back to therapy, and it's not a quick and easy fix obviously, but I've been talking about it and working on it, and I will continue to do so. The last thing I want is for my stuff to ruin something you love."

"Do you think you can trust me and my judgment when it comes to ballet?"

He nods. "I know it won't be perfect. I won't be perfect. But I want to try. I don't deserve a second chance from you, and I know that. But I want one, more than anything, and I will do whatever it takes to be worthy of that second chance if you can find it in your heart to give one to me." He cups my cheek in his hand. "You are more important than anything else, Allegra, and I want you in my life in whatever capacity you'll have me."

I bite my lip. It's everything I've been wanting him to say, and yet I know, even with my willingness to give him a second chance, this isn't going to be easy. "I was about to go out with the company to celebrate the closing of the show."

His face falls, and his hand drops. "No problem. I won't keep you any longer."

"Do you want to come with me?" It's the first test, to see how well he can assimilate into my life, my life that's centered around ballet, and will be for quite some time, hopefully.

It takes a second for the words to register, but when they do, a smile spreads across his face. "Would that be okay?"

I nod. "Of course, lots of people bring dates. And I'd like you to be mine, if you're up for it."

His arms snake around my waist, pulling me close. "I'm up for it."

"Good." I rise up on my toes. "I'm going to kiss you now."

"Thank god."

I press my lips to his, keeping it soft and sweet.

And then I tickle the seam of his lips with the tip of my tongue, so he gets a hint of what's to come later. After we celebrate with my friends. After I make it clear that Cord and I are together—and will continue to be. After I bask in the glow of a ballet I led, that I danced my heart out in.

Before we take the next steps toward the future. Together.

EPILOGUE

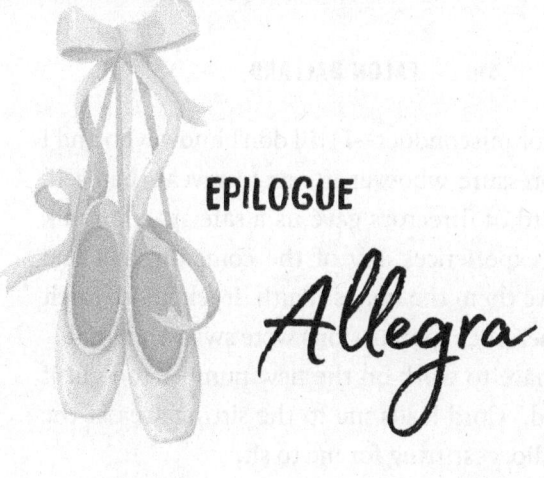
Allegra

One year later

I push through the door of the Six Pact studio, heading for the elevator because my legs cannot handle the stairs after a full day of class and rehearsal. I'm exhausted and sore, but the moment the door opens and I see Cord waiting for me, a rush of energy surges through my veins.

He greets me by sweeping me up in his arms before closing and locking the door behind me. For a minute, he just holds me, my arms tight around his neck, his face buried in the crook of my neck.

I sigh, letting out a long, content whoosh of air as the stress of the day leaves my body. "Hi," I say when he finally sets me down.

"Hi." He leans down for a soft, sweet, quick kiss. "How was your day?"

"It was good. Rehearsals have been no joke lately. Brianna runs an even tighter ship than David."

I don't think anyone was too sad to see David go when he turned in his resignation letter six months ago. Someone reported him for misconduct—I still don't know who and I would never pressure whoever it was to reveal themself. When the board of directors gave us a safe space to talk about similar experiences any of the company had had with him, I gave them the honest truth. It felt good. It felt even better when the repercussions were swift and final.

"We don't have to work on the new number tonight if you're too tired." Cord leads me to the sitting area at the side of the studio, gesturing for me to sit.

But I don't, instead slipping out of my bright pink joggers, the color more vibrant than the ballet pink I wore for so long. "I'm fine. I thought Noah and Lucy were going to meet us here?"

Even though David is no longer my boss, I've stuck to my word, no longer performing at Six Pact in the show with Cord. When Ivy moved back home, we taught the routine to Lucy, and when Lucy officially quit Ballet New York, she became a permanent cast member of Six Pact. She and Noah have been dating for nine months and when they dance together on that stage, the crowds lose their minds. And with good reason, those two are hot as fuck.

Cord takes my hand and pulls me to the center of the room. "I thought we could use this time just the two of us to work on the choreography. We can teach it to them later."

I smirk, draping my arms around his neck. "If you wanted to get me alone, all you had to do was ask."

He smooths the loose hairs back into my messy bun. "You've been working hard lately."

"I know." I rise on my toes to kiss him. "I appreciate you rolling with my schedule."

"Anything for you." He deepens the kiss, sucking gently on my bottom lip.

"I thought we were supposed to be dancing?"

He slides one hand to my lower back and grasps my hand with the other. He slowly leads us around the room, his lips never moving from mine.

"I talked to my landlord today." It's the one thing I can say to divert his attention, not that I don't want to lose myself in his kiss. But I've been keeping the news from him for almost twenty-four hours and it's been killing me.

Cord pulls away, hope shining from his bright blue eyes. "Oh?"

I nod. "I gave him my notice."

A small smile tugs on his lips. "To be clear, by that you mean?"

I grin, threading my fingers through the hair at the nape of his neck. "By that I mean I told him I will be moving out by the end of next month." I place a single kiss on his pulse point. "You wouldn't happen to know of anyone looking for a roommate, would you?"

He mock frowns. "Hmm. I'll have to think about it."

I swat his arm. "You've been begging me to move into your new place with you for months."

Once it became clear that I still had several years ahead of me with BNY, Cord sold his Hell's Kitchen apartment and bought a place in between the Six Pact studio and the BNY building. He asked me to move in with him as soon as he moved, but I've held off for the past couple of months, wanting to make sure it was something we were both ready for.

It hasn't always been easy, finding compromises that work for both of us, but we've been committed to each other, and committed to making it work for a year now, and honestly, even with the challenges, I've never been happier. I'm dancing better than ever before, and despite my advanced ballet age, I feel like my best performance years are ahead of me. I've been awarded several principal roles and have received stellar reviews for all of them. Not to take away from the hard work and dedication I've put into ballet since I was a child, but something about my time with Cord, the way he made me see and appreciate my body, it turned me into the best dancer I could be.

I also started therapy almost a year ago, and to say that it has been life-changing would be the understatement of the century. Turns out, I had a lot of deep-seated issues, with my body, with my mother, with masking my emotions. Talking about them once a week has done wonders for my mental health, so much so that when Brianna officially took over as company director, one of the first suggestions I made was for more accessible therapy. She happily obliged.

"Are you sure you're ready to live with me, Slippers?"

"That depends, are you going to leave dirty clothes on the floor?"

His nose wrinkles. "Ew. No. I don't do that now, why would I start?"

I laugh, pressing another kiss to his perfect lips. "I can't wait to live with you. I love you, Cord. So much."

His eyes soften and he pulls me closer. "I love you too, Allegra."

"Now. Shall we dance?"

He grins, joining our hands once again. "We shall."

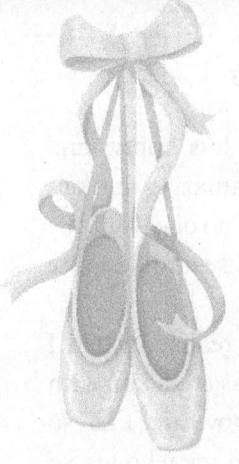

Acknowledgments

Not going to lie, writing the acknowledgments gets harder and harder with every book because I have more and more people to thank and it is my literal nightmare to leave anyone out! It takes a village to raise these book babies and I am so lucky to be a part of the absolute best village!

Thank you, as always, to my incredible agent, Kimberly Whalen. I was so excited when I got the chance to work with you five years ago now, and you have been such an integral part of my career. Literally could not do this without you by my side!

Kate Dresser, you have had such an impact on my writing and have pushed me in the best ways. I'm so grateful for the opportunity to work with you, and also so grateful you didn't have to mention the word "world-building" in your edit letters for this book.

Tarini Sipahimalani, you are a literal superhero and I am so thankful for all you do, and in awe of how easy you make it all look.

Kristen Bianco, Brennin Cummings, Jess Lopez, and Sofie Parker, if it weren't for you and the amazing marketing and publicity departments at Putnam, no one would be reading this book, so thank you doesn't seem like quite enough. But thank you. Seriously.

Speaking of Putnam, I don't think I realized when I signed my first deal in 2021 how lucky I was to end up with this incredible group of people. Now I know, and I am so thankful to have a team of people behind me who are so thoughtful, caring, smart, and creative. I truly can't imagine being anywhere else, so please don't ever leave me ☺.

Sanny Chiu, your art is a dream and I am so lucky to have it grace the cover of my book once again.

I never know who my audiobook team is going to be at this point in the process, but I feel like the PRH audio department deserves a major shout-out, especially Amber Beard for overseeing all of my audiobooks thus far.

I have some specific people who need to be thanked for this book in particular. Erika Lantz, who hosted *The Turning: Room of Mirrors* podcast and helped inspire this book. Channing Tatum, who danced a sexy duet in the rain and also helped inspire this book. Misty Copeland and Gelsey Kirkland, who wrote beautifully honest memoirs. Chloe Angyal and Deirdre Kelly, who wrote informative and insightful books about the world of ballet. Emily Waller, who came up with the name Six Pact. All the ballerinas on TikTok who share their lives and their talent with us. A million thanks to each of you.

I am so lucky (are you sensing a theme here?) to be surrounded by some of the best writers on the planet. Not only are their books amazing (you should read them), but they happen to be some of the kindest and most supportive humans I have ever met. Even if I only see you once a year, the conversations we have in person and online keep me sane. Endless thanks to Courtney Kae, Corey Planer, Kate Spencer, Elissa Sussman, Erin La Rosa, Susan Lee, M. A. Wardell, Holly James, Annabel Monaghan, Jody Holford, Hannah Bonam-Young, Jenny L. Howe, Jessica Parra, Gretchen Schreiber, Suzanne Park, Alexa Martin, Ali Hazelwood, Lindsey Kelk, Julie Soto, Denise Williams, Elizabeth Everett, Mazey Eddings. I know I forgot at least one person, and probably more than that, so to that someone(s), I'll buy you a drink to make up for it!

Let's stay on the lucky train! This book is dedicated to my readers because I would not still be doing this if you all didn't continue to show up for me. Getting to meet so many of you in person, or have chats in the DMs, is the highlight of my day/week/year. I cannot thank you enough for the love and support you have shown me. It means everything.

And speaking of love and support, I get an endless supply of it from my family and friends. You know who you are; I couldn't do it without you.

Canon, I'm writing this the day after your eleventh birthday, and I'm unsure how you have managed to turn eleven when I haven't aged a day. You are the best kid I could have ever asked for and I am so lucky to be your mom. I hope one day you think it's cool to see your name listed in these acknowledgments even if you're never allowed to read the books.

Matt, there is no one else I want to be on this adventure with. Thanks for picking me. Love you the most.

DON'T MISS FALON BALLARD'S OTHER FABULOUS ROM-COMS!

Available now from

DISCOVER THE BRAND NEW GORGEOUSLY SEDUCTIVE ROMANTASY THAT BLENDS *MACBETH* AND *MOULIN ROUGE*!

Available now!

RAISING READERS
Books Build Bright Futures

Dear Reader,

We'd love your attention for one more page to tell you about the crisis in children's reading, and what we can all do.

Studies have shown that reading for fun is the **single biggest predictor of a child's future life chances** – more than family circumstance, parents' educational background or income. It improves academic results, mental health, wealth, communication skills, ambition and happiness.[1]

The number of children reading for fun is in rapid decline. Young people have a lot of competition for their time. In 2024, 1 in 10 children and young people in the UK aged 5 to 18 did not own a single book at home.[2]

Hachette works extensively with schools, libraries and literacy charities, but here are some ways we can all raise more readers:

- Reading to children for just 10 minutes a day makes a difference
- Don't give up if children aren't regular readers – there will be books for them!
- Visit bookshops and libraries to get recommendations
- Encourage them to listen to audiobooks
- Support school libraries
- Give books as gifts

There's a lot more information about how to encourage children to read on our website: **www.RaisingReaders.co.uk**

Thank you for reading.

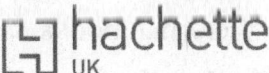

---

[1] OECD, '21st-Century Readers: Developing Literacy Skills in a Digital World', 2021, https://www.oecd.org/en/publications/21st-century-readers_a83d84cb-en.html

[2] National Literacy Trust, 'Book Ownership in 2024', November 2024, https://literacytrust.org.uk/research-services/research-reports/book-ownership-in-2024

FIND YOUR HEART'S DESIRE...

VISIT OUR WEBSITE: www.headlineeternal.com
FIND US ON FACEBOOK: facebook.com/eternalromance
CONNECT WITH US ON X: @eternal_books
FOLLOW US ON INSTAGRAM: @headlineeternal
EMAIL US: eternalromance@headline.co.uk